Lucy,
I hope you love
Hugh MacLeod as
much as I do!
Love,
Hilarie Alexander

Lost in Scotland

Lost in Scotland

HILARIA ALEXANDER

Lost in Scotland

Published: Hilaria Alexander 2017
hilaria_alexander@outlook.com
Editing: Editing by C. Marie
Proofreading: Author Services by Julie Deaton
Cover Design: Samantha Leigh Design
Photo: Adobe Stock
Formatting: AB Formatt

Prologue

I always enjoyed the train wreck that came with Hollywood's falling-outs, whether it was friendships, love stories, or simply superstars throwing shade at other superstars. I grew up in Los Angeles, so I was used to it; gossip was part of my reality. I loved the public, petty celebrity breakups, and more recently, the Twitter and Instagram bashing.

As much as they claimed to want privacy, celebrities could never seem to hold back. Things always got ugly, even with the biggest power couples.

Pretty much every divorce turned nasty, despite the A-listers being oh-so-concerned about "the well-being of the kids."

We were never short of drama in Hollywood, on or off the set.

I happened to be one of those who enjoyed the spectacle—that is, until I found myself in the middle of one and my name became a headline.

Admittedly, it was partly my own fault. I had decided reckoning day should be a public affair. I refused to take the high road. I had been given lemons, and I was going to serve lemonade.

Chapter 1

SAM

January

I had been dreaming of attending the Golden Globes since I was a young girl.

My parents worked in the industry for decades, and growing up, my sister and I always wanted to work in movies. While I was more of a behind-the-scenes type of girl, my sister enjoyed the spotlight, and she became one of the most beloved young actresses in Hollywood. At twenty-six years old, she was already a Golden Globe winner and an Oscar nominee.

The Golden Globes were one of my favorite awards shows.

I *loved* the atmosphere—it was always funnier and looser than the Oscars. The jokes were sharper, too, and usually included poking fun at the intoxicated attendees. I also loved the after-parties. I had gone to a couple of them in the past, thanks to my sister Amira, but this year I was attending with my boyfriend, Eric Oliveira.

The show we both worked on, which he co-created and co-wrote, was nominated for best comedy on TV. I was so proud of him. He had worked so hard to get there.

Hi, My Name is Georgia, was Eric's lovechild with actress Quinn Levy, and it had quickly become the darling of the critics. Ratings hadn't been great the first season, but thankfully the network had granted us a second chance.

Season two had been well reviewed so far, but once again, the declining ratings had brought us close to the brink of paranoia. We feared every day that the network would decide to pull the plug on us. Then, a month ago, we had woken up to the greatest news ever.

Georgia had not only been nominated for a Golden Globe for Best Comedy, but both the lead actor and actress had scored a nomination in their respective categories. Ratings started picking up, and even though the show was currently on Christmas break, our numbers on Hulu and Netflix were up as well. It seemed *Georgia* was finally getting the big break it deserved.

Quinn Levy played the part of the titular Georgia, on top of being the co-creator and co-writer of the show. Quinn was beautiful in that obnoxious typical Hollywood actress way—tall, skinny, blonde—but she had such a fantastic personality that it was basically impossible to hate her. She was funny, and she always had your back, a real team player. On set, she always tried to make everyone's job easier. In Hollywood, she was outspoken in the fight for women's equal pay.

If there was one thing she was *awful* at, however, it was *breaking.*

No matter how many times she rehearsed a scene, there would always be a moment, especially during late-night shoots, when she'd break out of character and start laughing while delivering the lines. She broke more than Jimmy Fallon on *Saturday Night Live*. One night, we had to shoot a scene almost a hundred and fifty times. Other than that, she was a peach. She was from Georgia, coincidentally, and she had the kindness and manners of a Southern belle.

She gave the funniest interviews, too—well, almost as funny as my sister's. No one beat my sister Amira—or Mira Farouk, as the world knew her—when it came to charming the press.

Quinn finished telling a joke from her early days as a stand-up comedian, and we all laughed. As they announced the beginning of the telecast, we all clinked our glasses and cheered. Eric hugged me and kissed my cheek.

"You look so damn sexy, Sam. I can't wait to fuck you out of that dress," he whispered in my ear, sending a shiver down my spine. Seven years as a couple—including two living together—and he still turned me on like the first day.

"You'll have to, since Amira's stylist sewed me into it," I replied seductively, looking up to him. His eyes went wide, and he replied with a deep hum as he scanned my body, which was wrapped in a tight red dress that exposed my back all the way down to my ass.

Eric and I had been together since one hot summer working on the same show seven years earlier. After resisting him for weeks, I had succumbed to his charm. To this day, our passion was incandescent. Everyone knew how fragile relationships were in Hollywood, and this was true for actors as well as people who didn't have a spotlight pointed at them at all times. Even my parents, after three children and many years of wedded bliss, had called it quits about ten years ago.

Fortunately, Eric and I were doing just fine. He was even more handsome after recently turning thirty. His hair was jet black, and his eyes were a beautiful emerald green. His skin was tanned, which added even more sex appeal to his whole persona. His parents were from Brazil and had immigrated to the US when he was a kid. When he was younger he was approached by a talent scout to do some modeling, but he turned it down. He could have probably been the male Gisele if he'd wanted to, but instead he decided to work in television. I gazed at his profile and he smirked when he caught me staring. I bit my lip in anticipation of what would happen later that night.

What seven-year itch? I was still completely smitten with him, and we were still having as much sex as we had when we started dating. We'd even manage to sneak around on the nights we worked late.

As a matter of fact, Eric seemed to be even more passionate as of late, maybe because things were going better with the show.

It was only a matter of time before he'd propose...at least I thought so.

I wasn't one of those women whose sole objective in life was to get married, but I loved my man and wanted to spend the rest of my life with him. I knew marriage was in the cards for us because he had been telling me so himself. He was the one to bring it up, explaining that he wanted to get married after he'd hit it big. He was ambitious and determined, and he knew it was just a matter of time before he would get to work on a hit show.

A win for *Georgia* would definitely secure his status, and maybe a ring on my finger, too.

A couple of awards and several drinks later, I waved at my sister from across the room as she walked back to her table after announcing the winner for Best Supporting Actor in a movie. She was sitting with the director and cast of her latest commercial success, *No Time Like the Present*. Amira and Ross David, the director of the movie, had become quite the dynamic duo in the movie industry. Ross called Mira his muse, purely because she was such a talented chameleon. In fact, Mira seemed to be able to slip into any role, no matter the challenge. I knew a lot of people in Hollywood speculated that Mira and Ross were a couple, but my sister assured me their relationship was purely professional; we didn't keep secrets between us. She was just three years younger than me and was my best friend. I knew there was nothing going on with the director, because I could always tell when she was lying. I didn't *really* have anything against Ross David—he was handsome and successful—but he was also fourteen years older than Mira. I wouldn't have wanted an old man dating my twenty-six-year-old sister, and our father wouldn't have either, that was for sure.

A few awards later, we all damned Gael Garcia-Bernal under our breath when Wilder Simmons, the male lead in *Georgia*, lost for Best Actor in a Television Series Comedy category—but only after making sure the cameras weren't pointed at our table. We all knew it was a long shot, and we were aware of how much buzz there was around *Mozart in the Jungle*. The Hollywood Foreign Press seemed to be completely smitten with it.

"I'm going to lose to Julia Louis-Dreyfus, I just know it," Quinn said as Seth Myers and Amy Poehler came out to introduce the Best Actress in a Television Series Comedy category. I saw her breathe nervously, and I wanted to hold her hand, but Eric was sitting by her and I couldn't reach her. We exchanged a look, and I gave her an encouraging smile. She nodded and smiled back, looking uneasy.

"And the Golden Globe for Best Actress goes to..." Seth Myers said.

"Quinn Levy for *Hi, My Name is Georgia*!" Amy Poehler yelled, and everyone at our table erupted into cheers and hugs, quickly stealing kisses from Quinn as she started making her way toward the stage from our table, which was way in the back.

We all listened to her speech with tears of joy in our eyes, and suddenly, the excitement in our hearts grew even bigger—maybe we had a chance to win Best Comedy, after all. I looked around at Eric and the cast and the producers sitting at the table; I knew we were all thinking the same thing, but no one wanted to jinx it.

When the time came, Eric held my hand in one hand and Quinn's hand in the other. When they announced the name of *our* show, Eric hugged Quinn first, leaving me dumbfounded for a second. Then he turned around, hugged me, and gave me a passionate, quick kiss before going with the cast and the producers up on stage. It was such an incredible moment, I felt overwhelmed with joy. I was smiling, but tears were coming down my cheeks, my heart drumming so loudly in my chest it almost overpowered the cheers and claps in the room.

Quinn was hilarious as she tried to thank everyone as fast as she could and then passed the microphone over to the producers of the show. They all tried to talk and give their speeches quickly because they knew the music was going to start any second.

Eric took over the microphone, and he looked so handsome and happy, it took my breath away. I loved him so much. He was brilliant and funny in his brief speech, thanking his parents and his teachers and everyone at the network that supported the show.

He didn't thank you.

Amira's text came through as soon as they started to leave the stage. She was right; he hadn't thanked me. The producers had made sure to say a quick thank you to their wives and children, but Eric said nothing about me. Sure, it stung a little, but it happened all the time.

Dude, remember when you forgot to thank your director?

Touché. Still, I don't see how I could forget my partner of the last SEVEN years.

Maybe he'll make it up to me. ;-)

I decided to forget about Eric's little mishap considering he didn't have much time left before the music started playing, and I went to stand outside the press room where they were giving interviews.

Best Comedy was one of the last awards, so everyone was about ready to get out of there and head to the Vanity Fair after-party.

I waited, leaning against a column because my shoes were already killing me.

Soon after, I saw everyone from *Georgia* walk by, but I couldn't spot Eric.

Or Quinn.

Maybe they were holding them back for another interview.

I looked around, trying to decide if I should go back to the table or not, and then I heard Quinn's laughter. I turned around, and that's when I saw him.

That's when I saw *them*.

And my whole world came crashing down.

A bullet to my chest would have hurt less, probably.

There was no way to explain how it felt seeing my boyfriend of seven years kiss his coworker, my boss.

A woman I thought of as a friend.

I hid behind the column as I spied on them...watched the love of my life capturing Quinn's mouth in a hungry kiss. He was holding her head just at the nape of her neck, and his other hand was looped around her waist. She raised her arms and wrapped them around his neck. It didn't even look like a first kiss; there was no hesitation. They looked too comfortable with each other's mouths for it to be the first time this had happened.

My eyes welled up with tears. My lips trembled. I was holding on to the column with my hands, feeling like my knees were going to give way at any moment.

I felt like sobbing, but somehow I managed to keep my mouth shut.

Don't move, I told myself. Then I got an idea.

Quinn caressed Eric's face, and then they kissed again.

I pulled out my phone and took as many pictures as I could.

They stopped kissing, and as Quinn fixed her hair and her dress, I hid behind the column. When I heard footsteps approaching me, I circled the column, trying to stay hidden. They laughed, walking back to the ballroom hand in hand.

My heart sank, and I finally let out the sob I had been holding in.

How long? How long had they been sneaking behind my back?

How long had Eric been cheating on me?

I started replaying the last few weeks, the last few months in my head, trying to remember a detail, a moment, or a situation when I should have been suspicious, when something strange should have tipped me off.

The late nights...but those were part of his job, always.

Writers always stayed up late writing scripts...and they weren't alone. *But they were together. Always together.*

I clutched my fists, and I ran as fast as I could in my high heels.

I locked myself in the nearest restroom, needing a moment to clear my head. I didn't know how I was going to face Eric again, but I couldn't confront him right then.

Not here. Not tonight.

I leaned my forehead against the door and took a deep breath as the tears kept coming down, falling everywhere: my cheeks, my chest, my dress.

Where are you?

The fucker texted me. I scoffed. Even seeing his name on the screen of the phone repulsed me. It's funny how quickly your perception of people can change. I didn't want to be anywhere near him, but I couldn't tell him what I'd seen—not yet.

Maybe not ever.

I looked at the photos of him and Quinn on my phone, and I could barely make out who was in the picture. Anyone who knew them could probably identify their silhouettes, but not everyone would recognize them. I exhaled, disappointed and angry. My evidence was crap. Then, an idea popped in my head.

It sounded dangerous and crazy, but oh so appealing. I could already feel it on the tip of my tongue—the sweet taste of revenge.

I sniffled and typed a quick text.

I'm in the restroom. I'll be right out.

Hurry. The broadcast is over. We're about to

leave.

I opened the door of the bathroom stall, looked at my tear-stained face in the mirror, and turned the faucet on to fix my makeup. I had left my clutch behind, like the idiot I was. Just as I finished cleaning up my tears, a crowd of cheerful, intoxicated women swarmed the place, and I headed back to our table. The ballroom was half empty, the remaining people scattered around the space, chatting and catching up.

Eric stood alone by our table, and as I walked in his direction, he turned around, as if he sensed me coming. He smiled warmly at me, holding up my clutch in his hand, and a bright smile stretched across his face. It felt like a blade cutting through my skin.

Liar. Liar. Liar.

I tried to reciprocate his smile, but my facial muscles felt stiff, as if I had just gotten Botox. I had to force myself to smile wider.

He handed me my clutch, and as I got closer, he placed a small kiss on my lips.

Judas kiss.

You're a pig, Eric. You're a fucking bastard. You're a liar. I'm done being your fool.

"Don't you have anything to say?" he asked with a smirk.

"What do you mean?" I said, confused.

"Sam, we won! A fucking Golden Globe! We've done it. The show won't get cancelled now."

Duh, of course that's what he meant.

"Yes! I'm so happy, honey. I'm so proud of you," I told him, caressing his face just as Quinn had done a moment before. I tried to smile again, but it felt like I was grimacing. Eric didn't seem to notice, just ran his fingers through my long dark hair and pressed his body against mine, giving me another kiss.

With tongue this time.

I closed my eyes, repulsed by his touch. I wanted to gag, but I couldn't let him know anything was wrong. I couldn't let him know *I knew*.

Still, I couldn't respond to his kiss as eagerly as I usually would.

Suddenly, he stopped.

"Babe, are you okay?" Eric asked, his brows furrowed, showing concern. *Fucker.*

I swallowed and shook my head. "I'm fine."

He tipped my chin up and studied my face.

"You look like you've been crying."

"Well, it's been an eventful evening, and I was so happy when we won, I couldn't stop the tears," I said, running a finger under my eyes, cleaning up the last few smudges of makeup. I sniffled. In that moment, he looked worried, handsome, attentive. In that moment, he was the perfect boyfriend—but in reality, he was a liar. He was a cheater. I wanted to scream in his face. I wanted him to pay. I wanted him to suffer. How could he do this to me? How could he cheat on me on a night like this? How long had he been doing it behind my back?

"Are you sure you're okay?"

"Yes, I swear I am! It's just...I'm a little drunk, and my emotions are all over the place."

"Yeah. Me, too," he said with a dreamy look, hugging me closer to him and grabbing a handful of my ass.

Fuck you. And fuck Quinn.

I wasn't going to go down quietly.

I was going to take everyone down with me.

"Ready to go?" he asked, and I nodded, a million different thoughts and scenarios running through my head.

Don't make rash decisions. As much as causing a

scene at the after-party sounds like a good idea, you're just going to end up looking like the crazy girlfriend.

Take your time.

What do they say about revenge?

It's a dish best served cold.

Eric held my hand as we walked out of the ballroom toward the valet. We waited outside the Beverly Hilton and then got in a car to head to the Vanity Fair party. Eric was busy checking his phone, and as I stared at him, so careless and oblivious, I felt sick.

My stomach was churning. We hadn't had anything to eat, and then I'd downed at least five glasses of champagne. I was lightheaded. I wanted to scream at Eric, sitting next to me as if nothing had happened, as if he hadn't just been kissing another woman half an hour ago. His eyes met mine, and I wanted to cry and let my disappointment spill everywhere. Instead, I looked away.

"Sam, what's wrong?"

"I don't feel good. I think I might need to go home." I couldn't bear the idea of partying with *him* and everyone else, having to pretend I was happy for all of us. I didn't want to be around Quinn and act like we were friends.

He scoffed at my words. "Sam, come on. You'll feel better later. How can you bail now? I thought you wanted to go to this party..." He searched my eyes but I looked away. He was right. I had wanted to go to the party.

Not anymore.

"I don't want to bring morale down, and I don't want to end up getting sick while I'm there. I know I'll be better off if I go home." He rolled his eyes and ran one of his hands through his hair, frustrated.

"What's gotten into you?" he asked, and for a moment, his eyes looked fearful, as if he knew I knew. Then, as the car stopped, he changed expression. He turned on the light and tipped my chin up, examining my face.

"You know, you do look a little pale. Maybe you're right. Maybe it's better you call it a night." *Right. This way, you'll be able to sneak around with your mistress.* He gave me a peck on the lips and another one on my forehead. I wanted to cry. I wanted all of it to be a bad dream. I wanted to wake up next to him as if nothing had happened.

I wanted to be able to love him and trust him again, trust him like I had just an hour before. He said good-bye, and as he left the car, I felt as if I had lost a part of myself. I felt as if a huge part of my life was suddenly over.

On the ride home, my feelings alternated between anger and sadness as the driver tried to make small talk. I replied to him absentmindedly, unable to think of anything but the scene of betrayal I'd just witnessed. I was heartbroken, but I knew I wasn't letting Eric Oliveira walk away unscathed. I got a text from my sister.

Where are you?

Not feeling good. Too much bubbly. On my way home.

What? That's a bunch of bullshit. You were so looking forward to this.

I overdid it with the champagne. Why does no one tell you you have to skip the red carpet to get served dinner in there?

I know. I've made the same mistake before, trust me.

I told Amira goodnight, but I knew I wasn't going to be

able to hide this from her. She could always read me like an open book, and my mother could, too. She was going to know something was up.

I needed to talk to her.

I called her and she answered after a couple rings.

"Mom, I need your help."

That night, I resisted the urge to break everything Eric owned or was sentimentally attached to. I resisted the impulse to set the house on fire. The fabric of the train of my designer gown rustled on the smooth floor as I paced the living room, trying to calm myself down and decide what I needed to do. I managed to get myself out of the dress and get ready for bed, never turning the lights on, enjoying the quiet, and I went to bed with tears streaming silently down my cheeks. I closed my eyes but couldn't sleep, so I lay under the sheets, naked, plotting my revenge.

Chapter 2

SAM

August

"It's so beautiful, Mom." I pointed the camera of my phone to the scenery in front of me.

"I can see that. It's just as stunning as you see on TV. So green."

"It's almost too much to take in all at once."

Scotland was intimidating in a mysterious kind of way. California was what I had known all my life, and I'd barely even spent any time around the United States. Save a few times in London with my father and my siblings to visit my grandparents, I hadn't been anywhere else in the world. Scotland was as foreign and new as it could get, but now, it was going to be my home for the next eight months. I switched the camera back to me.

"Have you met any of your coworkers?"

"Not yet, just one of Mira's friends, Lainey. She picked me up at the airport and took me to my place. I have a roommate, but I haven't met her yet. Some of the crew was out bonding last night. I missed it."

"Oh, well. You'll have time to get to know them. You're lucky you got this gig at the last minute."

"Yeah, I know."

"Samhain, everything will be fine. You're a talented makeup artist. You know you got this job because of your extensive resume and not just because of a phone call."

If you say so, I wanted to tell her, but I just nodded. I hoped my mother couldn't tell how scared I was. I knew I was overreacting—I was twenty-nine-years-old, for crying out loud. I was acting like a kid leaving for college, but this actually was my first time away from home, away from my family, my friends...my sister, my brother. I was going to miss them so much.

"Maybe I'll come visit you," my mother said. "I heard the male lead on this production is quite the hunk," she joked. I saw her wink through the screen, and just like that, she brought the smile back to my face and washed away my fears. I laughed and rolled my eyes.

"Mom!"

"What? I might be old, but I'm not dead. I can appreciate a handsome man when I see one." She shrugged. "Who knows, maybe you'll meet someone cute."

"I don't think so. My goal is to lay low for a while. Love only leads to drama." I knew that all too well.

"Oh, honey...I'm not talking about love—"

Oh, Jesus.

"Mom, come on."

"No, Sam, let me say what I have to say. Sweetheart, you're still young. Have your fun while you can. You know that's why I never liked the fact that you and Eric got so hot and heavy when you were just twenty-two. You spent your best years with a man who didn't deserve you."

I nodded and pressed my lips into a tight smile. She was right, of course—as was everyone else with their *I-told-you-so's*. I was the fool who had loved him blindly for too long, getting nothing in return. I had gotten my revenge on the cheating bastard, but it had kind of backfired in a way I hadn't expected. Now, for the next eight months, I would have to call Scotland my home.

I heard footsteps coming from behind me, and I turned around.

The hill I had *attempted* to climb was deserted. I was alone. In that moment, it dawned on me that maybe this hadn't been the smartest decision. I shouldn't have ventured out by myself; I was in a foreign country, and I didn't know anyone.

But the scenery had been so inviting.

I barely detected my mother saying, "What is it, honey?" I was too focused on the noise. A moment later, a tall guy in a baseball cap and athletic gear reached the small, flat spot where I had been chatting with my mom. He was wearing a windbreaker and shorts.

Shorts! I was huddled in a knee-length puffer jacket, and just the sight of him in shorts made me shiver. He lifted his head and the sight of his ice-blue eyes made me shiver again. He looked at me for just a second, nodding his head in my direction.

"Hello," he said in a deep, uber-manly voice, one of those that could make you swoon even saying the most boring and generic stuff. *He had me at hello.*

"Hi," I replied, frozen.

His eyes shifted to the phone in my hand. My mother kept calling my name from her office in Los Angeles. The stranger stared at me for another second, and then he gave an imperceptible shake of his head. The corner of his lips curled into a smile.

Ugh. Fucking embarrassing. I had been caught FaceTiming with my mom. This would be a really good time to lose reception, but noooo. My mother kept calling out to me, but I was sort of frozen on the spot, staring at the handsome stranger.

Yes, handsome. I stared at him all of five seconds, but that was enough to see his face—and what a face it was. He had the most perfect features: straight nose, strong jaw, high cheekbones. His eyes were sharp blue and gorgeous, and with just one look, they were melting my insides.

"Samhain! Are you okay, honey? What's wrong?"

"Mom, hang on a sec," I said, completely distracted by the vision in front of me.

He quickly walked past me and kept climbing up the steep slope, making it look so effortless.

"What is it, honey?" my mother asked again.

"Nothing, Mom. Just some mountain climber," I said in a lower tone, raising my eyebrows, hoping the stranger wouldn't hear me. He kept moving just as steadily as he had a moment before. He had to be a *pro*—he moved way too quickly to be a regular person. I was a fan of hikes, but my expertise was limited to canyons in the valley. This California girl was no match for real mountains like the peaks of Scotland. I had been out of breath in minutes. It must have been the altitude or perhaps the fact that my body was not made for strenuous exercise, no matter how hard I tried. I might not have had a lot of time to look at the stranger, but since I got to stare at his back for a little bit, I knew the rest of his body was as good-looking as his face. He had broad shoulders and muscular, lean legs—no wonder he made it look so damn easy, effortless even. His thin shorts revealed the curve of his ass and that alone was...*spectacular*.

I sighed. It had been too long, what felt like forever since I'd lusted after a guy. I guess I wasn't broken after all. *Good to know*. If I had more stamina and no shame, I would have followed him up the mountain. I would have committed to following that ass anywhere.

"Mom, I have to go. I need to get back to the townhouses. Maybe I can catch my roommate before my orientation."

"All right, honey. Text me, okay?"

My phone buzzed in my pocket as soon as I hung up the phone. It was my sister Amira. To the world, she might have been the talented Golden Globe and Oscar nominee Mira Farouk, but to me, she was just my little sister. She was only three years younger than me, but I had always been very protective of her, even more so since she decided at a young age that she was going to become an actress.

Did you find JAMMF yet?

WHO?

Jamie Alexander Malcom MacKenzie Fraser. Good heavens. How many times do I have to tell you, Sam? You really need to meet Jamie motherfucking Fraser.

Are we still talking about this? He's a FICTIONAL CHARACTER, Mira.

He is real! He must be. There must be a modern version of Jamie Fraser up there in Scotland.

Again, he is fictional, straight out of the mind of a very brilliant woman. That doesn't make him more real.

Book boyfriends are REAL, Samhain!

She typed, adding a slew of emoticons.

Mira, are you high?

Maybe. ;-) But, seriously! Why have you not read the books I sent to your tablet? How can you call yourself my sister?
You know primetime TV has a grueling schedule, and in the last few months, I couldn't bring myself to do anything.

I had been too busy vegging out on her couch.

You'll change your mind once you read the books! And then you'll realize how stubborn you've been all along. It's not fair that you're the

one who gets to go to Scotland!

Right. Lucky me. I would rather be in LA, working, possibly.
Not that I'm not thankful you got me this job. It's just...lots of changes.

Sam, I'm sorry...I didn't mean it that way. I'm sure you're going to have a lovely time. Annndd, I saw the pic of the male lead on this production. He is HOT!

God bless. Why had I not Googled the guy? First, my mother, and now my sister. Now that I thought about it, I was pretty sure even Lainey had made some comment about him. There I was and I hadn't even bothered to check him out. Truth be told, I had been busy the last few days, getting ready to leave on a moment's notice.

Okay, Mira. Calm down, all right? I promise to text back as soon as I find JAMMF.

I added a winky and a kissy emoticon and put the phone back in my pocket. A gust of wind blew through me, making me shiver inside my parka, and I shook as I tried to put my gloves back on. It was only August for crying out loud, and it was already cold. The next few months were going to suck.

Hugh

I felt as if I had been holding my breath for weeks, months even—probably ever since I had been cast as Abarath. Now that I was in St. Martin, I felt like I could exhale again. I hadn't been back there since I was a kid.

Scotland was my home. It was the place where I grew up, the place in the world I loved the most. Being in the mountains was one of the great things about working on this project, and I finally felt I was in my element.

Even as I climbed up higher and the altitude started affecting my lungs, I finally felt at peace.

For months, I had been afraid the project would fall through, scared the investors would back out. It had happened so many times before. I would get a part, one that was sure to help me getting noticed, and it never failed: either the show/movie/play got cancelled altogether or it didn't make as big of an impact as predicted.

I had almost given up on the idea of ever becoming a successful actor.

Year after year, I had been scrambling, jumping from gig to gig. A lot of times, I had to swallow my pride and take whatever was available just to keep going, to keep working. I had been in the business for a while, and yet, I could hardly make a living in my profession. It had been ten years since I had graduated from the Royal Scottish Academy. After that, I had also studied in London, auditioning for a few parts here and there. I had small arcs on soap operas, but there never seemed to be the right role for me, one where I could showcase my abilities. I was always told I was too tall, that I was too built to play a young boy and was too inexperienced to be cast as a leading man. I even spent a year in Los Angeles, vying for pilot season, but nothing good ever came along, and after a while, I had to make the decision to go back home.

In the end, it was better working on soap operas than nothing at all.

When I decided to start acting, I knew what I was signing up for. I was aware that this job was not going be easy, but I also knew that giving up on my dream would be the equivalent of giving up a part of my soul. There was nothing I liked more than being on a stage or in front of a camera.

Maybe one of these days I was going to make it. I knew I just had to stick with it and persevere. I had to remind myself that so many actors get their big break later in life. Sometimes, when I'd feel down about myself, I would resort to listing the names of all the actors that made it big after decades of being in the business. If they had done it, I could do it, too. I just needed to keep at it and work harder.

I couldn't allow myself to get distracted by anything else.

My craft was my only focus. Maybe one day I would get the role of a lifetime, like Jon Hamm in *Mad Men* or Christoph Waltz in *Inglourious Basterds*.

Giving up on acting was not an option.

When *Abarath*'s producers told me I got the role, I was elated—at first.

Then anxiety got the upper hand, crippling me with fear. I worried that the series would never happen, feared that production would halt before we even started shooting and the show would never see the light of day. For a while, the show did stall, struggling to get green-lighted. It was an ambitious project, and funding was crucial. So, as months went by, the tightness in my chest caused by stress and anxiety became more pronounced.

But now it was finally becoming a reality. I couldn't believe I was actually visiting the sets that were getting built and training for my role. What was even more exciting was that in less than two weeks, I would start shooting.

I was ready to show the world what Hugh MacLeod was capable of.

Chapter 3

SAM

After a while, I finally made it back to the townhouses the cast and staff were occupying. I had gotten there at the very last minute and had missed days and days of preparation and whatever bonding experience they might have had going on the night before. I was going to be the new kid from a block far, far away, and I was terribly nervous about screwing it up.

I hadn't worked since I had basically walked out from my last job and the scandal had broken. After that, I couldn't find another one.

For months.

Eric had told me he would make it hard for me to find a job, and he had kept his promise.

Asshole.

My career, at least for the moment, was going absolutely nowhere. My reputation was *ruined.* I had wanted my revenge, but now I was paying the price, and I'd had to resort to using my sister as a connection to get this job. I knew I had gotten lucky, but part of me still wished I could be in Los Angeles.

My parents had been in the business since the late '70s. My mother was a screenwriter before she sold her soul to *Gossip Gods* in exchange for a big, fat salary. My father was a cameraman, and he still loved his job as much as he had on his first day. I knew that because every time I asked him when he would retire, he'd tell me he didn't want to because he loved what he did so much. He used to work on movie sets a lot when I was little, but in the last decade he'd started working exclusively on TV dramas. He said he didn't mind the long hours, and he enjoyed that he got some of the summer off. That way, he always had time to travel a little bit and visit his family. I wished he'd done that when we were younger, because then me and my siblings would have had more chances to spend time with my grandma, who lived in London.

While my mother's family was originally from California, my father had moved to LA from London in 1976. His family had moved to the UK from Pakistan as refugees around 1965. I remembered him telling me how hard it was for both him and his family to start over. Even though Pakistan was a member of the British Commonwealth, there were so many challenges to face, the language being one of them. Although the first few years were tough, my father always told me how once he felt he had a better knowledge of the English language, he loved almost every minute of living in the United Kingdom. He had opportunities he never could have dreamed of if his family had stayed in Pakistan.

He started working right out of high school, and somehow he ended up at a TV station. He worked his way up from the mailroom, and in a few years' time, he found himself behind the camera. My father could go on and on about how much he loved movies and TV. He could remember hundreds of movie titles and knew all the names of the directors and actors. When Amira and I were little, we'd love to quiz him. We would browse through the TV channels and ask him all kinds of questions. He would hardly ever miss—the man was like a walking IMDB before the site was even created.

My father loved cinema so much, sometimes I was surprised he never tried to push his passion further. I often wondered why he'd never tried to direct or write anything. He and my mother could have even worked together on a project. They would have made a great team. Between the two of them, they had plenty of knowledge and connections.

Years later, I asked him why he never tried his hand at directing, and this was what he told me.

"Sam, directing is a little bit like storytelling. You need to know and feel the story you want to bring to the screen. You need to have a vision. I never felt I had a story to tell. I love to capture the scene, but I never felt the need or instinct to tell my version of it."

My mother, on the other hand, was completely in love with storytelling. She *lived* to write stories. I could still remember how excited she would get when she came up with an idea and started brainstorming. Sometimes, she would talk out loud in the car while driving around LA with Amira and me in the backseat, telling us the story as she made it up. But, bringing a script to life is much harder than just writing it. My mother was a gifted storyteller, but over the years, she lost her patience with the industry, and she got sick of Hollywood politics. At her house, she had a bookshelf full of scripts that never made it past a pre-production stage. She once told me that just twenty percent of what she wrote during her career as a screenwriter made it to film.

It was a pity to see how disenchanted she'd become over the years. So, when the opportunity came around to do something different, she took it. She started writing for scripted talk shows, and eventually, ended up with *Gossip Gods* right before the boom of Internet gossip sites. She was now in charge of their whole social media department. *Gossip Gods* was one of the "friendlier" gossip sites. Its content and articles were edgier than E!, but not as ruthless as TMZ.

Once Amira and I started working in the business, it became rather useful having someone "on the inside". My mother would tell us which places we should avoid if we were looking for a quiet night out and which places we should go to if we wanted to be seen. As far as I was concerned, I never wanted to be seen by anyone. I was—and still am—a quiet and reserved person who happens to work in Hollywood. However, in order for Amira's career to take off, it was helpful to be seen out and about, so a lot of times I would accompany her. It was thanks to some of the photos that circulated after one of our outings that I'd caught the eye of the only man I had ever loved.

I still remembered the first time Eric asked me out; it was also the first time I turned him down—the first of many. It was the summer after I graduated college and I had just gotten my first internship on a new small-budget series.

I was one of the makeup artists, and Eric was one of the writers.

Well, he liked to think of himself as one of the writers.

He was really more of an intern. They used him for all kinds of errands, and of course, they hardly used his suggestions or his knack for editing, no matter how much he tried to prove himself.

But, he didn't let any of that keep him down. Eric was driven, and he was as ambitious as he was handsome.

He was tall and lean with jet-black hair. He had bright, piercing green eyes that looked even brighter against his tan skin. He wanted to be a writer, yet his demeanor made him look like a bad boy instead of a nerd. His mouth was full and his lips were so defined, they looked as if they had been traced with a pencil. I tried to convince myself I noticed every detail of his features because it was my job, but it didn't work. The truth was that I had dreamed of kissing him long before he looked my way. It was true that I had noticed him before he "saw" me, but, unlike my sister, I was very shy.

A few weeks into my internship, some pictures of Amira and me were published on the US Weekly website. Pretty soon, everyone on the lot knew I was the sister of Mira Farouk.

Amira was just an emerging actress then, but her role in a gritty indie movie had created a lot of buzz. People were talking about her fantastic performance, and as proud as I was of her accomplishments, I was a bit uncomfortable with being put on the spot and being asked about her.

One day, Eric and I started talking outside the lot during a break. At first, I thought he wanted me to introduce him to Amira, but then he said he'd seen my photo in the magazine and told me how beautiful I'd looked—the night the pictures were taken, I had worn a skimpy outfit and a lot more makeup than I did when I was at work—and then he asked me out.

As flattered as I was, I was more concerned with doing

a good job and possibly get hired permanently, so even though I truly lusted for Eric, I turned him down.

For weeks.

He took it as a challenge. He could tell I liked him, so he made it his mission to convince me we should be together. After weeks and weeks of relentless flirting—and after I got hired to be the makeup artist on a different production that would start shooting in the fall—I caved in and said yes.

By the end of the summer, Eric and I had had sex all over Lot B.

Every corner, every closet. Even on the back of a golf cart.

We had sex breaks like some people had smoke breaks.

It was just the beginning of a mutual, unhealthy addiction that would last for several years.

Until he decided to cheat on me.

"There you are!" said a short blond girl with an adorable pixie cut and a thick British accent as I opened the door of our townhouse. "I am so sorry I missed you last night. I was looking forward to meeting you!" She came toward me and pulled me into a hug. I froze for a second, but then I managed to move my arms and hug her back.

"My name is Cecilia! And you must be Sam?"

"Y-yes. I'm Sam. Nice to meet you, Cecilia. Are you a makeup artist, too?"

"Yes, I am. Bloody hell, your skin is gorgeous. And your eyes, too! Oh, my gosh, your eyelashes are so long! Are they fake? We need to trade beauty secrets...wait! Do you use Botox?"

"No," I said with a laugh. "I want to keep my face intact for as long as I can afford it. Besides, it's not like I have to be in front of a camera."

"Well said! You were working in Hollywood, right? I always wanted to visit and maybe even work there," she said excitedly, clapping her hands together.

"Oh, well, it's not all it's cracked up to be, you know..."

"Nonsense! It's got to be far better than working in Borehamwood," she said. I stared at her in confusion, and then she added, "Borehamwood is the name of the studios where I worked. Just outside of London. Not quite Hollywood."

"Ahhh! I see. But, wait...that's where they shot *Star Wars*. And *Raiders of the Lost Ark*! It can't be that bad."

"Oh, look at you, so well informed! Well, I worked on TV sets and it was a real bore. Nothing exciting ever happens. I got so sick of it, I applied for every job with every production outside of London. Have you seen this place? Isn't it bonkers?"

"It's...beautiful," I admitted.

"It's *magical*," she said with a tone a Disney princess would use in a movie, excitement making her blue eyes shine brighter. "I cannot wait to learn some of their old legends. I can't believe I had never been farther north than Edinburgh. Silly me! Have you ever been to Scotland, Sam?"

"I haven't. This is my first time here, but I have been to London. My father's family moved to the UK years ago, and I visited my grandparents a few times before they passed."

"No way! I want to hear everything—but not now, because we have an orientation to be at in half an hour!"

"It's only a matter of time before everyone will forget about all these stupid rules—except for the non-disclosure agreement." Cecilia pouted, flipping through the pages of our massive orientation packet.

"What do you mean?" I whispered, brows furrowing. I didn't understand why they would put us through hours of this if it didn't matter.

"I mean, sure, they have to tell you about the sexual harassment rules and what will happen if you transgress, but pretty soon everyone will start getting busy around here, if you get my gist." She winked and then gave me a coy smile. "For example, I already have my eyes set on someone." She pointed her chin in the direction of a handsome guy with broad shoulders and tanned skin sitting on our right side. I could see just his profile from where I was sitting. His hair was as dark as mine, and his profile was gorgeous—straight nose, high cheekbones, and a strong jaw with a delicious hint of stubble.

Not bad at all. *Well done, Cecilia*, I thought, but then I worried about all the *rules* they had been dropping on us.

"Are you serious? What about the rules? I'm pretty sure it said somewhere that *fraternizing* was frowned upon."

She dismissed it with a wave of her hand. "I mean, I get that they want us to keep our mouths shut about production and the plot of the show and how it differs from the books, but see, my dear Sam, sooner or later we're going to get bored. We're going to be holed up here for months. It's only a matter of time before people start hooking up left, right and centre. They can't expect us to keep our mouths shut *and* our hands to ourselves," she said with a mischievous wink.

"Will people really do that?"

She looked at me in confusion. “Have you never worked on location?”

“No, not really. I’ve always been in LA.”

“Excuse me, are you trying to say crew members don’t hook up in LA? I’m not going to believe that.” She stifled a laugh.

Well, she was right, after all. I laughed, somehow embarrassed by my own faux pas. “Of course they do.” *Too much, too often.* “But I guess it’s different, you know? When you get off work, you go home...to your family, significant other, and so on.” *Or you stay at work and cheat on your girlfriend.* On second thought, I guess the situation wasn’t that much different. I was the one who had been too naïve.

“Well, here you’re far away from your family and friends. The staff is bound to become your family, unless you’re a hermit and you’re fine with being on your own all the time. And I don’t know about you—oh, wait! Do you have a boyfriend?”

“No.” My response came with an involuntary sigh, but thankfully, my colleague didn’t catch it.

“Neither do I! This is bloody perfect.”

“How so?”

“Well, because we will be the two single gals looking for some fun! It’ll be great.”

“I’m not so sure about that.”

“Oh, please! Don’t be so bloody chicken. Do you not fancy boys? Is that what it is?” I looked at her, frowning, and she suddenly looked so sorry, as if she had committed a terrible offense. “Oh, I’m so terribly sorry. I’m so insensitive. Here I am, talking about my fondness for cock and how we should make plans to score some and you—” I stopped her right then and held her wrist to get her attention.

"Cecilia, stop. I fancy cock...very much," I told her, a laugh escaping my lips.

She laughed, too, but unfortunately our giggling didn't go unnoticed. Suddenly, everyone was looking at us, including the lady who was leading the orientation, and she was saying or asking something...while looking directly at us. *Dammit.*

We both apologized and remained quiet. Cecilia's alabaster skin turned a bright red, while I was somewhat able to hide my own embarrassment.

"Now, if you two young ladies are done interrupting the orientation, I would like to encourage you to read the paragraph at the bottom of page forty-five..."

As the woman resumed her lecture, I glanced at Cecilia, who was pretending to read her booklet.

"Sorry, Cece. I don't want to get us into trouble."

"Cece, hey? You've already given me a nickname. We so are going to be best mates!" She winked then glanced at me and smiled mischievously. "You can make up for it by getting us into some trouble once we're out of here." I frowned, not quite getting what she meant.

"There's a guy staring at you. Two rows over, ten o'clock," she whispered in my ear. A moment later, I raised my eyes and noticed a handsome guy looking my way.

He had short brown hair and big, beautiful brown eyes. As his stare turned into a smile, my breath hitched—he had the most perfect smile I had ever seen. He had the smile of an actor, so what was he doing at a staff orientation? I smiled back instinctively, thinking about Cecilia's words.

Maybe she was right. Maybe soon everyone would start hooking up.

In that case, I wouldn't mind messing around with Mr. Perfect Smile.

Chapter 4

SAM

After another hour and a half, our orientation was finally over. My brain was fried from information overload, and I couldn't wait to go back to the townhouse.

Cecilia, however, had other plans.

"That's it! We're going to the pub for a pint! You need to come! You didn't get to meet anyone last night."

"Yes, because I got into town very late, which also means I am severely jet-lagged."

"That's such bollocks! One hour and a pint of beer are not going to make you feel any worse tomorrow. I'll make sure you go straight to bed as soon as we get back home."

"Fine! One beer!" I exhaled, and at the same time she elbowed me.

"Oh, look. It's the handsome stranger from the presentation."

"Ouch!"

"Oh, come on, Sam! I didn't hurt you, did I?"

"Did you? You just elbow—"

"Hi. Cecilia, right?" the handsome brown-haired guy asked my petite but very strong friend.

"Yes, it's me. Did we meet last night? Sorry, I was sloshed and I could hardly remember my own name."

Mr. Perfect Smile laughed, and now that we were up close, I noticed how beautiful his skin was. I blamed it on my job—it made me notice all the details of a person's face right away. He laughed nervously at Cecilia's words and kept glancing my way.

"No, actually, we didn't get introduced, but everyone was chanting your name..."

"Ohmygod! How embarrassing!" Cecilia cried, covering her face with her hands for just a second. She acted as if she was embarrassed, but I didn't quite believe it. She simply didn't seem the type.

"Well, anyway, my name is Jake." He stretched out his hand and she shook it. Jake turned my way and I stretched out my hand.

"Hi, I'm Sam."

"Samantha?" he asked, a charming smile stretching across his face.

"Just Sam," I replied. My name was too long of a story to get into. *Thanks, Mom.* Sometimes I wished I could switch with Amira. Sure, it was still an ethnic name, but I always felt it would have suited me better than my sister, especially with my hair and skin tone.

"Are you guys going to the pub?" Jake asked.

"Sure we are! Let's go!" Cecilia exclaimed excitedly, turning around to wink at me. I rolled my eyes and hoped it was just going to be one pint as she'd promised.

Cecilia told me that St. Martin, the town where we were staying, was an old fisherman's village on the East coast of Scotland and had been a ghost town for years. Locals had moved to bigger cities over the last thirty years, and the town was mainly rented by movie companies. She said that the staff of *Game of Thrones* had stayed in the townhouses we were occupying during season two and part of season three. The locals understandably loved the influx of cash big production brought in, and they were very welcoming of the casts and crews. It was a nice change of pace for the usually quiet town.

As a huge group of us left the building—an old movie theater that had been converted and was being used for the town's assemblies—I took in the atmosphere around us. It was so cheerful, it looked as if school had let out for the year. There was palpable excitement and joy, and everyone had big, happy smiles on their faces.

It finally hit me.

Working on this show was a big deal—a *huge* deal. First of all, it was a co-production between the US and the UK, and according to the projections, the show was going to be a hit. It was a mix of fantasy, romance, and adventure. The main hero was a warrior, a dragon slayer, and, from what I'd read, a bit of a Casanova. I was still working my way through book one. If shows like *Game of Thrones* and *Outlander* were any indication, this was going to be a worldwide phenomenon. The fans of the books were hardcore about the series, and according to what everyone kept telling me, the actor cast in the main role was hot as hell. I still hadn't Googled him since my cellphone reception was spotty at best—though, surprisingly, it had worked when I was FaceTiming with my mom. Anyway, as I slowly started pulling my head out of my own ass, I realized how lucky I was to be there. In Scotland.

Working on a mega production.

Which had been my dream before I'd gotten "stuck" working on primetime TV.

Before I graduated, my dream had been to work on movie sets. In fact, my degree was in prosthetics and special effects.

But then when Eric and I got together and got serious so fast, it was hard to stay away from Los Angeles. A year into our relationship, I had the chance to go work on a movie set in Morocco. Like the fool I was, I turned it down. I wanted to go, but I didn't want to leave Eric. It didn't help that he begged me to stay, and I decided to turn the opportunity down. So stupid. For a while, I used my degree and worked on special effects in California, but when other states started offering big tax breaks, a lot of productions moved elsewhere, and I started missing out on a lot of good opportunities.

Going away to shoot on location wasn't what I wanted anymore, and it didn't help that Eric guilted me into staying. We were crazy about each other, and because I was young and stupid, I refused to listen to anyone who told me to put my career first.

When Eric got his own show, it seemed only logical to start working with him, so we'd be on the same set. *Hi, My Name is Georgia* was about a quirky woman in her mid-thirties who shares an apartment with two guys, and after a one-night stand gone awry, she finds out she's pregnant. Besides a couple scenes with a pregnant belly here and there, there was not a lot of room for special effects. I missed working on what I thought had been my strongest asset, but I loved being close to my man, supporting him and sharing everything with him. Eric kept telling me he wanted to get married, and that once he had a well-received show under his belt, we would eventually move in that direction. When the show was nominated for three Golden Globes, we all cheered and felt so relieved, and I hoped that soon enough he'd propose and put a ring on it—but then he had to go and ruin everything.

Fucking bastard.

I clenched my fists thinking about how much I still wanted to punch that lying, cheating motherfucker while I walked behind Cecilia and a few other members of the staff.

She turned around and looked at me, eyes wide.

"What's with the murderous look, love?"

"Nothing...I was just thinking about my ex-boyfriend."

"Ahhh. Lying sack of shit, hey?"

"How did you know?" I asked her with a smile.

"Aren't they all? Fucking bastards—well, at least most of them. Did you give him a good bollocking?"

"A good *what?*"

"Did you make the bastard pay?"

"Oh, yes. I made him pay, all right."

A smile stretched across her face, and it made her blue eyes light up even more.

"Come on," she said in a cheerful tone. "Let's go get a drink and forget all about your wanker ex-boyfriend."

We spent the night with many of our coworkers and even met the senior makeup artists, Margaret and Blair, who were in charge of the male and female leads. Blair was a spitfire brunette with an amber complexion, while Margaret was tall, blond, and skinny...with a visible baby bump.

"I've been attached to this project for a while, and my husband and I had kind of given up on the idea of getting pregnant," she admitted. "I didn't think it was ever going to happen...but then it did."

"How far along are you?" Cecilia asked. Margaret had to be at least five months, and shooting was scheduled to require eight months with just a short holiday break in the middle.

"I'm twenty-four weeks along. I know what you're thinking: how is this going to work? I already talked to production and they will have one of the other makeup artists fill in for me when the time comes. We'll have to talk it out with the team and see who's the best fit to substitute for me. It might even be one of you guys."

That sounded like a great opportunity, but I wasn't that interested in having more responsibilities on set. I was just trying to cruise through the next few months without any accidents. After a while, we said good-bye to Margaret and Blair. Thankfully, I was able to drag Cecilia out of the pub before she ordered her third pint.

We said good-bye to the rest of our team, knowing we had several long meetings about our schedules and assignments the next day. Before we left, the key makeup artist, Gertie, said something about "assessing our skills" in the next few days, whatever *that* meant. Was there going to be a test? Were they going to make us compete and see who was the best? I hated competition. I was good at what I did, but I wasn't looking forward to being put up against any of my colleagues. I didn't have a competitive bone in my body. Maybe if I did, I would have tried to win Eric back—not that the fucker deserved it.

As Cecilia and I walked back to our place, I noticed a tall man with broad shoulders walk down the street. He was wearing a jacket that looked just like the one the guy I'd seen up on the mountains earlier in the morning had worn.

I wondered if he was the same guy, and I grimaced,

remembering how I had looked like a complete fool. Was he a local? Did he live here? Or was he here with our production? He hadn't been at the orientation with the rest of us.

Did that mean he was one of the actors?

I hoped I would find out soon.

Chapter 5

SAM

I woke up before my alarm that morning.

That didn't happen very often; usually, I loved to sleep in. I could only remember waking up early when I was about to start a new job.

I was nervous.

I was afraid to fail. Margaret and Gertie's words had gotten me worried. I was afraid I wasn't good enough after all, afraid what I had been doing the last few years was not enough. I didn't know if they were going to use me for regular makeup or prosthetics and special effects.

Just take a deep breath, Sam. You'll do fine.

I was happy to be there, grateful to be given the opportunity, but I did feel lonely. I couldn't help but miss my family and friends. I wanted to call my dad, especially after I found a note from him wishing me luck, but it was the middle of the night in LA.

Cecilia's bedroom door was open. I peeked in and saw she was still asleep.

I took a shower and got dressed, and when I went downstairs to the kitchen, Cecilia was dressed and chipper, sipping on a cup of tea.

"I wanted to make you a cup of tea, but something told me you're a coffee person." She winked, and I smiled at her.

"You got that right!" I turned on the coffee machine and checked the time to make sure we weren't running late.

"Is our first meeting at nine?" I asked.

"Yes," she said, stifling a yawn.

"Are you okay?"

"I couldn't go to sleep last night, even after the day we had. Usually, I pass out when I'm tired and have something to drink, but nooooo...I don't think I fell asleep before one o'clock."

"Why couldn't you go to sleep?"

"I don't know...I guess I was nervous. I am nervous," she admitted with a shy look and a shrug of her shoulders.

I smiled, suddenly feeling better. It wasn't just me—Cecilia had first day jitters, too.

"Can I tell you a secret? I'm super nervous, too."

She smiled, looking relieved.

"You know what we're going to do?" I asked.

"What?" She looked up at me from her cup of tea, her blue eyes bright and curious.

"When we get back tonight, we're going to start making this place our home."

"So, in the end they did test us! Those *slags*!" Cecilia laughed.

"What does slag mean?" I asked, rubbing my hands against each other. I had forgotten my gloves. *Dumb move, Sam.*

Cecilia gave me a sly look. "It means...bitches!" We both laughed, glad the day was over. We had been in meetings for over four hours, and then we'd done a few "test runs" to see how well we worked on prosthetics versus regular makeup.

It had been a long day. During the meetings, we went over our schedules for the next few days and all the things that needed to be organized before we would start shooting. We learned that the actors had already been there for a week so they could start training for horseback riding and sword fighting. Most of them had a lot of action scenes, and even though there were always stuntmen available, the majority was probably willing to do most of their stunts. Gertie told us we had two more weeks for rehearsals before we'd officially start shooting.

In the next few days, we would get to meet the actors and would be told whom we were working with. Makeup artists like me and Cecilia had a list of actors we'd work on along with the extras for each day.

Speaking of the cast, why had we not met a single actor yet? They'd had some extras come in for our "test."

"They seem to be particularly precious with the cast, don't you think? How come we haven't met any of them yet?"

Cecilia shrugged. "Well, we met them the other day at the party. You weren't here yet. It is a bit weird, though, you're right. They've probably been too busy training. I heard some of them had never been on a horse, and they have barely two weeks to *master* that."

"That's not a whole lot of time."

"It isn't, and on top of that, they must learn to sword

fight and stuff like that. Have you looked at our schedules for tomorrow? We might get to meet some of them. I think I saw something about a screen test."

"No, I haven't."

"So, what's making you so fidgety? Are you that impatient to meet McHottie? That's it, *innit?*"

"McHottie?" I frowned.

Cecilia pulled out her phone and showed me a picture of a shirtless dude with at least twenty pounds of muscles on his arms. "Yes, silly! McHottie. The star of the show. *This* guy!"

I leaned in closer and studied his face. Straight nose, piercing blue eyes, strong jaw. Yep, I recognized him. It was the guy I'd met on my failed hike.

"*He* is the star of the show?"

"The very same," Cecilia said with a long sigh.

"What's his name?" I asked.

"You haven't looked Hugh MacLeod up yet? Bloody hell, Sam! You need to study up!" she said, giving me a playful slap on the arm.

"I've been...preoccupied." More like my head had been somewhere else entirely. I felt as if my body was in Scotland, but my mind hadn't caught up yet. Between jet lag and training, I felt like a spaz. Plus, to be completely honest, I was still nursing my wounds. It had been months—when was the bitterness of my breakup going to go away?

"What the bloody hell is that?" Cecilia asked as I opened a package from Amazon a day later.

"Watch and learn, young Brit. This is called a *Crock Pot*." I pulled the black pot out of the box and placed it on the counter.

"And what are we doing with that?"

"We're cooking."

"In that?"

"Yep."

"You know, when I said we should make this place a home, I thought we would go down to IKEA in Edinburgh and pick out a few throw pillows. I never thought it would involve cooking."

"I saw a nice little market not far away from here. They probably have local produce and—oh, are you vegetarian or vegan?" She shook her head no. "We can have some nice stew cooking for us while we're still at work, and then we'll come home and ta-da! Dinner is served."

She rolled her eyes as if I was missing something. "Two words, young American: catering service. We don't have time to cook, Sam, or even have a life by the look of things—not for a *long* time. We're going to be working ten to twelve hours a day, five days a week."

"You're right, but aren't we going to get tired of catering services? It'll be nice to have a home-cooked meal every once in a while, you'll see."

"Whatever. I'm going to see if I can order throw pillows from IKEA and maybe a cozy blanket," she replied, waving me off.

"We're just going to show her how wonderful you are," I said out loud, talking to the Crock Pot. I was talking to inanimate objects...yeah, I needed a drink.

The next morning, I got up early again. It wasn't even light outside; I figured I was still jet-lagged. I had only been there a couple days, and I had yet to sleep eight hours straight. Cecilia's door was closed, so I went downstairs as quietly as I could.

I put my sneakers on and got the warmest jacket I had. I grabbed my gloves, shoved them in my pocket, and headed out. I wanted to run, but I hadn't scouted out a good place to do that. I decided to go on a walk and study the area where I was going to live for the better part of the next year.

A gust of chilly wind blew in my face just a few seconds after I headed out, waking me up completely. I started walking as fast as my legs could go. I didn't have a set destination in mind, but I found myself at the bottom of the trail I'd checked out a few days prior.

As I watched the valley in front of me and felt the wind blow through my hair, I thought about the feeling of recklessness when you go down a hill on your bike—the wind on your face, the feeling of lightness. I thought about going fast and feeling like you could crash any minute if you weren't careful enough. When it came to dangerous stunts, that was as far as I'd go: going fast, down a hill, on a sturdy bike. Overall, I had always been a safe person. Maybe it was because I was the oldest and always felt I needed to watch out for my siblings. I never felt the need to be reckless; out of the three of us, I was the nurturing one.

Amira was the true daredevil of the family.

A lot of times, I would go along just to make sure she didn't get into any trouble. Soon, Rob followed her lead, even though he used to be a real crybaby when he was little. He had sure gotten over that—these days he was all about extreme sports.

He spent all his time exercising, lifting weights, doing yoga, and rock climbing—which was kind of surprising since he was one of those techy developer guys. Rob developed apps, and although he still hadn't come up with something as big as Snapchat, I was sure it was only a matter of time before his big break would come.

Amira always said that Rob was the perfect package: smart and good-looking. As much as I hated to even remotely think of my brother that way, I had to admit she was right. If only we could find guys that were as handsome and smart as him.

Unfortunately, finding someone worthy of her time seemed to be hard even for my sister, the movie star. In truth, Rob was no saint. He was just like all the other men—a goddamned player.

When the three of us got together, we basically tortured him, lecturing him about not being just another douchebag on the dating scene.

I laughed to myself, realizing just how much I missed my brother and sister.

I hadn't thought I would feel this way so soon, and I wondered if it was just because I knew I wasn't going to be able to see them for a while. I had no idea what my actual schedule was going to be for the next few months or if I would be able to go home at all.

Maybe I could get them to come visit me. Rob would love Scotland.

I had no idea what Amira's plans were for the holidays. It seemed that every single year she was in the running for some award, so she always spent November and December promoting a new movie or campaigning for a prize. A lot of times, we had to fly across the country around Thanksgiving or Christmas in order to spend a holiday all together. Our parents were divorced, but somehow we still managed to get along. The willingness to make it work was one of the things I loved the most about my mom and dad.

Anwar and Kathleen Farouk decided to split up when I was eighteen, and it took all of us by surprise. Amira and I were pretty self-absorbed with our teenage lives, and Robert was just a kid. We didn't understand why. Our parents hardly ever fought, and our father worshipped our mother, treated her like a goddess who walked on water. At the time, Amira was fifteen, and Robert only thirteen. He was the one who took it the hardest; it was no wonder he didn't care about being in a committed relationship. We were all in shock for weeks and felt hopeless.

For a while, I worried that one of our parents had cheated on the other. Even though my father was truly in love with my mom, that didn't mean he couldn't have cheated on her. I suspected my mother, too, and even followed her a couple times, but I didn't find anything out. When I tried to talk to her, she simply said that she had fallen out of love with my dad and that instead of making the rest of his life miserable, she wanted to give him the chance to find love again. I thought my father appreciated her candor, but he was still crushed, and for years, he never seriously dated another woman, hoping my mother would eventually come around.

But she didn't. Around the time of her separation, she had become more closed off toward me. I remembered noticing how weird it was, and since I was eighteen, I took it personally. I was upset. I didn't understand why my mother was trying to shut me out when growing up, she had been my best friend.

I asked her so many times to tell me what was going on. I didn't understand why she was taking the divorce so hard when it had been her decision in the first place.

A couple years after the divorce was finalized, my mother confessed to me the real reason she had divorced my father: she had fallen in love with a woman, a coworker of hers.

Initially, she had tried to dismiss her feelings as a

crush. She never intended to leave my dad, but no matter how hard she tried to fight her feelings, they wouldn't go away. She assured me that nothing happened between them while she was still married, but her feelings for this woman had become so strong, they made her question her sexuality. She felt guilty, and she thought it was unfair to her husband. She cared for him and wanted him to live a good life. Even after the divorce was finalized, Kathleen Farouk, née Smith, still wasn't at peace with herself.

She told me she was seeing a therapist, and it was slowly helping her come to terms with who she was. On a sunny afternoon in Venice Beach, my mother confessed to me that she was bisexual and that she had recently figured out that she had been for most of her life. She had suppressed her feelings and her nature for a long time, for fear of being judged.

I was proud of her and sad that she'd had to keep it to herself for so long, sad that she couldn't truly be herself. It had to be a terrible feeling to live with such a secret, a horrible thing to feel trapped in your own skin, to live your life feeling like you needed to hide your true nature from everyone you love.

My heart ached for her and for everyone who had to go through that in life. I'd always been of the opinion that everyone should be able to love whomever they decided to love without having to hide it.

Amira and I were extremely supportive of my mother. Rob was just a teenager and was a bit confused, struggling so much with his feelings that for a while he moved in with our dad. As much as it hurt my mother at the time, it ended up being just what she needed. Amira and I were out of the house, and with Rob living with Dad, she could focus on herself and figure out what she wanted. A few months later, we welcomed her girlfriend, Christina, into our family.

Eventually, Rob came around.

My father moved on and married someone else, Rita, a woman he'd met through work who had also recently gotten divorced.

I wondered why I was giving so much thought to my family; maybe it was because I felt like I was starting over, just like my parents had not that long ago.

I started climbing the mountain again, wanting to get a little higher this time.

I noticed a piece of sparkly granite stone and grabbed it. I cleaned the soil off and felt it in my hand, admiring how shiny it was.

The rock was green with variegated white stripes and a certain shine that I knew came from the crystals present in granite. *Oh, the random things you remember from school.* I looked at the steep hill in front of me, then checked the time. It was barely six forty-five, and the sun was just now coming up. I felt wide-awake, and I hadn't even had any coffee before heading out. Even so, I knew I was probably going to get sleepy again later during the day. Jet lag sucked.

I kept putting one foot in front of the other, trying to be careful. I was still getting used to the altitude since it was so much higher than what I was used to in LA, and it basically took no time at all for me to feel out of breath.

I heard some noises and spotted someone climbing up, getting closer and closer.

I stopped in my tracks.

I turned around and looked down at the man climbing up the hill.

It was hard to see his face because it was partially covered with the hood of his jacket, but I recognized him.

"Hugh MacLeod," I said out loud, and his eyes shot up and met mine, wide and alarmed. As he kept staring at me, I realized what I had just done, and I wished I could just dig under the rocks and make my own resting place right there, right then.

I had said his name out loud, as if I knew him. *Could I be any stupider?* It was one of the dumbest things I had ever done. I didn't think I had ever embarrassed myself like that in high school nor any time in all my years in Hollywood.

"Do I know ye?" he asked in a deep voice laced with a beautiful Scottish accent. As he climbed closer to me, his eyes studied my face. "Have we met?" he inquired when I didn't answer. I felt tongue-tied. *Snap out of it, idiot.*

"Y-yes...no...I mean—" *Good grief. Get it together, Sam.*

"We've met. Here. On this hill...right? The other day?" he asked, his brows furrowed. By the look in his eyes, I knew he remembered me. I nodded, still unable to say anything. "You were FaceTiming with your mum." My face fell. *Great, he remembers that.*

"Um, yes," I said, looking down to avoid his unsettling blue eyes. "Sorry, I didn't mean to bother you. I...I just didn't recognize you the other day." He gave me a quizzical look. "I'm not a weirdo, I swear. I'm one of the makeup artists. I'm here to work on *Abarath*," I explained.

"You're not a weirdo?" A wide smile stretched across his face, and he pulled his hood down.

"You know what I mean," I explained, closing my eyes in embarrassment. He laughed, the sound warm and hearty. Apparently, being a goof was a good way to break the ice. The sun rose behind me and suddenly everything around us was colored in a soft orange glow, making the color of his hair look closer to copper than the brown I had seen in his pictures. He wasn't wearing a hat today, and his hair fell on his forehead. It was just slightly wavy on top with soft curls around his ears and neck.

"What's your name? I don't think we met the other

night at the party."

"No, we didn't meet. I had just gotten in town that night, so I missed the party." I stretched out my hand and shook his. He held it and smiled at me, his gaze warm, friendly. I finally started feeling a little more at ease, although I couldn't quite hold the intensity of his eyes. They were studying me. I felt them *everywhere*, and somehow, I wasn't even a little bit upset about that. Heck, I had been the one checking out his butt the other day.

He looked at me, still holding my hand, and I realized I still hadn't told him my name.

"Sam," I replied. "I'm Sam Farouk."

"Ye don't seem to have either a British or a Scottish accent. Where are ye from, Sam?" he asked, eyebrows pulled together, the corners of his lips curled up.

I pressed my lips together. "Los Angeles, California."

"Really? That's a long way from here," he said with a mix of surprise and excitement.

"It sure is," I replied with a smile.

"And what are you doing up here this early in the morning?"

"Turning my stupid jet lag into a workout, I suppose."

"I'm going a little bit farther," he said, pointing up. "Would you like to join me?" His accent sounded heavier on the last two words, and I smiled. He responded with a smile of his own, and his eyes, dark and questioning a moment before, turned bright and inviting.

How could I say no?

"I would love to," I replied.

Chapter 6

SAM

"I'm sorry I didn't recognize you the other day," I said, trying to catch my breath.

We had been climbing up for just a couple of minutes, but I felt the need to fill the silence. I knew he was the star of the show, and I needed to address that. Some actors lost their goddamned mind if you didn't recognize them or if you didn't rain showers of compliments on them. Others were cool and humble.

I didn't know which category Hugh MacLeod belonged to yet.

He gave me a look and then smirked, making me feel more at ease.

"Why should you be able to recognize me? I'm not famous," he said with a shrug of his broad shoulders.

"Yet," I corrected him.

"Yet," he replied with a nod, his lips in a tight line. He had a bit of scruff that framed his pink, full lips so perfectly. Now that the sun was up, I could see his hair was indeed a light brown with red highlights, and his scruff was about the same color with a bit of red and gold in it.

"You know, usually I'm better prepared when I start working on a new project. It's just that this gig was very last minute, and I barely had time to get my shit in order before flying out here," I confessed. *Wow, Sam, forming full sentences—way to go.*

After talking to Cecilia the night before, I'd finally looked him up and checked his IMDB page. Hugh MacLeod had been in a few things here and there, some UK movies, some minor roles in some US indies, but this was the very first big thing he'd been cast in.

I found an article that said how many other actors he'd beaten for the role, and the showrunner, Nora Peters, was quoted saying how perfect he was for the part.

I had yet to finish the first book in the series, but it was true that he matched the description of the main hero to a T.

Abarath was tall and muscular, with light brown hair and icy blue eyes, a mix of Braveheart and Beowulf—and way more handsome than Mel Gibson in his prime, if you asked me. Abarath was a warrior and dragon slayer in a fantastic version of Scotland circa 1345. He was born a sickly child, but his mother's prayers to the Celtic gods granted him health and the strength of Hercules. He was also a ladies' man when he wasn't busy protecting Scotland from evil dragons. At the point I had gotten to in the story—which wasn't all that far—he had *three* different love interests. Quite the Casanova, indeed. When I checked the IMDB page for the show, I saw that the actresses they had cast as his love interests very much resembled the book characters, on top of being exceptionally beautiful women.

The story was long and intricate, and apparently, the author of the series was set to release three more books. If the show worked out, Hugh MacLeod was going to be busy for the next few years and would be making the big bucks.

"There seems to be a lot of hype about the show," I said, glancing his way to see his reaction. His lips pressed in a tight smile, and he gave me a curt nod—not the reaction I was expecting. "Did I say something wrong?"

"No, you didn't," he tried to reassure me, but I wasn't buying it. I cocked one eyebrow, giving him a look.

He let out a deep breath. "You didn't say anything wrong. It's just...it's just that a lot of times it's not a good thing when there's too much hype, whether it's a book, a show, or a movie. A lot of times, when there's too much hype, there's too much pressure to deliver, and it becomes hard to focus on what's important. People forget it's about the story, versus making a lot of money. The true meaning of everything gets washed out."

I looked at him and frowned. I could see where he was coming from, but it was surprising to see this reaction. I had never seen an actor not excited about his new gig turning into a huge deal.

"I mean, don't get me wrong, I am happy. It's just...Abarath is a great story. I'm just worried that all the publicity, all the *hype* will take away from the story a bit. I don't want that to happen. I want this to be for the fans and to be done right, rather than becoming some phenomenon with very little substance. I want the story to be told the way it should be. Fortunately, I think Nora is the right person to accomplish something so...*big*."

He was right. Nora Peters was a badass, one of the few successful showrunners on TV. She'd had a couple good runs on HBO, and now she had a fantastic deal with the Constz (short for Constellations) channel.

I tried to keep up with his pace, but he was too fast for me. On top of that, we had been talking, so I was even more out of breath than usual. I put my foot forward, trying to keep up with him, but I miscalculated and almost slipped. Hugh quickly turned around and grabbed my hand, preventing my fall.

"Thank you," I exhaled. His hand was warm, the skin a little rugged, and I loved the way it felt.

"What brings you to Scotland, Sam?" he asked, turning to look at me.

"Um, work?"

He laughed and bit his bottom lip. "I mean, why here? You were working in LA before?"

"Yes, I was."

"TV or movies?"

"I was working on a TV series."

"And the show you were working for...did it get cancelled?" *Yes, but that isn't the reason I don't have a job anymore.*

"Sort of...yeah." I could feel his eyes on me, and when I met his gaze, he gave me a strange look. "Ultimately, that's what happened."

"You don't talk much, do you?" he teased.

"I'm not an actor," I joked. "I'm not used to hearing myself talk."

"Har har." He smiled, still holding my hand, helping me up.

"You know, this is another level of hiking for me. I thought I was a hiker—back in LA, I mean—but I was damn wrong. Going on strolls in the canyons around LA can hardly be called hiking."

He paused and exhaled, making me realize it wasn't

quite as easy for him as he made it look. "*This* is definitely a different level of hiking. As a matter of fact, I'm out of shape myself."

"Out of shape? I don't think so," I said, giving him a once-over then immediately wishing I could take it back. Was I flirting or just being terribly blunt? I glanced his way, and he smiled at me. His eyes fell to my lips, and I realized how surreal this whole thing was. We were two strangers climbing up a hill, hand in hand, and somehow, I didn't feel uncomfortable, not a bit. I felt safe with him, and if I could have suppressed the jolt of electricity running through my body when he looked at me, I could have almost sworn that Hugh MacLeod and I were going to be great friends. There was an easygoing quality about him; I couldn't put my finger on what it was, but I had a feeling. The alarm on my phone rang, and when I grabbed my cell to turn it off, I realized I would have to tell him good-bye soon, and I didn't want to. It was such an odd feeling. I wanted to stay and talk to him at least a little longer.

He was still holding my hand, but I stopped climbing and disengaged myself from him—reluctantly.

"What is it?"

"I need to start heading down soon. I have all kinds of stuff lined up for today. I probably should have realized I wasn't going to have enough time for the whole hike this morning, but I woke up and couldn't go back to sleep. My first meeting is at nine, I believe." I felt his eyes on me and caught him staring. What was he looking at? I had no makeup on, and I had hardly brushed my hair. I probably looked like crap. "Don't you have some training session to attend, too?" I asked him, squinting my eyes now that the sun was so much brighter.

He smirked. "I do," he replied, and even the way he said one-syllable words did things to me. "But I think ye should go a bit farther up with me."

"Why? Is there something I should see?" I frowned. What was up this hill and why did Hugh think I needed to see it? He didn't elaborate, just nodded with a tight-lipped smile in place. His eyes were so beautiful, almost the shade of quartz. His face looked as if it had been carved out of marble, and his cheekbones were simply too perfect. His nose, his chin...hell, his entire face was. I told myself to look away and not stare. He stretched out his hand and I took it, as if it was the most natural thing in the world, and we started hiking again.

"So, you really won't tell me why you're here for work? I'm sure you had your pick of jobs to choose from back in LA." His smile was tempting, inviting. Maybe I should have just told him the whole truth. After all, we were going to be working together for the next several months. But, it was a long story, and unless people looked up my name and found out what happened, I usually preferred to give the CliffsNotes version.

I sighed and bit my lip, debating if I should tell him or not.

"What?" He laughed. "Is that such a loaded question?" he asked, his Scottish accent thicker out of the blue.

I hated to say *his* name this early in the morning, let alone think about him *at all,* but I also didn't want to come across as snotty. I took a deep breath and let it all out.

"My boyfriend of seven years cheated on me with his coworker, who also happened to be my boss."

I noticed his eyes widen in shock, and he inhaled a deep breath. "I'm sorry," he said, his eyebrows pulled into a frown. I expected more questions from him, but he didn't press me. Instead, we climbed our way up in silence, and even though I had just revealed something about myself I didn't like to get into, I didn't feel uncomfortable about it. I could feel his eyes on me, and as we walked closer, I became aware of other details I liked about him—his scent, for example. It was clean and musky, and I felt surrounded by it.

"So, this is your chance to start fresh, aye?" he asked, giving my hand a small squeeze.

"Aye," I replied, mimicking his tone, and we exchanged smiles. "I am. I'm starting over." He cocked one eyebrow, trying to get my attention, and I frowned.

"Look to your left."

I turned around and saw the sun was up high in the sky, shining all over the valley. I believed in Scotland it was called a *glen*. There was a line of huge, beautiful mountains in the distance, but that wasn't what made the view unique. The entire valley and the surrounding smaller mountains were covered in lilac flowers.

"Lavender?"

"Heather," he replied. It was breathtaking. Mountain after mountain was covered in purple flowers, alternating with the deep green of other peaks. The view was majestic, one of those moments that made you think God had to exist, whether you believed in him or not. It was simply too spectacular.

"Good God, it's beautiful." It was. It was one of the most beautiful things I had ever seen in my life. It was so gorgeous, my chest filled with a strange, warm feeling, and tears threatened to escape my eyes. I found myself fighting to hold them back. I looked up to him, and he smiled proudly. From the way his eyes shined, I could tell he was equally moved by the astonishing landscape.

"You've made the right choice, Sam. Scotland is the perfect place to start over."

The first few days on set were brutal for several reasons.

The main one was that we were still adjusting to our new schedule. We woke up early in the morning, went to the set, and got started on our to-dos, which would go on and on all day—get the actors ready, then the extras, then all the touch-ups throughout the day. When we got home, we were exhausted. Cecilia went straight to bed the first three nights. Another reason was the weather. Scotland was showing off its range of moody weather all at once or so it seemed.

I realized, in hindsight, that the beginning of August had actually been fairly forgiving. Toward the end of the month, it started raining more and for longer periods of times. "It's Scotland, what do you expect?" people said, but it was hard for someone like me to get used to it. It rained every motherfucking day, and it seemed there wasn't a way to escape it. The rain was there, greeting us when we'd leave for the set in the morning. It was there on and off during the day, a lot of times affecting our shooting schedule. I felt like I was shivering constantly.

I shouldn't have been complaining because the actors and the extras were the real troopers. They were the ones wearing costumes that weren't waterproof, and they had to deliver their lines in awful, frigid conditions. I sighed with relief whenever we had interior scenes to shoot. It made everyone's job much, much easier.

We had been preparing for about two weeks, but things were different when cameras started rolling. Even though we had been trying to get ready for this, we were suffering. No one talked about it, but you could see the exhaustion all over people's faces. After spending the first ten days hanging out in a pub almost every other night bonding with the crew, Cecilia and I made the decision to abstain from alcohol all week until our days off and to supplement our diet with several vitamins. Just like the actors, we couldn't afford to get sick, and we had to keep our energy levels up. It was vitamins and unlimited cups of coffee that got us through the first grueling days.

There were two hundred people in the crew alone, so even though we technically met everyone at some point, we couldn't actually say we knew each person working on the production. Little by little, we got to know most of the crew and the actors.

One morning during our first week, Hugh walked by my station with a towel still around his neck to protect his costume from the makeup Margaret had just applied. He noticed me and said hello.

"Hi," I replied with a smile. It was a simple *hello*. Unfortunately, it didn't go unnoticed. As soon as he was out of earshot, Cecilia came up to me.

"I thought you didn't know who he was," she teased.

"I Googled him since then. Plus, we met a few days ago."

"Boo! You whore. When was that?"

"It was early morning, and I couldn't sleep. I went out on a hike, and I met him while he was out."

"And you chatted him up? Well played, Sam. I didn't know you had it in you. You look all shy and quiet, and instead, you've already put the moves on him," she said, giving me a once-over.

"I did not put *the moves* on him. We just had a conversation for crying out loud." I felt my cheeks redden, and I looked down. I didn't want to be teased by Cecilia about Hugh. I loved her spunk, but she liked to talk. The last thing I wanted was to become the subject of gossip the first week on set. I was determined to stay *out* of trouble.

Our days went pretty much the same way every day: we got up early in the morning, spent all day on set, and dragged ourselves home in the evening. Most times, we were utterly worn out. After a few weeks of this, Nora noticed morale was down, and she tried to get us together on Friday night so we could all unwind and socialize. The local pub—the biggest one in town—was the one chosen for our meet-up, and it just so happened that Friday night was karaoke night. I didn't think anyone in our group was that shy to begin with, but when Nora told us we would have to pay for a round if we refused to sing, everyone was game. As much as I didn't enjoy the limelight and never cared to be onstage, I was a sucker for karaoke. Karaoke mania had exploded everywhere when Amira and I were children. Our dad got us a system, and we had dozens of tapes. We'd sing every day, much to the dismay of our poor mother. I believed that was when Amira's star quality began to emerge. She would be the one encouraging me to learn songs and practice duets and routines with her. It was one of our favorite things to do, and I had so many great memories of us putting on shows for our parents.

Because no one wanted to put up with having to pay for a round for such a large group of people, everyone got over their presumptive shyness rather quickly, and as beer and whisky kept flowing, our group became rowdy and loud.

I was drinking with Rupert, Cecilia, Altus, and Oliver. Rupert was a lighting director, and Altus and Oliver were lighting technicians. The three men were engaged in a heated conversation about Chelsea, Manchester United, and some other soccer team I had never heard of. Cecilia was listening to their conversation, and she chimed in from time to time to talk about one of the teams and their players. She seemed to know names, roles, and whatnot. I, on the other hand, didn't have a clue about soccer.

Cece and I were drinking our pale ale and waiting for our turn to sing. A lady named Miranda was singing a near-perfect cover of Mariah Carey's "Heartbreaker," and a lot of people were singing and dancing along. I couldn't help thinking of the heartbreaker I had left behind. I looked to my right and spotted another one.

Jake had been buzzing around me for the first couple weeks, but because I didn't give it up to him fast enough, he had moved on to an attractive redhead who worked as a set decorator. I was neither jealous nor looked at it as a missed opportunity, which told me I had made the right decision by not dropping my panties for him. He didn't look like Eric at all, but there was something in his mannerism that reminded me of him—his ambitiousness, maybe, or the way he almost *demanded* attention.

Cecilia pointed her chin in their direction, getting my attention.

"He could have been yours, Sam. Why did you let him go? Did you not fancy him?"

"He's a good-looking guy, but that doesn't mean he's the guy for me."

"Not even for a little bit of fun?"

"I don't know if I'm looking for fun right now."

"I thought you just got out of a long-term relationship."

"I did," I sighed.

"Don't you want to forget about your ex with a hot rebound?" she asked, raising her voice over the music. In that moment, everyone around us seemed to look our way. I rolled my eyes. She somehow always seemed to draw attention to us at the worst time.

Life on the set was already complicated as it was, and everyone tended to get nosy about everyone else's affairs.

"Could you please lower your voice?" I asked her, my voice betraying irritation.

"Sam, come tomorrow, no one is going to remember anything."

"I seriously doubt that," I grumbled.

"I guarantee it. You clearly haven't seen how *pissed* British and Scottish people can get. Everyone is going to have a major hangover, and no one will remember what they overheard at the bar. They won't even remember their own embarrassing karaoke performances," she said, pointing at the guy from the lighting department who had decided "I'm Sexy and I Know It" was a good song choice. I laughed and shook my head.

"They'll just remember they had a good time. Nora was right, we needed bonding time."

"I guess so. Do you know what you're going to sing?"

"Did I put in my request? Oh, yes I did," she teased, and I raised my eyebrows at her, curious. "Oh, I couldn't possibly tell you. It's a surprise," she said with an air of mystery, fluttering her eyelids, shimmying her shoulders.

"Oh, Cece! You're such a tease!"

"Okay, so...if Mr. Perfect Smile is not your type because he's a bloody womanizer, what would the guy for you be like?" she asked with a flirty smile.

"Loyal."

"I meant looks-wise."

"I don't really have a type. I like men who know how to

treat a woman and that are not cheating bastards. They don't have to look a certain way."

"All right, so you want someone who's loyal. What else? There's got to be more than that. Go on."

"Humble. Someone who doesn't take himself too seriously. Someone who's protective of his partner but who also encourages them to reach new heights."

"Got it." She looked behind me and waved. "Hey, Hugh!"

I turned around and found Hugh right behind me, hanging out with some other actors.

"Cece, Sam," he said, giving us each a nod of his head. How long had he been behind me? And had he heard what I'd just said? I gave Cecilia a look, and she responded with a sly smile. What game was she playing? I loved her, but sometimes she drove me crazy.

"Hugh!" she called him again. "Could you keep my girl company for a bit? It's my turn to go up there to sing, and these blokes are no fun with their soccer talk. Plus, I'm about to give you two something to talk about, aye?"

My jaw dropped at her bluntness, but I quickly tried to recover. I heard Hugh laugh behind me.

"I'll keep Sam company. Don't worry, Cece, she's in good hands."

Cecilia winked at him, and then poked Oliver on the arm. "You better watch, mate."

Hugh leaned closer to me. "What is she going to sing?" he asked.

"I have no idea. She didn't say, that little minx."

"Are you two getting along?"

"Very much so. She's a spitfire, but I like her. I think we're a good combo. She's vivacious, and I'm quiet. How about you? How are you getting along with your costars? I got to talk to Melissa yesterday, and she's a sweetheart."

"She is," he replied, but his eyes never left me. I liked Hugh, but when I was around him I felt uneasy, though not in a creepy way...more in a *I wouldn't mind having some fun with you* kind of way, despite what I had just told Cecilia. I was attracted to him; I couldn't help it. He was handsome, and from the few exchanges we'd had, he seemed kind and down to earth. His eyes were magnetic, and I found myself fantasizing about him more often than not.

In fact, ever since our hike on that early morning, he had become a fixture in my dreams. It got even worse after I saw him act on set one day—shirtless, nonetheless—as I was on standby for touch-ups. Because of Margaret's pregnancy, we had been training with Margaret and Blair, so we had been working closer to the main cast.

Unfortunately, because of the growing crush I had on Hugh, I had a really hard time making small talk, which probably made me look either stuck up or plain stupid, especially since he was always so nice when we crossed paths.

The music started, and I found myself mouthing an *Oh my God!*

Cecilia was singing "Diamonds Are a Girl's Best Friend," but it was the cover from Moulin Rouge, the one that's a mashup with Madonna's "Material Girl." My petite roommate was even more of a firecracker when she held a microphone, apparently.

She crushed the song, and everyone cheered her on.

"What are you going to sing?" I asked Hugh.

"Oh, no. Didn't you know?" he said with a frown, eyebrows pulled together. "Actors are exempt from Nora's rule."

"You're so full of it! Actors are not exempt. Alyssa was one of the first to sing tonight!"

“That’s because Alyssa loves the spotlight,” he said, cocking one eyebrow, his voice deep. Alyssa played one of the three love interests, the sexy seductress. The female roles in the books were a bit stereotypical for my liking, but I was hoping that as the story progressed, the main actresses would have more substantial material and would be able to give their characters a little more depth. Alyssa Northam had a Broadway background so, yes, *technically* she was showing off a bit with her “Everything’s Coming Up Roses” song from *Gypsy*, but she was always very nice to everyone, and I liked her even though she sometimes sounded like Jenna Maroney from the show *30 Rock*.

“You need to sing. I’ll make you.” I poked Hugh’s rock-hard bicep with my finger. Apparently, a glass of whisky was all I needed to be able to hold a conversation with him.

“I am a terrible singer.” He sighed.

“You’re an actor. I’m sure you could make these people believe anything, including that you know how to sing,” I told him with conviction.

He laughed. “And how am I supposed to do that, exactly?” he asked with a look that was a mix of amusement and confusion.

“I mean...you could pretend to know what you’re doing. You might not have the strongest voice, but I’m sure you could disguise it somehow.”

“I wish, but no amount of *acting* could disguise my *singing* voice. I’m doing everyone a favor by sitting this one out, Sam, I swear.”

“I find that hard to believe. Nora is trying to build comradery, and you refuse to participate. You’re not helping.” The alcohol in my system was making me feel all happy-go-lucky, and I poked his bicep again. *Damn*. It was hard as a rock. He watched me with a serious expression. *Oops*. Maybe I was crossing the line.

He's cast, and you're crew—remember that.

"Maybe one of these days you could sing with me? We'll do a fun duet."

He laughed at my insistence. "Are you always this persistent? Didn't you just call yourself a *quiet* girl a minute ago?"

"I said I was quiet. I didn't say I was *good*." I winked, and he seemed to be taken aback. That was definitely the alcohol talking. He inhaled sharply, and then gave me a flirty, tight-lipped smile. There was a certain twinkle in his eyes, and I found myself fantasizing about kissing him—but the enchantment was broken rather quickly, thankfully. As soon as Cecilia's song ended, they called my name to sing the next song.

Chapter 7

SAM

We were bonding, all right.

I had just started singing "Don't Stop Me Now" by Queen, and someone had passed along a fake mustache for me to put on. I already had on my leather jacket, and apparently, someone thought I needed to get into character. I groaned.

Show people—they were the goddamned worst!

"Good grief! Who goes around with fake mustaches in their pockets? Damn makeup artists!" I yelled into the microphone, and everyone laughed.

"You're missing your cue!" Margaret yelled with a laugh.

"Freddie Mercury didn't have a mustache when this song came out!" I protested. Queen was one of my favorite bands, and I knew for a fact that when the video for this song was shot, Freddie Mercury was clean-shaven. The mustache came later on.

"Just put the damn thing on!" someone else chimed in.

"You're all going to pay for this," I said into the microphone while pointing my finger at everyone who was yelling for me to get a move on. I shook my head at Margaret and Cecilia, who were nearby and put the mustache on. Whoever oversaw the karaoke machine even had the balls to restart the song.

Fine. I glared at all of them, but they laughed and cheered.

I put the mustache on and more cheers followed. *Drunktards*, I thought, but then I smiled under my mustache. As I started to sing, I did feel more and more in character. I commanded the audience as Freddie Mercury himself would have. Amira used to say that when I sang, it was as if I shed my skin and left it behind, revealing a completely different side of my personality. I loved music, and I loved the way it could make you feel brand new and fearless. I loved the way it made you feel connected to other human beings, and that night, even though we were just singing silly songs at karaoke, we were connecting. I didn't have a particularly good voice, but I knew I was an okay singer. I could keep a tune.

I hit *almost* all the notes, and I gave it a bit more by adding a few of Freddie's signature moves. At some point, someone hustled me up on a chair, and I found Hugh in the crowd. I pointed to him and gestured for him to come join me, but he just shook his head and smiled broadly. The way he looked at me made my stomach fill with butterflies. I didn't care that I had everyone else's eyes on me. That didn't make me nervous at all. The way Hugh was looking at me, however, was unsettling.

I had to look away to keep my nerve and finish my song, but I felt his eyes on me the whole time, and when I was done, I could see him cheering and clapping from the corner of my eye. I turned in his direction for just a second and smiled big, and then I took a theatrical bow worthy of Freddie Mercury and made my way back to him.

Nora had been right—karaoke night did help. We got to know people outside our department, and we were now more familiar with people we hadn't known that well before. After my ballsy performance of "Don't Stop Me Now," I had gained the nickname Freddie around the set. I wasn't mad about that; being nicknamed after one of my idols was the least of my worries. Work was still stressful, and we were still striving to find a balance. Karaoke night had been fun, but I felt we needed to do more as a group as much as our schedule would allow us.

So, after discussing it with Cecilia, we invited a few people over for a small get-together at our place. Despite her initial reluctance, Cece had become quite fond of the Crock Pot and liked to come back to the townhouse to find a hot meal just for me and her. Word got around, and after the first little dinner we had with Margaret, Blair, and a few others, we found ourselves hanging out with almost thirty of our closest coworkers. Our townhouse looked like a commune with everyone sitting on the floor cross-legged, pouring wine, and telling stories. Pretty soon, everyone knew about Cecilia and Sam's (very informal) *dinner parties*, including the cast.

"Why am I never invited?" Hugh asked one morning, piercing me with his sky-blue eyes. In the last week or so, Cecilia and I had been working even more with the main cast. I had the luck to be assigned to Hugh, shadowing Margaret. She was due in about ten weeks, and I knew production wanted to make sure we'd be covered. To be honest, I was surprised they hadn't called someone else with a résumé like Margaret's, but I was glad I was being given the chance to shine, and I didn't want to throw it away.

As such, I had convinced myself I had to abandon all the dirty thoughts I had about Hugh MacLeod at once. I wanted to lock them up in an ancient trunk and throw them in the ocean. Unfortunately, when I was close to him and we happened to be alone, it was hard to keep myself in check.

I stopped applying fake dirt to his face and looked at him, pretending I didn't understand what he'd just asked. "What do you mean?"

"Your crew parties, why am I never invited?"

I stifled a laugh. "Well, they are *crew* parties," I said, smiling down at him, my lips pursed together. "You know...for the *crew*."

"Mostly crew," he said, smirking. "I know of a few cast members who have been invited." He was right about that. A few cast members had been invited.

"Why not me?"

"You know, I've been in this business for a while, and I've always been told cast and crew shouldn't mix." More specifically, I'd always been told the crew should not try to mix with the cast unless invited.

"That's bollocks." He shook his head, his lips pressed in a smile.

"It has nothing to do with the fact that we don't want you over. You're the star of this thing. People know you have long shooting days, and plus, don't you work out in the evenings? And you have to learn your lines. I'm sure everyone is just trying to give you space and leave you alone."

"Oh, how thoughtful. But you see, the other day I was walking to my place, and I heard all this laughter," he said, pointing his finger at me. "And it was coming out of your townhouse." He gave me a serious look, and I sighed.

I tried to justify myself. "We didn't mean to hurt y—" I said, but he lifted a finger and asked me to let him finish.

"Now, I understand you guys were trying to be respectful, and in some cases, yes, you might be right about cast and crew not mixing. God knows I have been in productions where they made sure they let you know what your place was," he said, letting out a deep breath. "But, if, as you pointed out, I am the star of this thing, shouldn't I receive preferential treatment? Shouldn't I be invited regardless of if I accept or not?"

"Do you really want to join us?" I was surprised by his insistence and couldn't help but smile.

"Sam, I grew up with four brothers. Believe it or not, even though I have been on my own a long time, it still feels kind of weird to go back to an empty house. I could use the company."

"*Four* brothers? You mean there are five boys in your family? Your poor mother!"

"We weren't that bad." He shrugged.

"Says you! I bet she would beg to differ."

"Maybe one of these days you'll get to ask her yourself and find out," he joked, and I narrowed my eyes at him.

"Is she coming to visit and watch you be a badass?"

"Maybe," he replied with a coy smile.

Margaret came back to the trailer.

"Is Hugh ready to shoot?" she asked a bit curtly. She looked tired.

"Yes, I am almost done with him."

"Hurry, Sam. They're ready for him." She left, and I let

out a sigh.

"Sorry. I didn't mean to get you in trouble," he said, grabbing one of my hands, his voice soft and gentle. I nodded and gave him a small smile. I resumed applying dirt to his cheeks, and then tipped his chin up and locked eyes with him.

"It was not my intention to hurt your feelings." His eyes grew warmer. "I'll make sure to let you know when we have our next get-together, okay?" I told him with a nod of my head. He nodded and gave me a lopsided smile. God, why did he have to be so damn attractive? "Close your eyes," I ordered him. Hugh hanging out at my house? Yeah, that sounded easy peasy. How was I going to keep my dirty thoughts away then?

The more I worked with Hugh in the following days, the harder it became to be indifferent to him. Most days, he was polite and chatty and all-around one of the best people I had ever worked with. Some days, he had to sit in a makeup chair for about three hours, like when we had to apply the scars to his chest.

He was kind, and he always told funny stories about the many acting gigs he'd had to take during his years as a struggling artist.

On set, everyone loved him, and not just because he was the main character. He was respectful and humble and was always nice to everybody, even after long hours on set when everyone had had it and was just itching to be done for the day.

There were also the times when he had to focus on the role or when he had a difficult scene coming up. On set, we all knew that some days were easier than others.

We knew that, on some mornings, Hugh—along with the other actors—just needed to concentrate, so we moved around them accordingly, trying to work as quietly as we could, focusing on not disrupting their concentration.

On those days, the change in him was so drastic, I almost felt as if I didn't know him at all. I noticed that on some mornings when he got into character, he wasn't the cheerful, gorgeous man I often chatted with.

He was Abarath, the brave, sometimes arrogant hero with a dark past.

As a matter of fact, we had just started working on some flashback scenes that were going to reveal part of his past. Sometimes we had to be on standby for touch-ups, especially for the fight scenes that were always particularly bloody, and we had to wear rain suits to protect us from the weather. I liked that the Gore-Tex material kept me warm and dry, but it never failed to make me feel like a bulky robot when I walked around. I hated it.

"You!" said the director who was working on the current block, some guy I had never seen on set before. "Find my lead actor." No *please,* no *thank you* came out of his mouth. What an asshole. I was tempted to remind him I wasn't a production assistant and that it wasn't my job to fetch things or people.

One look at this guy and I understood the type: arrogant director prick of the Michael Bay variety. We'd had such nice directors so far, and thankfully, he was only scheduled for the current block, so we'd just have the pleasure of working with him for two episodes.

Where was Hugh, though? It wasn't like him to not already be on set after he got called on. I had seen him ready at least half an hour ago. I had been busy all morning getting a couple extras dirty and bloody. I looked for his assistant,

Kevin, but I couldn't find him anywhere near the trailer. I knocked on the door, and no one answered. I knocked again and when there was still nothing, I decided to open the door. I didn't want to go back to Mr. Michael Bay empty-handed. Hugh was sitting on a couch, one arm propped on his knees, holding his head up. He didn't look up immediately, but he did a double-take when he saw it was me. The expression on his face was unreadable, and for a moment I thought maybe it would be better to go back to the asshole director without the lead actor.

"I knocked," I explained. "Twice." He gave me a silent nod and exhaled a deep breath through his nose. He made a sign for me to come to him. "Is everything okay? They're waiting for you on set." My voice was low and tentative; I was nervous.

He had mostly been pleasant with me, but actors were moody sons of bitches, and yes, I included my darling sister in that category. He was obviously distraught about something. I didn't know how he would react. This was just another reason why I never ever wanted to work overseeing production. It seemed like an endless pain in the ass or maybe I should say *arse.* (I loved saying *arse.*) I let out a breath, and he looked back up at me as if he had just remembered I was standing there.

I chose the gentle approach. It looked like someone was having a bad day, and theoretically, our day hadn't even started yet. Better get this handled now or we were going to be out there for longer than required. *Brrr.*

I knelt in front of him and took the hand he had been resting over his knee between mine. Our eyes met, and he gave me a wary look.

"What's going on, Hugh?" I asked.

He didn't respond immediately, as if he were working up the nerve to tell me the truth. His brows furrowed, his eyelids shut, and I fixated on his impossibly thick, light brown eyelashes. I often wondered why guys were always the ones with better eyelashes. Was it a genetic attribute to get the woman to fall for the man, much like a male bird's feathers were brighter and more colorful than his female counterpart's? What was with male eyelashes, really?

"Hugh, are you feeling okay?" He nodded. "Tell me what's going on. You can talk to me." Just then, he looked at me, eyebrows raised in surprise. He exhaled, and when his warm breath caressed my face, I realized how close we were. I was on my knees, in front of him, our faces just a few inches away from each other. "It's nothing, Sam. Dinna fash yourself," he said with a small smile, trying to hide what was anguishing him. "I guess it's just a little performance anxiety." He was supposed to shoot a pivotal emotional scene that day, when Abarath comes back home after a mission only to find death and destruction at his parents' estate in Broochmar.

"Stop it, Hugh."

"Stop what?" he asked.

"I know this is not my area of expertise, but I believe you're overthinking it."

"Am I?" He raised both eyebrows at me, his jaw taut, his lips pressed together.

"You so are. Now, I may not be the actor here, but I grew up with one, which means I do have some experience in the matter." I gave him a convincing smile, and he stifled a laugh, smiling back at me.

"You do?"

"Yes, my sister is Mira Farouk."

"Mira Farouk is your sister?" he asked in a tone of surprise, his eyes widening. "Why have I never made the connection before?"

"Because we look nothing alike. Yes, she's my sister,

but we don't have time for that right now. We need to get you ready for your next scene."

"Okay, so what have you got for me?" I quickly glanced at my phone. We were running late.

"Well, I know that your next scene is pretty dramatic and emotional—"

"Correct. So, what's yer advice?" he asked with a smug smile.

"I am not going to tell you to do what Lee Strasberg recommended."

"Which was...?" he asked with a hint of amusement.

"Pull a hair out of your nose," I deadpanned, and he laughed. "No, seriously, he really said that! It's supposed to help you cry. You can thank Amira—I mean Mira—she's the reason I even know any of this."

He seemed to be a little more relaxed; the frown between his brows disappeared for a moment, and his shoulders sank. "What else do you know?" His voice was low, but his tone was so deep it felt like a low rumble in my ears. Gahh, it was so sexy. He could have read me anything, any time.

I pressed my eyebrows together, trying to remember what I had learned through my sister. "Well, there are actors and coaches who do not believe in rehearsing.'"

"Do you believe that?" He cocked one eyebrow at me.

"Yes and no. There are many acting teachers who swear by preparation, and many others who just believe you should jump into a scene." He nodded and remained quiet, his eyes fixed on me. "Now, what I think we have here is a severe case of *head-stuck-up-your-arse,"* I told him, pronouncing the last word with a British accent. "Jokes aside, I think your brain is playing tricks on you. You just need someone to talk some sense into you." He hung his head, and I placed my hands on his shoulders, shaking him lightly so he would look at me. He did, and I felt his eyes piercing me. "You're a trained actor. You've worked your ass off for years. You are perfectly capable of going out there and slaying this scene." I stretched my arm and pointed outside. "You're going to go out there and *murder* this scene." *Over and over and over, no matter how many times that prick out there wants you to repeat it.* "And I guarantee you, by the end of the day, there will not be one dry eye. Everyone is going to lose it when they watch the dailies." I fixed the lapels of his coat and grabbed his chin in my hand, realizing too late I shouldn't have done it. *Oh, well.*

"You got this." I wasn't just telling him what he needed to hear; I honestly believed what I was saying. I had seen enough from him to know he had range, and I knew he had it in him. He'd just gotten stuck. It happened to all of us. I was sort of stuck myself. I had been living the last few months on autopilot, and I was just now feeling like I was grasping the steering wheel of my life again.

His smile returned, and this time it reached his beautiful eyes. We stared at each other for a few more seconds, and I felt as if his fiery-blue depths were able to reach inside of me. My heart started galloping within my chest, and I let out a breath.

He stood up and stretched out his hand to help me get up. We left the trailer and walked toward the set.

"Thank ye, Sam." It was a simple expression of gratitude, but the look in his eyes was so intense, it could have set my panties on fire.

"You got it. I'll send you an invoice for my services." That earned me another laugh from him, and the kindling fire inside my chest started burning a little brighter, a little stronger.

Hugh

It had never happened to me before to get stuck like that. I'd always looked forward to a challenging scene. I had never experienced that kind of panic, and I would have hated for anyone to witness it. I didn't want anyone to question my capabilities or think I wasn't up to the task, but somehow I didn't mind that she had seen the state I was in. When she accompanied me to the set, I felt a renewed sense of calm, a peace, and a confidence I had been longing to find all morning. She had helped get my head out of my arse.

"Thank ye," I told her again before I said good-bye.

"I didn't do anything. Go out there and kill it."

I nodded. "Will ye stay here? For a little bit?"

"Okay." She smiled at me, and my chest felt suddenly warmer, filled with something I couldn't explain. It was a feeling that encompassed both hope and excitement. I had felt it before around her, but I thought it was just because she was attractive. I could have stared at her brown eyes all day, but the director had already acknowledged my presence, and the assistant director was ordering everyone around to take places.

I took a deep breath and paced a few steps, emptying my mind of everything: my sudden nervousness, the pressure I felt I was under, the way Sam's eyes affected me...the way her presence affected me.

I walked to the spot the production assistant pointed to and stood there, head down, focusing on my breath, trying to get in the zone. Someone called "Action!" and in that moment, I became Abarath again.

SAM

There it was. It was what I loved the most about this job: the moment when everyone shut their mouth, the camera started rolling, and the actor became the character. I loved that moment, the moment when fiction became something tridimensional. No matter how stressful and draining working on set was, moments like these were what I did it for. This was why I loved my job so much.

Being able to witness a story brought to life, just like this, before anyone else could see it unfold? It was priceless. No matter how many people were around, from light technicians to camera operators to sound techs, everything disappeared the moment the actor said his lines. I was completely enthralled by that magic. It was as if everyone were collectively holding their breath as fiction made its way into reality.

I couldn't tell how long I stayed out there watching Hugh; there was a small part of my brain telling me I should probably go back to my quarters, but I couldn't walk away, and I didn't want to, especially after he'd asked me to stay. My heart broke when he shot the scene the first time. I knew what was going to happen, and yet I wasn't ready for it. My body shook as he cried out when he found and embraced the dead body of his mother, and tears started rolling down my cheeks as they shot the scene for a third time. Time after time, his performance was nuanced by a different subtle shade of heartbreak, and my own heart could not take it.

The director called for a break and then touch-ups, and it took me a few seconds to snap out of my daze. Thankfully I had my kit on me, so I walked over to him as someone handed him a bottle of water. He took a swig and nodded in my direction, acknowledging me as I approached him. I replied with a small smile, careful not to say anything to him, not wanting to distract him with small talk.

I took his chin in my hand and started fixing the smudge of blood that had dried out. I could feel his eyes on me, but I didn't want to meet his. There were at least thirty people around us, and I suddenly felt exposed. I wanted to tell him how great he'd been, but I knew better. I was going to wait until later, when the day was over. From the corner of my eye, I saw him lift his index finger. He wiped one of my tears away, and I closed my eyes, relishing his touch. I told myself it was small and insignificant, but my heart wanted to turn it into something bigger. Our eyes locked, and I smiled shyly at him. He looked as if he wanted to say something, his lips slightly parted. His breath was warm and ragged, his eyes wide and bluer in the sunlight. The day's weather was some of the best I had seen: chilly, but with a bright sunshine. It created a stark contrast with the macabre scene we were shooting.

That was why it was even more crucial for Hugh to nail the scene, because the result of it depended exclusively on his performance, with no help from his surroundings. He couldn't count on the elements to make his delivery more dramatic. There was so much I wanted to say, but I bit my bottom lip, holding back my words, hoping he could read them in my eyes.

I patted him on the chest. "All good," I mumbled, but just as I tried to walk away, his fingers grabbed mine for a second.

"Later," he said between his teeth, his eyes scanning the set to see if anyone was paying attention to us. He glanced down at me, the look in his eyes dark and impenetrable, charged by all the words we couldn't say. I gave him a silent nod and walked away.

Chapter 8

Hugh

At some point during the day, she disappeared and was replaced by Margaret. Although I knew she was probably busy with something else, I missed her presence.

"You shouldn't be out here," I told my very pregnant friend. I had known her since I'd attended the Royal Scottish Academy, and she'd never been more beautiful than she was now with a baby bump.

"I wanted to give Sam a break. She's been out here most of the day. Besides, the weather's nice. I could use some Vitamin D," she said, patting her growing stomach.

"Are you doing okay? How are you feeling?"

She replied with a smile. "I feel fantastic, thank you very much. How are you?"

"Great."

"You've been bringing the house down today, so I've been told. Nora said the director only wants to do a couple more takes."

"Sounds good."

I listened to Margaret make small talk, but my mind was elsewhere. I knew the next few takes would probably not get used at all. I wasn't usually so presumptuous about my skills, but I knew I had already given the right performance three or four times during the day. Now that my chest didn't ache with performance anxiety, I was occupied by thoughts of Sam. I didn't understand why I was longing to see her again. I had always been okay with hookups, but I had never fallen for anyone. I never wanted to let anything distract me from my career, and no one really held my attention for too long, anyway.

I had plenty of chances to be around gorgeous women, but most of the actresses I had encountered so far were fickle and always a bit too manipulating, just looking for a partner that could help them establish or further their status. I certainly wasn't famous enough to gain them more exposure, nor I was interested in playing whatever media game they had in mind. All I wanted was to act; the rest was just icing on top. I wasn't interested in Hollywood politics, didn't care for the fame game, but according to my agent, I would have to learn to navigate it soon enough. Things were finally going to change. According to everyone's predictions, I was going to be famous.

I was going to be a star. I had been an actor for years, but so far I had lived a pretty quiet life.

Was I ready for things to change? Was I ready to sacrifice my private life to be a successful actor? Part of me still feared the show was going to flop. If, however, it was a success as everyone predicted, I hoped I'd be able to handle my newfound fame with confidence and class.

As the sun started its descent, we stopped filming. Margaret said good-bye, and after I took off my costume, I went to the makeup quarters instead of my dressing room.

I didn't even realize where I was going until I walked through the door. Sam was there, as was Cecilia, although she seemed on her way out.

Cecilia's eyes widened as she saw me enter the room. I would usually just wash my makeup off with a shower, but I wanted to have an excuse to see Sam.

"I-I'll go ahead, Sam. I'll see you at home." She said good-bye and hurried away.

"Hey," Sam said with a tip of her chin when we were finally alone. "What can I do for you?" She put some makeup brushes away and gave me a furtive glance.

"Well..." I hesitated, a few scenarios running through my head, none of which were very gentlemanly. She was wearing a tight white T-shirt and black jeans that hugged her curves, leaving very little to the imagination. My palm twitched, needing to touch her. I made up an excuse. "Margaret was saying it's bad for my skin to wash the makeup off in the shower." She frowned and gave me a perplexed look. "She said there might still be makeup residue after I wash."

"That's true. Sit down." She patted the chair next to her and I took a seat. The smile she gave me was sweet, but there was a certain wariness in her eyes. She bit her bottom lip and leaned closer to me, putting a paper towel around my T-shirt to keep it clean. She applied some cleanser on a cotton pad and started wiping off all the makeup and fake grime that was layered on me. I closed my eyes. It was quiet around us, except for some music coming through from a phone docking station.

"You were great today," she said. "You had nothing to worry about." My eyes were closed, but I could hear the smile in her voice.

"Only because ye told me to get my head out of my arse," I replied with a laugh.

"You know I didn't mean it that way!" She slapped me playfully on my arm.

"Yeah, ye did."

"I was joking! You just needed to put things into perspective. I knew you had it in you."

"I'm sorry I made ye cry."

"I'm not. It was a heartbreaking scene. You'd have to have a heart of stone to not feel anything."

"You were the only one crying." She stopped cleaning my face. I opened my eyes and found her glaring at me, a murderous look in her eyes. "What? I'm simply stating a fact."

"Shame on you. It's not very nice to make fun of my sensitive soul." She cocked one eyebrow at me, but the tone of her voice was playful.

"I wasn't pointing it out to make fun of you—quite the opposite."

"And what exactly do you mean by that?"

"I liked that you were so into it. It gave me confidence, and I felt I got even better after a couple of takes," I explained. Her eyes softened and she reached for my jaw, turning it in her direction brusquely to resume cleansing my skin of the leftovers of the day. I didn't take my eyes off her.

When she glanced back at me, she said, "Take number three was my favorite." She smiled, and I couldn't help but grin, letting out a breath of elation. She leaned down over me, carefully wiping the skin around my eyes. I felt her warm breath wash over me, and her closeness caused my heartbeat to accelerate, running off like a wild horse. I closed my eyes again.

I recognized "Killer Queen" by Queen playing through the speakers of the dock. Soon enough, Sam started singing along, her voice barely audible even though she was so close.

"You can sing if you want, you know. You have a nice

voice."

"Thanks, but I don't really want to shout in your face." She laughed, and I loved the sound of it. It made me feel lighter, in a way I hadn't felt in a long time. Suddenly, I felt like I wanted to be the one to make her laugh, the one to make her happy.

"You like Queen a lot, don't you?" I asked her.

"My dad used to live in London in the '70s, and he saw them live a couple times. Can you believe that? I'm so jealous," she said with a small shake of her head. "So, yeah. He's a big fan, and I grew up listening to Queen a lot."

"What does your dad do? When did he move to the US?" I was honestly curious. Sam was unlike any other American girl I had met so far. She had a slight California vibe, but there was also something different about her, something more—some part of her makeup made her different and unique.

"It's a long story. Are you sure you want to hear it?" she asked bashfully.

I stared at her rich brown eyes. I wanted nothing more than to know more about her. I smiled and replied, "I would love to."

SAM

"Is Sam short for Samantha?" Hugh asked casually one morning while I was applying his makeup. His eyelids fluttered open, his piercing blue eyes framed by thick brown lashes. Sometimes they startled me, seemed to reach inside of me, as if they were capable of knowing all my secrets. His eyes alone made me feel things I shouldn't have been feeling. It was hard to keep it professional around him, because he was always so friendly. I lifted my gaze and found a producer staring at us, narrowing his eyes.

"No," I replied with a shake of my head, afraid I would get in trouble for being too cozy with the lead actor.

"Sorry, I bet you get asked that a lot." The look in his eyes told me I had been too curt with him. I felt the need to apologize. From the corner of my eye, I saw the producer leave the room.

"No, it's not that...it's just...my name is short for *Samhain.*" He frowned. "Ugh, I'm pronouncing it wrong. What I meant was *Sow-een,*" I said, hoping my pronunciation was somehow correct. His eyes widened, and he let out a chuckle of surprise. Clearly it wasn't the answer he'd expected, which happened all the time. I gave him a tight-lipped smile and a slight nod of my head.

"Yep, that's right."

"Your full name is Samhain?" My name in his mouth, said the right way, sounded completely different. *Sow-in.*

"Weird, I know. You can thank my mother for that."

"Do you mean your name is Samhain as in Samhain *the* Gaelic festival?"

"The very same," I said with a heavy sigh. Usually people didn't know why I was called Samhain or what Samhain was, but I was in Scotland now, and people there were more inclined to know what it meant. Samhain was the Gaelic festival marking the end of the harvest season and the beginning of winter. It was celebrated between October 31st and November 1st. I had asked my mother many times why she'd decided on that name, and she always said "it felt right" since I was born on October 31st. I mentally scoffed at the memory.

"I thought your father was from Pakistan."

"Yeah, my father is from Pakistan, but my mother is a hippie from the valley—from LA, I mean," I corrected myself, realizing only Californians would get that reference. "Let me rephrase that...she used to be a hippie when we were little. She was obsessed with Gaelic myths when she was pregnant with me." His eyes kept studying me, making me more and more nervous. "My mother and I don't look anything alike. You would never guess I came out of her womb," I blabbered.

"Why? Is she not gorgeous like you are?" he asked with a laugh, a bright smile stretching across his face. My breath hitched, and my eyes widened before I could control my emotions. A rush of heat traveled from my chest to the rest of my body, and my throat felt suddenly dry; I quickly swallowed and tried to regain my composure. I gave him a small smile, ignoring my heart beating as loud as a drum in my chest. Things had been different between us lately. Ever since the day I'd barged into his dressing room to help him get his shit together, he had been friendlier, trying to stop and chat whenever he could.

I thought there was something else, too. He seemed to look at me differently. There was an intensity, a curiosity in his eyes every time he glanced my way. I was rarely working with him, helping Margaret from time to time, but when we'd cross paths, he would smile at me in a way that was so warm and genuine, it made my heart flutter. It felt like the sun peeking through the clouds. I could feel the warmth of it even during those dreadfully cold Scottish days. Some part of me wanted to believe he regarded me more than others, but the truth was that he was amiable with everyone on set. I wanted to keep my feet firmly on the hard-ass Scottish rocks, but when I was around him, I couldn't help but fantasize about the possibility of something more between us.

He just said I was gorgeous.

Stop. Everything.

Breathe. And smile.

I wanted to pause time and start doing a little happy dance on the spot.

A bright smile stretched across my face, and he seemed delighted that I appreciated his compliment. He rewarded me with a sly grin. "No, I mean...my mother looks like a total California girl and I...well, *I don't.* Amira—I mean Mira, looks more like her." I had told him everything about my famous sister the other night when he asked about my dad. He was a fan of hers, of course, and he talked enthusiastically about some of her movies. Nothing about his demeanor told me that he'd made the connection about me and what happened back in LA; I was surprised. When things went awry with Eric a few months back, my revenge plan blew up across social media partly because I was Mira's sister. So far, no one on set seemed to know who I was or what I was "famous" for—or *infamous*, depending on how you looked at it—except Nora and Lainey. I was glad no one knew, and I wanted to keep it that way.

"I think your name fits ye perfectly." His voice was deep and seductive and made me snap out of my inner ramblings. His compliments ignited a chain reaction inside my body—my heart started beating faster and faster, blood rose to my cheeks, and there were also other areas that responded enthusiastically to his compliments. I sighed and then tried to say something; I couldn't take his eyes staring at me like that any longer.

I frowned and bit my lip. "Why do you think it fits me perfectly? She gave me this Gaelic name, supposedly on a whim, and I don't look *Gaelic*...at all."

He laughed, and the rich sound vibrated through my body as if we were much, much closer.

"Are you done laughing about my misadventures?" I asked him with a smile.

When he finally stopped, he got all serious, his eyes dark, fixed on me. It wasn't just a look—it was a smolder. The way he looked at me made me feel all hot and bothered, and wetness pooled between my legs.

"Sam, ye might not look Gaelic, but you must know Samhain means 'darker half of the year'."

"Yeah...so? What's your point?"

He took a deep breath and then his blue irises stared into my eyes for what felt like forever. He finally looked away and his hand went into my hair, his fingers weaving through it.

"Well, your hair, your eyes, your skin...every part of you is dark, *neach-gaoil*. That's why I say your name suits you perfectly," he said almost in a whisper.

"Neach...?"

"Gaoil."

"What does that mean?" I asked him.

"It means *sweetheart.*"

I swallowed in an attempt to contain every emotion his words were igniting, but then I licked my lips and his eyes fell to my mouth. I thought it must be what hell feels like—burning with no way to extinguish the fire. Being around him every day was torture. If we had been anywhere else, if we had been alone, I wouldn't have thought twice about kissing him, right there, right then.

I had a feeling he wouldn't have been upset about it at all.

But this job was important to me, and I didn't want to lose it because I had a crush on the man I had to literally *work on* from time to time. I told myself I had to get over every compliment, every sweet, sexy word he was aiming at me.

"Thank you?" I didn't mean for it to, but it came out as a question. He just smiled and bit his bottom lip, drawing my attention to his beautiful mouth. *Dammit.* I lifted my eyes to meet his, and he gave me one of the intense stares he usually reserved for his love scenes. *Damn him.* He closed his eyes and I leaned in closer, pinned his hair away from his forehead, and proceeded to apply the rest of the makeup.

Chapter 9

Hugh

On Sunday, I found her sitting on the side of the valley, in the middle of a patch of heather, her hair tied in a side braid, her black sunglasses on. She was enjoying the sunshine. The weather had been beautiful all morning, and that's why I had decided to come up for a hike. I stared at her for a while, fighting the impulse to call out her name. I should have left her alone, but I couldn't stop myself.

"Sam! What are you doing down there?" She waved at me and smiled brightly. I looked down, trying to find a path to her. In one way or another, it seemed I gravitated toward her. I had thought about her often since the first time we had spoken, up on this very hill. The mysterious California girl with the melancholic eyes had made an impression on me, and each time I saw her after that, she revealed a trait of her personality that surprised me. There was a softness in her manners, but she could have a hard edge when crossed—I had seen her get frustrated on set from time to time. She was shy, but there were certain situations where she would shed her skin and act with a confidence she didn't always display.

She reminded me of some graffiti I had once seen in LA that read, *She is beautiful and terrifying at the same time, like nature itself.* She was quiet most of the time, but there seemed to be an underlying fierceness trapped under all those layers.

Speaking of layers—she was always wearing too many clothes. I found myself fantasizing about her body. She was someone I worked with; I shouldn't have thought of her that way, but she made it impossible. She was sexy in an almost effortless, natural way.

I walked to the spot where she was sitting as she took her sunglasses off and smiled at me again. She had the sweetest smile, and as my eyes closed in on her, a smile of my own stretched across my face.

"What are ye doing here?" I asked as I sat down next to her.

"You're not the only one who's fond of the outdoors. I love it up here...even though it's still a bit of a walk for me. Plus, someone told me I better enjoy the sunny days, because they are few and far between."

I nodded and smiled. I had said something to her in that regard, and she'd scowled at me.

"It almost feels like a spring day today. It's so nice, and the sun is so...*bright* out here. It feels different than on the West Coast."

"Yeah, but winter is coming," I joked, quoting the House Stark's motto from *Game of Thrones*.

"Shhh. Don't rain on my parade." She shook her head slightly, looking as if she wanted to scold me, but then her expression turned into a smile. She pointed at something out in the valley. "Have you seen that cottage? I had never noticed it before."

I narrowed my eyes and focused in on a small white cottage with a dark grey roof on the other side of the valley.

"That's because it was hard to see all the way down there from this hill," I said, pointing toward where we had hiked before.

"Do you think anyone lives there?"

"Hard to tell," I replied. "Want to go check it out?"

"Another time, maybe. I kind of like sitting here in the heather," she said, giving me a look.

"Aye, you better enjoy it now, because it's not going to last long." She glared at me. "What did I say?" I asked with a laugh.

"Winter is coming. I get it, okay? California girl here, have some mercy," she said as she pointed at herself, a smile stretching across her beautiful face.

"Fine. I won't mention it anymore. Do you want me to leave?" I asked, and her smile fell. She shook her head.

"No. I don't want you to leave. Stay." Her voice sounded sweet and...sincere. She took something out of her bag and handed it to me. "Peanut butter and jelly sandwich?"

"Thank you." I took the sandwich from her hand. Her skin was soft, but cold. "Would you like to trade your sandwich for an apple?"

"Why, yes, I would," she replied. "Thank you."

I bit into the sandwich she had given me as she bit into the apple I gave her in return. My eyes focused on her mouth, on her soft lips pressed against the skin of the apple, and I had to make a conscious effort to direct my gaze elsewhere.

"This is delicious, by the way."

"Thanks," she replied.

"How long have you been up here?" I asked her when I

was nearly done.

"A while. All the girls went to Edinburgh, but I wasn't in the mood for it. I felt like I needed to spend some time by myself." A patch of clouds covered the sun, and she frowned, looking at me as if I had brought them on.

"Wasn't me, I swear."

She laughed, and I loved the way she tilted her head back as she did. I found myself studying her profile, her beautiful, impeccable caramel skin. Her bright smile created such a stark contrast with her skin and black hair, and her hair framed her face so perfectly, especially now that it was tied in a pretty braid.

"So, you wanted some alone time. Are you sure you want me to stay? I completely understand if you don't want me here. 'I love man no less, but nature more.'"

She frowned, her eyebrows pulled together. She gave me a long look, seemingly trying to figure out whom I was quoting.

"Lord Byron."

She nodded, and then smiled with a light shake of her head. "Handsome, chivalrous, and quotes poetry—what else?"

"Aye, Lord Byron was of Scottish descent. It's basically a sin not to know his verses." Then, I thought about what she had said, and I suddenly felt my cheeks redden. "Chivalrous?" I asked her.

She shrugged. "You helped keep me from landing on my face a few days ago up on this hill, and then you held my hand the entire time. That counts as chivalrous in my book." Her eyebrows shot up, a flirty smile illuminating her face. I hadn't thought about it at the time—had done it simply because it was the right thing to do—but then I'd kept holding her hand because it felt *right*. "And I've seen you taking care of Margaret on set, always making sure she's all right," she added.

I shrugged. "It's the least I can do," I said, looking down, feeling suddenly shy. I looked up, and our eyes met. The amused gaze in her eyes puzzled me.

"What is it?" I asked, my voice coming out huskier than I intended.

"This blush," she said, reaching for my cheek and brushing my skin with her forefinger. "It's the cutest thing." I smiled, letting out a shaky breath, and I looked down, mostly afraid that my blush would deepen. "I didn't mean to make you uncomfortable. I was just trying to pay you a compliment," she added.

I grinned, and her smile widened.

"Thank ye," I told her with a grin, still red in the face, and she laughed. "So, how are you liking Scotland?"

"It's beautiful. I love it here." She let out a breath, but her eyes were betraying something else: longing.

"Do you miss yer family?"

"I do, actually, more than I ever thought possible." She looked to her side and cut off a small branch from a heather plant next to her. She fiddled with it between her fingers. "I know it sounds silly. I'm an adult, and I have the chance of a lifetime working here."

"It doesna sound silly to me. It's nice that you have such a strong bond with your parents and your siblings. I miss my own family, and they're just a short trip away."

"I guess I hadn't realized how hard it would be to keep in touch with the time difference. I'm used to talking to my sister on a daily basis, but I don't want to complain. This is what's best for me. I needed a break from LA, anyway." She looked at me and frowned. "Do you like LA?" she asked with a curious look on her face.

I let out a breath and smiled. "I mean, don't get me wrong, it's the *United States*—the land of opportunity. For an actor, Los Angeles is like Mecca. It doesn't get better than that. I do like the city, but I guess if I had to consider it without thinking about the business side of it, I would pick New York over LA in a heartbeat. It's just an older city, and it has so much history. I don't mean to offend you in any way. I'm probably missing out on something special LA has to offer. After all, I just spent about a year there."

"No, I get it. You're right, sort of. It's a tough city to live in, especially if you have no ties to it. I guess I love it more than any other place because it's home. And of course, I've been lucky, growing up in a family that has been in the business for so long...I have so many wonderful memories of visiting my parents on set. From a child's perspective, it always looked so magical. *I loved it.* I have been chasing the magic ever since." The tone of her voice was nostalgic, but the smile on her face was so bright, it reached her eyes.

"You're beautiful. Why not try acting?" The words were out of my mouth before I could realize what I was saying. Her eyes widened, but she gave me a small nod, ignoring my compliment.

"Acting is not for everyone," she said shyly.

"True, but you've been around the business your whole life. You never had any desire to try?"

She shrugged. "I don't know," she said with a small smile, her eyes fixed on the branch of heather between her fingers. "I suppose I found the magic somewhere else." She glanced my way and raised an eyebrow. "What you create on set, it's beautiful. It's an enchantment, really. Actors are like magicians, but I love the magic that happens backstage. That's what I fell in love with when I was a little girl—the chaos, the preparation, the moment before everyone is ready for a scene, the very instant before someone says 'Action!'"

I nodded and stared into her eyes, captivated by her

words.

"Besides," she continued, "I did take acting classes with Amira. It wasn't for me. I froze on more than one occasion. I wasn't able to evoke emotion, and I hated having everyone's eyes on me."

"But you don't mind singing in front of a crowd?"

"I don't mind singing in front of *friends.* I could never act in front of strangers."

"So when did you realize you wanted to choose this career?"

"I narrowed it down when I was in high school. I knew I wanted to either be a makeup artist or a costume designer, and let's just say I found out rather quickly I was better with the brush than I was with the needle. Did you always want to be an actor?" she asked.

"Aye, for as long as I can remember."

"This must be a dream come true for you. It's the role of a lifetime."

"It is, and I'm determined to make it great. I want to make Abarath unforgettable."

SAM

I used to be a person who enjoyed being on her own. I was in a relationship for what amounted to almost a fourth of my life at that point, and I loved being by myself from time to time. However, as of late, I had a hard time being on my own. Maybe it was just because I was homesick and was still getting used to being there. I was surrounded by people all day long, yet I dreaded the moment I'd be alone.

After Eric and I broke up, I had the hardest time sleeping on my own, and it was safe to say I was still not used to having the bed all to myself.

Lately, I didn't enjoy my company as much. I noticed that my mind would sometimes go to a very dark place. Occasionally, the memories of that night at the Golden Globes would flash in front of my eyes.

The betrayal, the heartbreak, the anger—I relived it all over again.

I replayed the whole breakup, including the mayhem of epic proportions that followed a few months later. Eric firing insults at me in a conference room filled with attorneys, their blank stares...I had wanted to feel vindicated, and yet, I felt humiliated.

My heart felt as if it had shriveled to the size of a prune. It felt smaller, but heavy as lead. I had been living with that feeling for weeks.

I felt smaller. I felt *insignificant.* I felt as if I didn't matter.

And to think I had been so ballsy when I'd delivered the blow. In the aftermath, I looked like the wounded one.

Earlier in the week, I had made plans with Margaret, Blair, and a few other girls. I suspected Cecilia and Oliver were finally hooking up, even though she hadn't confessed yet. I believed I was right simply based on the fact that she hadn't been around all weekend.

When I woke up on Sunday morning, I was in one of my dark moods, and I felt the need to come to a place I knew would make me happy. I had been thinking about the heather-covered glen for days, ever since I had been up there with Hugh. I had been longing to go back, but the weather had been horrible. Finally, it was a fabulous, almost spring-like day. It seemed to be the perfect time. I felt sure going up there would help me get out of my dark mood.

And it worked. The hills covered in purple flowers had such a soothing effect on my soul. Being out in the wilderness seemed to have a calming effect on me. As hippie as it might sound, I felt in sync with nature and all the elements.

I hadn't expected to see Hugh up there, much less that he would come sit down with me. My body hummed with excitement at his nearness. I got heady just on his smell, musky and masculine, tinged with peppermint.

We were alone. Completely alone.

Our shoulders were less than two inches apart. He only had to lean in and kiss me. He only had to make a move, and I would be his.

I wouldn't have minded rolling in the heather, kissing Hugh MacLeod.

Too bad he never did.

There are certain patterns you fall into when you live your life away from home. Some people take a lover, like Cecilia did, while other people surround themselves with friends. I found both things to be appealing. I would have liked to have a lover—Cecilia seemed even more cheerful than usual—and yes, I sort of had my eye on one guy in particular, but I enjoyed the fact that I relied on my colleagues more than I'd ever thought. We were a tight-knit group, much more than all the other people I had worked with in the past. We were all quite different, each one with a different story and upbringing, yet we seemed to get along better than most families.

When I was surrounded by the amazing women I worked with, I suddenly didn't feel lost or homesick anymore. It didn't matter that we were born decades and continents apart; there were other things that united us—a love for storytelling and for movies, for one, as well as a passion for anything regarding our craft. Of course, what united us above everything else was the desire to make this one of the best shows ever. We shared other passions, too: an unhealthy love for food, wine, and chocolate—although some of my colleagues did prefer whisky—and a passion for music. Along with wine, music was what helped us unwind the most. It wasn't unusual for some of us to start singing and dancing even when it wasn't karaoke night.

Music helped us forget everything. Tiredness and frustration would automatically be washed away with a good sing-along.

It was during one of those nights after a long work day that we found ourselves at the pub, and Adele's "Send My Love (To Your New Lover)" came on. As soon as the first notes came through the speakers, everyone cheered and Blair asked Angus, the owner of the pub, to turn it up. Everyone around me started swaying and singing immediately, trying to mimic Adele's moves from the video. We all sang together at the top of our lungs without a care in the world. All the people around us stopped and stared, but we didn't mind. We were enjoying the moment too much, singing a song that was sort of a kind diss to an ex-boyfriend. We were different, yet we were the same. I looked at the women singing around me.

We had differences, but we all had one thing in common.

A broken heart. A love story that had left us scarred. A lover who didn't deliver on a promise. We'd all been there.

Heartbreak, the universal denominator.

A couple weeks passed, and I longed to see the valley

covered in heather again, but I didn't get another sunny Sunday. It had rained so much in the last two weeks, we had to reschedule a shoot in Gullane, on the west coast of Scotland. Thankfully, a few days later, the forecast improved and production told us we'd be heading out early the next morning. The producers were confident we would get everything we needed in one day. We were scheduled to shoot on Gullane's beach first and then by the remains of St. Andrew's Church. There was only a small group of us, a skeleton crew compared to our usual numbers. Still, we needed two buses to fit everyone.

We were up at four, and by four thirty, we boarded the bus that would take us there. You could tell no one wanted to be up that early. The crew was usually so cheerful in the mornings, but it was too early for that shit. People couldn't stop yawning, and as soon as they took their seat, many closed their eyes and dozed off. Cecilia and I took a seat across from Margaret at the back of the bus.

Gullane was about an hour and a half from where we were staying. It was still dark outside, and after we left, the bus driver turned the lights off.

Cecilia was asleep in no time, resting her head on my shoulder. I leaned my head on top of hers and tried to get some sleep, too.

I napped for a while, but then Margaret's voice startled me.

No, I realized it wasn't her voice that woke me up, it was her breathing. It was harsh, labored. Her eyes were closed, and her brows were furrowed. A few seconds later, she started complaining in her sleep. Her voice was barely audible, but she looked distraught, and she clutched her belly.

"Margaret," I said softly, stretching my arm to reach one of her hands. Cecilia's head fell off my shoulder, and she grouchily leaned against the window, never opening her eyes. "Mags," I said again as I placed my hand on hers.

She opened her eyes, and her frown deepened. She took a deep breath.

"Are you okay? You were talking in your sleep."

"Y-yes...I'm okay, I think. Just tired. A bit of cramping," she said, massaging her belly.

"Is that normal?" I asked.

"Yes...I think. The doctors said they're called Braxton Hicks. I've had them before. It felt just like this. It's nothing...I just need to drink more water. Yell at me if I don't, okay?" she said as she kept massaging her belly. She gave me a small smile and then added, "I'm going to try to sleep some more."

I fell asleep again and only woke up when the bus started moving back and forth to park on what looked like a dirt road.

The location scouts had rented an old, empty farm-style house so we could put all our equipment inside and get set up for wardrobe and makeup.

I grabbed a couple cases of our things, and Cecilia grabbed the rest, then we both followed Margaret inside the house.

It was cold as hell, and I shivered inside my jacket.

It didn't even look like the place had electricity, but as Cecilia turned the switch on, I was pleasantly surprised to discover that it did. I stopped a production assistant and asked them for a space heater or something to make the place more comfortable. I was freezing, but I was honestly more worried about Margaret. I knew she had just reached the thirty-two-week mark, as she'd told me herself a couple days prior, so she still had eight more weeks to go. She had been trying to do less and just supervise our work, but the long schedule was hard on most of us, and I couldn't imagine how hard it was for her—we weren't the ones growing a human inside our belly. I was honestly worried that our long hours would eventually affect her pregnancy.

Margaret sat down and started organizing all our tools. We set up different stations so we could start calling in the actors who were going to be shooting that day.

We only had about a dozen between cast and extras, and the most tiring part would probably be staying out for touch-ups. I went into another room of the farmhouse and noticed that the catering people were setting up for food and drinks. We were going to need coffee and herbal tea for Margaret; it was going to be cold on the beach. I made a mental note to volunteer to go out so Margaret could stay inside.

I spotted Hugh on the way back to the makeup room. He was rehearsing his lines and staring out a window. He looked so serious, so different. I smiled, pressing my lips together. He looked regal and beautiful in his costume, his kilt wrapped around his shoulder, making him look even taller. I didn't want to interrupt him, so I looked away and went back to my team.

We had to wait for the extras to come out of wardrobe and hair first, and once we were done with them, we had the main cast come in. There were no prosthetics to apply to any of the actors, so it was just simple makeup. We weren't shooting a fight scene, so we didn't even need to work all day with synthetic blood.

It was going to be a long day, but an easy one overall.

Or at least it was supposed to be.

Margaret had managed to do most of her work sitting on a stool. It didn't look comfortable at all, especially with her growing belly, but she kept saying she felt fine. Every once in a while, she would grab her bottle of water and make sure to take a couple of sips.

When we were finally getting Hugh and two more actors ready, I noticed a weird expression on her face. Hugh was cracking jokes as usual, but the smile on her face was strained. She wasn't as relaxed and playful as she usually was, and even Hugh started noticing, since everyone in the room except for Margaret was laughing.

She stopped what she was doing and covered her eyes with her hand.

"Mags, are you okay?" Hugh asked her.

"Yeah, just give me a sec. I think my blood pressure is a little low."

"I'm going to get you something to eat. I'll be right back."

"There's no need," I heard her say before I left the room.

It took me no time at all to grab a few crackers and a banana.

"Please eat. I can finish up here," I told her. "Why don't you sit on that chair over there? You should really just be supervising us anyway, not doing all the hard work," I said, pointing to a folding chair that looked a lot more comfortable than the stool she had been sitting on. Thankfully, she listened to me.

"Thank you," she said softly, giving me a small smile.

I looked down, and blue eyes were staring at me.

"Hey." I smiled.

"Sam," he said with a nod, and that was all he had to say to make me smile.

"I'm going to finish up Margaret's masterpiece, okay?" I said with a wink. I dabbed the sponge with the foundation Margaret was using and applied it all over his face, making sure the coat was even and spotless all over.

I kept an eye on Margaret as I applied some brown eye pencil on Hugh's eyes and smudged it around the corners.

She had eaten a couple of crackers and taken a bite of the banana, but she didn't look any better. In fact, her face seemed even more tense, and she stopped eating altogether. She placed the rest of the food in her lap and kept massaging her belly.

"Mags...are you feeling okay?"

"Yes," she said as she stood up slowly. "I just need to use the restroom." She got up from her chair, holding the bottom of her belly. She noticed me staring at her, so I looked away and turned my attention to Hugh.

She walked out of the room, looking for the restroom.

"Should one of us go after her?" Cecilia asked. "I'm done here with Marcus anyway," she added.

"It's probably not a bad idea. Go check on her," I replied.

"What's going on?" Hugh asked.

"She's been acting weird all morning. I'm just worried, that's all. She still has eight more weeks to go, but has been acting really strange. I just want to make sure she's okay." I glanced down at him, and he gave me a worried look as I fixed his eyebrows.

"Cecilia, I told you, I'm fine!" Margaret said, exasperated. She walked back to her chair as Cecilia followed her closely. We exchanged a look, and just as Margaret was sitting down on the chair, she let out a sharp cry, clutching her belly.

We all ran over to her and she said, "Either I just peed my pants or my water broke."

Chapter 10

SAM

We wasted time trying to decide if we should wait for the ambulance or if we should use one of the buses to take Margaret to the nearest hospital, which was in Edinburgh.

"Just call the goddamn ambulance. I want to make sure she's properly taken care of!" yelled Nora, making her way through the crowd of people that was surrounding us and Margaret.

"Everyone! We're going to have a baby! Now, please resume your duties or the light is going to change and we'll have to have this field trip all over again." She commanded the crowd and, with a smile, gestured for everyone to leave the room.

Everyone had left, and it was just me, Nora, Margaret, Woody—an executive producer—and Hugh. Nora knelt in front of Margaret.

"You're going to be okay, sweetie," she told her with a smile. "How do you feel? How far apart are your contractions?"

"Not sure. Not that close, though...I think. Every few minutes, maybe."

"The ambulance is going to be here in thirty minutes. The hospital is forty minutes away," said Nora's assistant Ian as he barged into the room.

"See? You and the baby are going to be okay." Nora kissed Margaret on the head.

"Hugh, I think we're ready for you. Is he ready?" Nora asked, turning in my direction.

"He is," I replied.

"Sam, please go with Margaret to the hospital." I nodded. I had already decided I wasn't going to leave Margaret's side until she could get ahold of her husband. "Mags, do you want us to call your husband?" Nora asked.

She shook her head and smiled. "No, thank you. I'll do it."

Thirty minutes later, the paramedics were ushering Margaret into the ambulance, and I took a seat next to her. Even though Nora had told everyone to resume their duties and take their place, there was a small crowd waving us good-bye. Even Hugh came to see us off, and before the paramedic closed the doors, he jumped in the van.

"Good luck, Mags. I can't wait to see the little brat!" he told her with a grin, squeezing her hand.

She smiled back and said, "Be nice or I'll send you a picture of her covered in blood and birth goo!" He smiled brightly and nodded. He then turned to me and tipped my chin up with his finger. My eyes widened, and my breath hitched. His gesture shocked me.

"Take care of her. I'll call ye later." His eyes pierced mine with their intensity, and I couldn't manage a single word. All I could do was nod. My eyes widened even more when he kissed me on the forehead, but my brain was still processing what he'd said about calling me.

He's going to call me?

We had never exchanged numbers.

He jumped out of the van, and the doors closed. Soon we were moving, heading toward the hospital.

"Boy, you pulled quite the stunt to get out of work today," I joked, stifling a yawn. "You owe me some coffee, woman."

"I think you'll end up owing me, *lass*," she joked, rolling on her side, trying to get comfortable on the stretcher. "I'm getting out of your way just in time for you to make your move," she said with a smile, and I frowned. What did she mean? Did she think I was gunning for her position? That I was glad she was having this baby early so I could take over?

"What? Mags, no. I have no desire to take your job."

"I'm not talking about my job, although I already told Nora you should take over my responsibilities for the rest of this season. I'm talking about Hugh, silly. This way you can stop dancing around each other like fools."

"What? No! You've got it all wrong."

"Sure." She smiled, and then her face contorted. She was having another contraction.

"Breathe. Inhale and exhale slowly. Isn't that what they

tell you to do?"

"I don't know," she confessed. "I was supposed to start some online Lamaze classes in a couple of weeks, but I guess it's too late for that."

I smiled at her, trying to reassure her. "You'll be okay. You're getting to meet your baby early, that's all."

"So, you and Hugh..."

"You're mistaken. We're just friends."

"Sure, because friends touch friends like this," she said, stretching her arm across to tip my chin up the same way he had. "And friends kiss friends on the forehead. I saw that. Don't bullshit me."

"Seriously, there's nothing going on. We're just friends."

"Has he kissed you yet? I've been told he has mad kissing skills."

I pressed my lips together, hoping to hide my embarrassment. "Would you stop? No, he hasn't kissed me, and he probably never will."

"Oh, he will. It's just a matter of time. I've seen how he looks at you. I've noticed how he lights up when you're around. He might not have made a move yet, but he likes you."

"Shouldn't we be talking about your baby right now? Shouldn't we be calling your husband?"

"Fine. Oh, shite. Beckett is going to be pissed off. Or excited. Or both. Would you pass me the mobile, please?"

I looked in her bag and placed the phone in her hand. She wrapped hers around mine.

"Tonight." She pointed her finger at me, eyebrows raised, a playful smirk in place.

"What?" I asked, confused.

"I bet you twenty pounds he's going to kiss you tonight."

I stayed with Margaret in the room and held her hand as her contractions got stronger and stronger. Beckett, her husband, was in London and wouldn't be arriving before late afternoon.

"I am fine, Beckett. They said it's going to take hours, so don't you bloody rush with that damn car. Yes, someone is here with me. I'm in good hands," she said, glancing my way. "I will see you later." She hung up the phone and tensed up as another contraction ran through her body.

"Breathe," I reminded her, and as the pain got stronger, the nurses gave her some pain meds, and I massaged her back, trying to relieve the tension.

I didn't know how strong the drugs were, but soon she started blabbering, telling me how much she loved me and how she couldn't wait to meet her baby. She also kept talking about how Hugh and I would make a lovely couple. I played along, occasionally laughing at her silly predictions.

When Beckett finally made it to the hospital, Margaret was dilated almost seven centimeters. She had asked for an epidural, and they had given her one. She said she could only feel a little pressure, nothing like the pain of earlier in the day. She was mostly herself now, but at times she still talked nonsense.

"Sam is going to get kissed tonight," she told her husband as he placed a kiss on her forehead.

"What?" Beckett asked, confused.

"It's nothing...just an inside joke. I'm going to wait outside so you two can have some privacy." I hugged Margaret and kissed her on the forehead. "It's almost over. You'll do great, Mags."

"He's going to kiss you tonight," she whispered in my ear.

"Okay, okay." I laughed.

Beckett pulled me into a hug.

"Thank you for being here with Margaret."

"It was my pleasure," I replied.

I left the room and checked my phone. I had shoved it in my backpack and completely forgotten about it.

I had messages from Cecilia and Hugh, asking about Margaret and the baby.

Judging from Cecilia's last message, they were almost done in Gullane. In all the commotion of the day, I hadn't had time to think about how I would get back to St. Martin, but now I had to come up with a solution. It would have been nice if someone were going to send a company car to pick me up; it had been a long day, and I was worn out.

A few minutes later, I got a message from Cecilia.

We're sending someone to pick you up in a little bit.

She added a winky emoticon at the end.

Thanks. I don't want to leave until the baby is born, anyway.

You'll like your driver. He's hot.

I rolled my eyes but played along. I looked like crap, and the last thing I wanted was a really hot driver I'd feel uncomfortable around.

Really? Please, do tell.

Oh, you'll see for yourself soon enough.

Tease!

A couple hours later, Posy Lake was born in the Royal Edinburgh Hospital.

Beckett and I hugged again, relieved and happy. Unfortunately, Margaret barely had the time to hug her daughter before the nurses took her away and placed her in an incubator. Posy wasn't presenting any serious issues, but because she was premature, they had to keep her in an incubator for a few weeks. A while later, Beckett pushed Margaret to the neonatal intensive care unit in a wheelchair, and I followed them. I watched Margaret hold the hand of her preemie, and for a second, I felt as if I were intruding on a family moment.

"Sam," said a deep voice behind me. It felt like a caress, and I smiled and bit my lip before I even turned around. I knew exactly who it was. Cecilia's messages made sense now. Did this mean Cecilia was trying to tease me just as Margaret had been?

"Hey." I turned around to look at him, and he smiled.

"I saw you guys walk down the hall, and I followed you

here. Is the baby okay?"

"She's fine. They have to keep her in the incubator as a precaution, something about her body temperature with her being a preemie."

"She's a wee bairn, isn't she? What did they name her?"

"Posy." I smiled. "Her name is Posy Lake."

"Posy," he repeated. "I like it." He took a step forward and stood right beside me, watching the brand new parents interact with their baby.

I looked at Hugh. "So, are you here to pick me up?"

"Aye."

"Cecilia said my driver was *hot.*" I gave him a flirty smile, and he grinned.

"Aye, that's me. I hope you weren't expecting someone else." He had missed my gist completely. *Men.*

"I was not. I was trying to pay you a compliment, by the way, and you totally missed it," I joked, bumping my shoulder against his.

His eyes widened, and his mouth opened slightly, but he didn't say a thing for a couple seconds. Then, his shock turned into a cute, uneasy smile.

"Ah! I get it now. Long day, ya ken."

"I ken," I replied, smiling. He did look tired. He was even talking like his character. We stood in silence, watching Margaret and Beckett for a few more moments.

"I have to confess something," Hugh said. I turned my head in his direction and looked at him curiously. The smile on his face was loaded with mischief. "I might have volunteered to come pick you up. I wouldn't do it for just anyone, you know."

I smiled and looked up at him through my lashes. "Is

this your way of telling me I'm special? You came because of me?"

He nodded. "Well, the official story is that I came so I could congratulate the new parents."

I breathed out a laugh. "Of course."

"Nora said you'll be taking over for Margaret. Sorry to break it to you, but you'll have to work with me a lot more," he joked.

"That's what Margaret said." I tried to sound as neutral as possible, as if it didn't matter to me in the slightest. I glanced his way again, and he looked like he had expected a bigger reaction from me.

"Is that all you have to say?"

I closed my eyes and smiled, looking down. When I opened them again and turned to look at him, he was grinning. Were we really doing this? Was he really flirting with me? Maybe Margaret was right.

"Well, what I really wanted to say was, 'Yeah, that sounds *bloody* awful,'" I joked and rolled my eyes.

He smirked. "Awful, you say."

"*Bloody* awful." I matched his smirk with one of my own.

"Oh, I'll show you bloody awful." His eyes were bright and excited at the opportunity to tease me some more. He wrapped one arm around me and started tickling me around my waist with the other hand. I squealed, and it must have been loud enough for the parents to hear it because Margaret and Beckett looked our way. *Shit.* I hadn't meant to be so loud; we were in a hospital, after all. However, neither Margaret nor Beckett seemed too concerned—they just waved at Hugh, and then Margaret gave me a not-so-subtle thumbs up and a wink. *Seriously, Margaret? Not helpful.* I could feel Hugh's eyes on me as soon as she did that.

"Okay, let's lay down the law here, mister. You are not allowed to tickle me—"

"In public."

"In public," I repeated. *Wait, what?* I looked at him with a confused expression, and he laughed in my face.

"That look is one of my favorite things," he said as he put his index finger between my furrowed eyebrows.

What in the world is going on? I shook my head and decided to dismiss his words, at least for the time being.

"Really, let's be serious for a moment here," I said, turning around to face him. "You better be very nice to me, mister," I teased, giving him a look and raising my eyebrows.

"Oh, I plan to," he said in a low, gravelly voice that sent a shiver down my spine. He leaned in closer, his face just a few inches from mine, close enough that I could raise myself on my tiptoes and kiss him. "I'm going to be...*verra* nice to ye, Sam," he said, his accent stronger than usual. His eyes were dark for a couple of seconds, long enough to stir my insides, long enough for dirty thoughts to send a wave of heat between my legs. Then, he turned the smolder down and winked at me, reaching out with an arm and hugging me closer to him in the process.

He was so damn dreamy, even after a whole day on the set, and I seriously could have fainted in his arms. I realized I must have looked like a mess. I'd had a super early morning, a long day, and no makeup on my face whatsoever. Yet, he was here, hugging me, and I hadn't even asked him to. Maybe he did have a crush on me. I relaxed in his embrace and leaned my head against his shoulder.

Did he know I liked him? Did he know how much? Did he know I wanted to be around him all the time? As I started thinking about all the questions I didn't have answers to, my head started spinning, and I felt like I might really faint.

I placed my head against the nursery's glass window.

I was exhausted, but more than anything I knew I felt faint because I was thirsty and hungry.

"Sam, are ye okay?"

"Yes...just give me a second."

"Are you tired?"

"Y-yes...no. I'm not tired...I'm starving," I said with a laugh. "I didn't have a chance to eat anything."

"Let's go, then," he said, touching my elbow. "It's late, but this place I know should be open."

"Where are we going?" I asked, turning my head to face him.

"I'll take ye to the best kebab place in Edinburgh."

"So, you're saying Abarath shouldn't end up with Penelope?"

"I'm saying Leonia is his only true love. Come on, it's obvious," I argued.

"I don't know. He seems to be equally attracted to all of them," he said, taking another bite and cocking one eyebrow in the process.

I scoffed. "What? You've read the book, right?"

He looked offended for a second. "Of course. Many times," he said with a playful scoff.

"Then how can you say that? Abarath and Leonia belong together."

"I don't know. He's attracted to Penelope just as much."

"And Faroah," I added.

"And Faroah."

"But Leonia is his only true love. I know he's attracted to all three of them. Penelope is the smartest and Faroah is the most beautiful, but what he feels for Leonia is the purest form of love." He gave me a funny look as I argued my points, smirking behind the napkin as he cleaned his mouth.

I picked up one of the fries and tossed it in my mouth, then grabbed my soda, and took a drink. I could feel his eyes studying every single one of my movements.

"The purest form of love ye say," he muttered. His eyes were suddenly dark when I looked up at him, which caused my heart to do somersaults. The ache between my legs became more pronounced, and I wondered how much longer I'd be able to resist before I'd throw myself at him. *Dammit.* I bit my bottom lip, and that only seemed to make his eyes more intense. *Stop looking at me like that, Hugh, or I might jump your bones right here in this diner.* The kebab place was almost empty, but the owner had been staring at us since we'd gotten there.

"Leonia is the one he loves."

"But she's a princess, and he doesn't have much. Doesn't have a title. They can never be together. Their love story is doomed."

"But doesn't he save her kingdom from a dragon attack? That ought to count for something!" I explained, lifting my hands in frustration.

"Hold on." He pointed a finger at me and narrowed his eyes. "You said you only read the first book. How do you know Abarath saves Leonia's kingdom?"

I looked down, almost embarrassed, and brushed a strand of hair behind my ear. I closed my eyes and let out a deep breath.

"I might have looked online, okay? I couldn't wait to see what was going to happen!"

"Ha! You cheated. You're supposed to read the books," he teased.

"Yes, professor, I know that, but have you seen my schedule for the last five weeks? I can hardly keep my eyes open when I get back to the townhouse. How am I supposed to make it through multiple eight-hundred-page volumes?"

"Ha! Have you looked at our schedule for the next five months?"

"My point exactly." I smiled at him, and he smiled back, relaxing against the leatherette of the booth. I loved being there with him. It was easy; it felt natural. I could have continued teasing him all night. I sighed and looked away.

He cleaned his hands with a napkin. "Are you ready to go back?"

I nodded, pursing my lips.

"What's wrong?" he asked with a frown.

I shook my head. "It's nothing."

"Come on. Tell me." His voice was low and deep, and although he was not close to me, I could almost feel it on my skin. Being around him was intoxicating. Everything about him drove me crazy. I shivered, imagining us in a more intimate setting, preferably naked…

I dismissed the thought as I took a deep breath.

"I almost don't want to go back. I'm tired, but I'd like to take a walk around Edinburgh," I confessed shyly with a shrug of my shoulders.

He stood up, locked eyes with me, and extended his hand. "Let's go, then."

Chapter 11

SAM

Much to my dismay, he didn't kiss me that night.

We walked to Edinburgh Castle, and it was a chilly but lovely evening. The sky was clear of clouds, and the moon was out, giving the city an even more alluring glow.

Hugh pointed out his university, which was a couple blocks down the road.

"That's the Royal Scottish Academy where I studied drama. I used to live in an apartment two streets over. It was a hole in the wall, but it had this tiny balcony and you could see the whole city from there. I don't know how many nights I spent looking at the city, wondering if my dreams would ever come true, if I would ever be able to support myself as an actor." His voice was low, and his words almost sounded like a confession. He told me about his struggles and how he was glad he hadn't given up on his dream.

I was standing against a short wall on the bridge that led to the main entrance. I was listening, drinking him in.

I couldn't stop staring, marveling at every detail of his beautiful face, and I was itching for his lips to touch mine.

It was the perfect setting. As if he could read my eager eyes, he suddenly stopped speaking. His eyes grew darker, and he took a step toward me, leaning his head down.

Lights. Camera. Action.

"Samhain," he said, cradling my face with his hand. He didn't need to say any more, because I knew that from there on out he was going to let his lips do the talking. I arched my body against him, parted my lips, and closed my eyes. I felt his breath on my face, his lips kissing my cheek—but just as he was about to close the distance between our lips, his phone rang. We both opened our eyes, startled by the sound, and he grabbed the cellphone from the pocket of his jeans.

"It's Nora," he said. He pressed the green icon to accept the call. "Hello? Yes. No, we're still in Edinburgh. Yes. Yes, I know." I could hear through his phone what she was telling him.

Have you guys left Edinburgh yet? You need to get home. We have another early day tomorrow. You know I didn't agree about you driving over there to pick her up. Hugh let out a deep breath as he ended the call. His jaw was taut, and he had lost the seductive look he'd had just a moment before. I sighed.

"I'm sorry, Sam."

"Don't be. I guess we need to get back now?" I asked, looking up at him.

He gave me a silent nod and then tipped his head to the side. "Come on, let's go."

I started walking after him, my feet moving unwillingly. I wasn't ready to let go. I wasn't ready to go back.

Who knew when we'd get another chance?

I decided to seize the day.

"Hey, Hugh," I said, stopping in my tracks.

He turned around, his eyes soft. "What is it, Sam?" His voice was sweet, and there was a hint of a smile on his face. I stepped in closer and embraced him, running my right hand up the back of his neck, my fingers combing through his curls. We stared at each other for a second; I wanted to make sure I wasn't making a mistake. His eyes widened in surprise, and his lips parted just slightly. I closed the distance and pressed my lips against his.

My kiss was shy at first, wanting to make sure it was what he'd had in mind. My lips were still for a couple seconds, just relishing the feeling of his warm, soft mouth under mine. Then, his arms enveloped me, holding me tight against his body. His teeth bit my bottom lip before searching for my tongue, and my heartbeat quickened as warmth spread through my chest all the way to my fingertips, a pleasant contrast to the chilly air I breathed in. His tongue skillfully danced around mine, releasing all the tension and pent-up sexual frustration of the last few weeks.

"Sam, I've wanted to do this for so long," he said breathlessly as he leaned his forehead against mine.

I hummed happily.

He kissed me again, slow, deep, and all-consuming. His scruff was tickling my skin, heightening all my senses, but then he stopped.

"Don't stop." My voice was heavy with need, and that caused a smirk to appear on his face. I looked up into his eyes, which were charged with lust, yet playful, and wetness pooled between my legs.

"If we don't stop now, I might not be able to control myself. We could get arrested for public indecency."

I licked my lips and gave him a flirty look. His eyes grew a darker shade of blue.

"Don't they say you should try everything at least once?" My tone was serious, and he raised one eyebrow. I dropped the façade. "I'm kidding."

"That's too bad," he replied with a low growl, and when my jaw dropped at his statement, he tipped my chin up, closing my mouth. "If I weren't attached to a multimillion-dollar project, I would totally make love to you in front of Edinburgh Castle, public indecency be damned."

I inhaled sharply, still feeling heady, still turned on, needing more of his kisses.

As if he could read my mind, he kissed me again, soft and sweet this time, and when he broke the kiss, he laced his fingers with mine.

"Let's go."

When we got to the car, I sent Margaret a text.

He didn't kiss me tonight. I kissed him.

Hugh

I enjoyed being reckless when it came to sports, but I liked being safe with everything else. When it came to Sam, however, I felt like throwing caution to the wind. I was trying to keep my focus on the road, yet I couldn't stop fantasizing about taking her in the backseat of the car I had gotten from production. I couldn't stop imagining her naked against the supple leather of the luxury sedan.

She tried to stay awake for most of the ride, making small talk, telling me about helping Margaret through labor. She curled up on the seat, using her puffer jacket as a blanket as she told me stories about her sister and brother, and I told her about growing up with Declan, Tamhas, Fergus, and Ewan.

She fell asleep after a while, and although I was keeping my eyes on the road, I couldn't help but steal glances her way every so often to marvel at her beautiful features. Her face was a perfect oval, with thick eyebrows and high cheekbones. Her nose was a straight line pointing at her full, soft lips, which were pressed together in a slight pout as she slept. Her hair was as dark as the sky out on the Scottish Highlands, as dark as the night of Samhain. On top of her stunning features, her caramel skin drove me mad.

I wanted to take it slow, wanted to be a gentleman, but I'd have been lying if I'd said I didn't want to undress her and explore every inch of her skin.

She was poised most of the time, but I sensed a deep-rooted electricity buried in her that kept calling my name. I wanted to see her wild beauty come undone.

I just hoped I could manage to keep an appearance of self-control around her from now on. I knew things were going to be difficult for both of us if I let myself slip.

The boys and I had been out on a bike ride and came over to the pub for a beer and a bite to eat. It was one of those Scotland days when you'd have three types of seasons at once. It had started chilly in the morning, the wind blowing strong. Biking in Scotland was already not an easy feat, but with the wind it was twice as hard. Sometime around nine in the morning, the clouds had parted and we'd been able to enjoy a few hours of sunshine, but we'd had to cut our ride short because the weather started changing again, and soon it started pouring. We were already on our way back, but it was hard to ride with the rain impairing our vision.

We ordered some food at the bar, and I headed for the restroom to clean up. On my way back, I noticed Sam sitting in an armchair in a secluded corner of the pub, her eyes fixed on a tablet. She looked like she was reading. She was fiddling with her long black hair, which was tied in a low ponytail at the nape of her neck. The middle part highlighted the perfect oval of her face even more, and I remembered the way she looked when she was asleep next to me in the car. She was wearing a black turtleneck, yoga pants, and sneakers, the clothes hugging her body in all the right places.

It had been a torturous week. I had been hoping we would have time to talk about what had happened in Edinburgh, but we never seemed to be alone or have the time to meet up after hours. Every night, I hoped I would have a few minutes to call her and ask her to meet me at my place, but the writers had been rewriting the episode we had been working on, and I had a bunch of lines to learn. On the nights I wasn't busy with work, it seemed I couldn't get rid of my costars.

I longed for some time alone, and I was still hoping Sam and I could talk about what had happened at some point. My attraction for her hadn't changed—if anything, it had gotten stronger.

A lot of times, I had to keep my eyes shut when I was around her, not just because she had to work on my face, but because I had to concentrate on not getting a hard-on. Not only did she have a beautiful face and killer curves, she rendered me powerless with her sweet smile. Her voice was like velvet, soft as a caress, and one morning I woke up from wet dreams I'd had about her. On top of everything else, I couldn't get her smell out of my head. I had come to find out she wore freesia essential oil on her wrists, and it had become one of my favorite smells.

I realized it was as good a time as any to tell her I needed to talk to her. I knew she was probably confused by my behavior throughout the week, but she didn't let it show. When she looked at me, I saw the same desire in her eyes that was consuming me.

She hadn't noticed me yet, still immersed in her book. I didn't know why, but it made me smile. Her eyebrows furrowed, and then a smile stretched across her face. She laughed, covering her mouth with her hand.

God, she was beautiful. I had a last-minute impulse to turn around and go back to my friends, but it was too late, because just then, she looked up and her eyes met mine.

"Reading something good?" I asked.

Her eyes widened, and she looked embarrassed for a second, but then a wide smile illuminated her face.

"Very. Actually, it's *verra* good." She grinned.

"What is it?"

"*Voyager*, the third book in the *Outlander* series."

"Ah! I'm afraid Abarath can't hold a candle to that Jamie Fraser guy."

"Yeah, unfortunately, he can't. It's not Abarath's fault, though. Jamie Fraser is just a rare type of fictional hero. They are both charming, though."

"What is it about Scottish men, huh?" I teased.

"What is it about *fictional* Scottish heroes?" she corrected.

"Are you insinuating that real-life Scottish men are not as interesting as fictional Scottish heroes?" She looked down and smiled, shaking her head ever so slightly.

"I'm not saying that." Her eyes met mine for a brief second and then looked away. Mine fell to her pink lips, the curve of her neck, and her breasts, which were hugged so perfectly by the snug wool turtleneck.

"Well...we are talking about fictional characters. If you do know anyone who's a little less Casanova than our Abarath and more of a one-woman man like Jamie Fraser, kindly point me in his direction." There was a gleam of amusement in her eyes, but then it changed into something else, something darker, sadder. Who had hurt her? It had to be that fucker who'd cheated on her.

"Sounds like you ran into your own Abarath."

She shrugged. "Well, Abarath is not such a bad guy. He's not tied to any one of his love interests, and so far, I haven't seen him making promises he didn't keep—unlike some men. Also, I'm pretty sure fictional Scottish heroes don't send mixed messages to their love interests," she said, giving me a pointed look.

"I am sorry. It's been a lousy week. I have been slammed with rewrites every night. They have changed their mind so many times this week, they are driving me mad."

"Why didn't you tell me? Why didn't you text me?" she asked, her voice low.

"I wanted to, believe me. Have ye noticed we were never alone the entire week? Trust me, I did. I wanted to talk to ye so many times, Sam." She closed her eyes, as if she didn't want to listen to my reasons. "I'm not trying to make excuses for myself, but I probably should have texted ye."

"You should have." The tone of her voice was hard, and her eyes looked as if she wanted to shoot daggers at me.

"You don't understand," I tried to reason.

"Oh, I don't? Enlighten me then," she challenged, waggling her eyebrows.

I leaned in closer and lowered my voice, afraid someone might overhear. "Sam, trying not to think about you is one of the hardest things I've ever done. You have no idea how hard it is for me not to get turned on when you're around. I knew that if I started texting you at night, I would have gotten nothing done. When I have ye in my arms again, I'm not going to be able to let you go."

I saw her swallow, her eyes fixed on mine. I grabbed her wrist and felt her pulse quicken as her lips parted slightly. I almost forgot where we were when she licked her bottom lip. I wanted to kiss her, grab her, drag her on top of me. I wanted to feel her skin on mine. I wanted to undo her ponytail and have her hair falling on my face.

But this was not the time or place. I had to think of something else.

"By the way, what are you doing here? Wouldn't you be more comfortable reading at home? People's voices don't bother you?"

"Luckily, I can tune them out." She laughed. "What I can't seem to tune out or escape—even with the use of headphones—are my roommate's loud moans."

I thought I'd heard wrong, but the embarrassed look on her face told me otherwise.

I laughed. "What? Did I hear you right?"

She nodded. "Cecilia...she finally got together with Oliver, the guy from the lighting department. She's been lusting over him ever since we got here. You would not believe the things I have heard in the last ten hours," she said, shutting her eyes and making a face.

"*Ten hours?* Who is this guy?"

"Well, thankfully they went to sleep at some point, but they started all over again, hence my hanging out here. Some of the other girls went out of town, and I have nowhere else to go."

"I'm sorry, Sam, but you really shouldn't be eavesdropping," I said with a stern look.

"Eavesdr—" she said in an accusatory tone, but when she saw me laughing, she smiled and shook her head.

"Forget about Cecilia and her lover boy. Why don't you join us? It's me, Mick, Frank, and Marcus." I pointed at the guys on the other side of the bar.

She peeked at them curiously and then leaned back in her armchair.

"That sounds great, but I really have to finish this book, today if possible."

"Why today?"

"It's a long story," she explained. "My very competitive sister has been asking me to read these books for the last two years, ever since we started watching the show, and now that I am in Scotland, she said it's *unacceptable* that I haven't read them yet. So, she upped her game and challenged me to a dare."

"What's the dare? What happens if you don't read them?"

"She's given me a deadline for each one of them. According to her, I should be done with the books by the time we wrap season one, but I don't see how it's possible. Each one is a thousand pages! She wants me to be done with this one by the end of today. I'm at five hundred pages now, but there's no way that I can read another five hundred by the end of the day."

"What happens if you don't finish it tonight? What's the dare?"

She looked down and blushed. "I can't tell you."

"Come on, what is it? It can't possibly be that bad."

She shook her head and straightened herself up as if she was about to leave. I grabbed her arm.

"Sam, there's nothing you can't tell me. What are ye

supposed to do?" I asked. I was genuinely curious, partly because these two sisters seemed to take dares very seriously, and partly because she seemed rather distraught.

"She dared me to kiss a Scottish man. Can you imagine? What am I supposed to do, go to any guy and just say 'Hi, I'm supposed to kiss you for a dare'?" She looked around as if she were looking for a viable candidate.

"Sam, I'm offended. We kissed," I said in a low voice, unable to hide the frown on my face. "Don't I count?" I felt a little hurt, but I still managed a small laugh.

She blushed. She looked very cute when she was flustered.

"I told her I had already kissed a Scot, but she said it didn't count because it was in the past. I guess I'm going to finish these five hundred pages today." She made a face and raised her eyebrows.

I cleared my throat. "Ye wound me. I would gladly offer my services to get ye out of a dare."

She narrowed her eyes at me. "I'm not sure that after this week you deserve to come anywhere near my lips." *Ouch*. That hurt, but I kept my sexy face on and gave her an intense look.

"Oh, please. Quit it with the smolder, will ya?"

"Ouch! I must be losing my touch." I pouted, and she laughed at my dismay. I loved seeing her laugh. Then, I had a brilliant idea.

"How about this? I will give you some time to think about it."

"Oh, how generous of you. No than—"

"And you can go read at my place. You will definitely be more comfortable there." She frowned. "Here," I said, placing my keys on the table. "I won't be home for a few more hours."

"Oh. That's awfully nice, but I don't think I can do that,

Hugh."

"Why? You need a quiet place, and I'm offering you a quiet place. I guarantee there will be fewer distractions than there would be there."

"Okay then...thank you," she said, grabbing the keys off the table. She stood and put her jacket on. She moved closer, and I got a whiff of her heavenly scent. "Look, I appreciate the offer, as long as it comes with no strings attached—understood?"

"Understood," I replied absentmindedly, imagining all kinds of scenarios with strings attached. Was she really going to make me suffer for keeping my distance this week? I knew I sort of deserved it, but I needed to know if there was a chance she'd reconsider. I watched her walk away then joined the guys at the bar. They quizzed me about Sam, asking me what was going on. I was able to deflect some of their questions by ordering a couple of rounds of whisky, and when the first soccer game of the day came on, they were distracted enough to forget all about it.

Later that afternoon, I went back to my place, and it only occurred me when I was right outside the door that I didn't have my keys since I had given them to Sam. I rang the bell multiple times and started yelling her name against the door, feeling intoxicated. Multiple rounds of alcohol will do that to you, but I wasn't *completely* pissed, though; I was just on the edge of happily inebriated.

She opened the door, and I fought the impulse to take her in my arms and kiss her right then. She had been on my mind all day, even after she'd left the pub, and the alcohol only made me feel more reckless. Maybe it was just the right amount of reckless... I wanted her, and I knew she felt the same way. Even today, when she had been trying to resist me, I could see it in her eyes. She wanted me just like I wanted her. Why should I stop? Why should I stop myself when I wanted her so badly?

"Hey! You're back." She closed the door behind me, and I took my jacket off.

"How did the reading go?" I asked her in a low voice.

"I only have two hundred pages left. You were right—I just needed a quiet place. Thanks for letting me crash. I'll go back home now."

"No!" I said a little too loudly. "*Stay*. You don't need to go anywhere. I'll...I'll just go take a shower upstairs. I won't bother you."

"What? This is your place. I'm the one who doesn't want to intrude."

"And I don't want you to lose your bet." *Or do I?* "Stay. It's no problem, really."

I went upstairs and took a shower. I resisted the urge to stroke my cock under the warm water, but I couldn't stop myself from fantasizing about her body. I couldn't stop fantasizing about touching her...everywhere. So, inevitably, I got a hard-on, and I had to switch the water to cold to make it go away. Part of me was afraid she would leave while I was upstairs, and I still wanted to find an excuse to hang out with her, especially since I never got the chance to spend any time with her away from the set.

Did I need to be more straightforward with her and show her how much I wanted her? I hadn't been with anyone in a while, but being charming was never an issue for me—so why did I feel so nervous around this woman? My stomach was in knots, the anticipation killing me. She piqued my curiosity like no one else had. She was beautiful, but there was also an air of mystery about her. She was fun to be around, but her eyes were occasionally veiled with something I couldn't quite put my finger on.

When I went downstairs, she was still sitting on the couch, and I exhaled a breath of relief. I wanted to hang out with her, even if she didn't want to kiss me.

She smiled as I took a seat on the couch next to her, and in that moment, I decided.

Last time, she'd initiated the kiss. This time, I would be the one to kiss her.

Chapter 12

SAM

I was sitting next to Hugh MacLeod. Reading. On his couch. In his townhouse. When I'd woken up earlier that morning to Cecilia's moans and her bed frame thumping against the wall, I'd thought the day was going to be shitty from beginning to end.

Instead, I rather enjoyed the turn of events. I'd been able to knock out a lot of chapters, but now that Hugh was here, I couldn't concentrate on reading anymore. I was too distracted by him, and I read the same line over and over. He was watching TV but had turned the volume very low so it wouldn't bother *me*.

When I kissed him in Edinburgh the week before, I knew he wanted me. I could feel how turned on he was by the way he kissed me, the way he touched me. I could still remember how his body felt against mine, could still remember how it felt to be wrapped in his strong arms.

Mother of pearl, I would have seriously fucked him in the back of that sedan if he'd been up for it, but we'd had to head back, and there was no time...and I needed to take my time with him. I needed to explore every inch of his marvelous, statuesque body. I'd expected we'd resume the conversation during the week, but he had kept his distance. It was true that we had virtually no time and were never alone all week. We had been shooting away from the set, and he had been sharing the trailer with other actors to facilitate things. He could have texted me, but he didn't at all, which made me think he didn't feel the same way I did about him. It was his turn to show me he wanted me.

He had taken a shower, and now he smelled even better than usual, the clean scent pervading the space between us. His brown hair fell on his forehead; it was getting longer, and although it was overall wavy rather than curly, it formed small curls on the back of his neck. A few strands were still wet, and I fought the impulse to run my fingers through it. He hadn't shaved and was sporting the couple-days-old stubble I was all too familiar with. It was the length we usually kept it at for continuity purposes. He had changed into a black tee that said *Slay Hard* with the name of the show underneath, one of the promotional items the network had sent over. It stretched across his biceps, which was another reason I couldn't stop looking at him. He was wearing loose black pants that sparked my curiosity. I hadn't had sex in months—it was only normal to be curious and fantasize about his package, right? Listening to Cecilia getting some had only gotten me hornier. I couldn't help it. I wanted him to throw me across the couch and take me—if that was what he wanted. I needed him to be the one to make the first move this time.

I considered leaving before I did something stupid, like throwing myself at him—again. However, I had just tried to do so a few minutes ago, and he had told me to stay. It would have been rude to try to leave again, wouldn't it?

I lifted my eyes from my tablet and looked in his direction again. I stared at his beautiful profile, his straight nose, his jaw—I wanted to run a finger along the length of it. He looked so stoic and absorbed in what he was watching—some Formula One race by the looks of it—and I smiled to myself. I didn't peel my eyes from him fast enough, and he caught me. He raised both eyebrows at me, his eyes dark, and then he let out a deep breath as his lips curved in a smile.

I reached for my mug and took a sip of my drink.

"Oh! I didn't think about it—would you like something to drink?"

"You're offering me something to drink...in my house?" he asked, raising one eyebrow, one corner of his mouth tipping up. "I'm a terrible host." He frowned, looking truly disappointed in himself.

"No, no. See, I grabbed some vodka and orange juice on the way over—actually, I stopped at the house to get it, and...you don't want to know what I had to listen to," I said with a laugh. "Seriously. Those two need to tone it down a notch. After tonight, I'm having a talk with Cecilia." I walked to the kitchen with my glass in hand and grabbed the orange juice out of the fridge. I poured the vodka in a glass and mixed it with the juice, then made myself another round in my mug. "Hopefully, they'll stop going at it like rabbits," I said, rolling my eyes and handing Hugh his glass. He was laughing, and his eyes looked so beautiful when he did, shining even brighter. As he took the glass from me, his fingers brushed over mine, sending a jolt of electricity down my spine. *I need him to touch me.* I sat down on the couch and raised my glass in his direction.

"To your hospitality," I said.

He laughed. "To a perfect guest," he replied. We clinked our glasses. "Slàinte."

"Do dheagh shlàinte," I told him. I knew it meant something like *to your good health*; Rupert had taught me that.

"Very good, Sam," he replied with a wicked smile. We took a big sip of our drinks. "We really should be drinking whisky, though. Next time, maybe." *Next time.* Was there going to be a next time? His words made my heart do somersaults in my chest.

"How many more pages?" he asked as he placed his drink down on the coffee table. I did the same.

"Errr...a hundred and eighty-four. I can make it."

"That's too bad," he replied in a grave tone. He gave me a look so dark and intense, it could have easily melted my underwear. His words confused me, though.

"Why is that?" I asked with a frown.

"Because I would have willingly helped ye with your dare." His eyes never left me, and now they were fixated on my lips. He took the tablet out of my hand and placed it on the coffee table. He did want to kiss me then, and I wanted him to, although I did want him to grovel a bit for the radio silence he'd given me all week.

He scooted closer to me on the couch.

I had fantasized about kissing him again—*a lot*—but

now I couldn't move. I was petrified. He ran his fingers across my cheek, and just the feel of his skin on mine sparked a wave of heat in my belly. He loosened up my ponytail. I licked my bottom lip and leaned in closer, and he did the same. My breathing became faster and labored, my heart playing a rhythm that resembled some kind of tribal-like tune inside my chest. I thought I knew his face so well, but now that we were sitting like this, I caught other details I tried not to focus on when I was doing my job. The specks of darker blue in his irises, the lines of the tiny wrinkles around them. The translucency of the skin under his eyes. The red and the gold in his stubble. Our noses brushed, and I looked up at him, serious and impenetrable. His lips parted slightly, and I almost wanted to bite him, but he needed to take the lead. He tipped my chin up with a finger before pressing his lips on mine. This was it. We were kissing. *Again.*

His lips didn't leave mine for a few seconds. He cradled my head at the nape of my neck just as the tip of his tongue parted my lips, finding mine. Adrenaline coursed through my body, and I felt a rush from my head all the way to my toes. My tongue wrapped around his eagerly, kissing him back in slow, long strokes. His stubble tickled my skin, and I ran my fingers through his hair, holding him close, not wanting to let go.

He broke the kiss and pressed his forehead against mine, and I cradled his jaw.

"There, you fulfilled your dare."

My dare? Was this just about the stupid dare? My face fell.

"Fuck—"

He pressed a finger against my lips, silencing me with a teasing look. "No, that's not the only reason I did it. I haven't stopped thinking about kissing you again since last week, Sam, and now that I had another taste, I dinna want to stop. I want to kiss ye again and again, until ye beg for mercy," he said, his voice low and seductive, sending a shudder down my spine. My breath hitched, and I met his eyes, which were charged with intent. A moment later, he grabbed me by the hips and pulled me on top of him as if I weighed nothing. He marveled at my closeness, his hands running up and down my sides, his eyes full of excitement, as if he couldn't decide what he wanted to touch first.

I pressed my hands into the couch on either side of him to keep my balance and then teased him, offering my mouth and then pulling back. The smirk that appeared on his face was worth it. I lowered myself again and kissed him, this time taking control, exploring his mouth, licking his lips, biting gently on the soft skin of his bottom lip. I could feel him hard against me, and I grinded my hips against his. He moaned in my mouth, and adrenaline rushed through me.

We were making out, and if I let things progress, I could end up in his bed. *Tonight.* I really, really wanted to, but I was afraid it would make things complicated at work, and at the moment, I didn't need complicated. I needed simple.

But...I also needed a man. I needed *this.* Flesh and bone under my fingers. Muscle. So much muscle. Damn, he was so sexy, and he was such an amazing kisser. If this was the way he moved his tongue, I couldn't wait to see what else he could do with it.

I clearly wasn't the only one to have these kinds of

thoughts—his hands were all over me. He grabbed my ass, pushing it down on him, kneading the skin with his hands. His impatient fingers skimmed under my turtleneck, caressing my skin, going up, all the way to my breasts. He touched them gently and gave them a soft squeeze.

He broke the kiss, breathing heavily. He rested his head on the couch and looked at me with heavy-lidded eyes. He caressed my face and ran his fingers through my hair.

"You're so fucking sexy, Sam. I've wanted ye since the first time I laid eyes on you."

"The first time? When I was talking to my mom?"

He laughed. "Okay, maybe the second time, when you called out my name as if ye knew me."

"An honest mistake."

"A beautiful mistake. I have been fascinated with you ever since, and I can't even count how many times I've wanted to kiss you."

My eyes widened in surprise, and a small laugh escaped my mouth. I covered my face with both my hands, a mix of embarrassment and amusement coloring my cheeks. He captured both of them and wrapped them around his neck, bringing my face closer to his.

"What? Ye mean you never thought of me that way?" he asked, cocking one eyebrow. The smile on his face told me he didn't believe me. He wasn't wrong.

I rolled my eyes, letting out an awkward laugh. "A lot, actually—more than I'd like to admit." A big, bright smile stretched across his face, and I leaned down, kissing him as if it were the first time all over again. As he continued his exploration of my skin, I raised my arms and took off my sweater. I made him take off his shirt, and then I kissed his shoulders and traced the line of his chest, marveling at the beauty of him. I trailed kisses on his neck, down to his chest, the fresh scent of his skin tingling my senses. His fingers traveled into my pants, underneath my underwear, caressing my ass. He teased my wet center from behind while moving his other hand to my front, stroking my clit. I stared into his eyes, determined, dark with sheer desire. *To hell with everything.*

I wanted him, and as risky as it was, it felt right.

The flickering of his fingers against me increased just as a buzzing sound made the couch tremble with vibrations.

My phone.

Dammit.

I decided to ignore it, and after a while, it went silent.

"Keep going. I want you," I whispered.

A moment later, it started buzzing again.

"Fuck!" I muttered.

Hugh laughed softly. "Maybe you should answer."

I grabbed my phone from under the pillow. It was Cecilia.

"Hello?"

"Sam! Where the bloody hell are you? You're not at the pub."

"Uh, I left."

"Want to have a sarnie together? I'll come meet you."

I hesitated for a moment and tried to come up with an excuse, but I was drawing a blank. "Uh, I'm just walking around town. I'll come meet you. Stay put." It was the first thing I could think of.

"See you in a bit."

I hung up the phone, realizing I had just said I would

meet her at the pub. I wasn't going to have sex tonight. Stupid me. Missed opportunity.

"I have to go meet her or she'll wonder what I'm up to—"

He nodded.

"I'm sorry," I said.

"Me, too," he replied with a small smile, looking up at me. I leaned down and kissed him again...and again.

"You're a really good kisser, by the way."

His lips curled up in a smile. "Years of practice," he replied with a laugh. I pulled myself off him unwillingly, and I put my sweater back on.

"I'm going to use the restroom," I said. I fixed my hair back in a ponytail and washed my face. My lips were a little red, but it wasn't anything a little ChapStick couldn't fix. My eyes, though—they were wide and excited as if I were high. Well, in a way I was. *High on Hugh.* Although part of me knew it was better this way, I was sorry to leave.

I found him standing in the middle of his living room, hands in his pockets. He'd put his shirt back on, unfortunately, and I sighed. He smiled at me, and I fought the impulse to run and wrap my arms around him. Before I said good-bye, though, I did caress his face, and when he leaned down, I kissed him again. This one was hard and fast, a kiss driven by the fact that neither one of us wanted to let go.

"I can't wait to see you tomorrow," he whispered against my lips.

I begrudgingly let go of his hand and left to go meet my pest of a roommate.

A few steps down the road, I pulled out my phone to

send a text to my sister.

Dare fulfilled. Scot kissed.

She replied a few minutes later.

You're a lousy reader.

I am so not, but I found a Scot who's possibly as dreamy in person as Jamie Fraser is on paper.

Where did you find such guy?

On set, duh.

Oh, Sammy. I thought you didn't want to go there.

I didn't, but he started it.

Oh, this is good stuff. I'm calling you.

Chapter 13

Hugh

Things were good for all of two days. Granted, it was neither my fault nor Sam's. The circumstances sucked, and it only got worse.

I didn't seem to have a choice when it came to Sam.

For years, I had avoided any distraction and only focused on work, but now I couldn't push my thoughts of her away. I knew this wasn't the time to chase after someone, yet my heart wasn't listening.

It was a daily struggle to be so close to her and not being able to do anything. Even when we weren't together, I could see her. I could feel her. If I closed my eyes, I could picture her moving around me in that certain way she seemed to move. She looked like a panther around set, moving swiftly from one station to another. Black hair, dark skin, and black clothes; she was sinuous and sexy—at least when she wasn't wearing big coats that swallowed up her figure.

I could see her beautiful mouth and her sweet brown eyes, which sometimes turned as dark as the blackest coffee. The air of mystery about her was one of the things that attracted me the most, and her soft voice was another, but the way her eyes seemed to look right through me was what was most unsettling.

On top of that, when she smiled at me, I felt powerless. I didn't have a chance against her. I had to give in. I wanted to fall for her, follow her anywhere.

We tried to behave for the first two days of the week, but then I made a mistake. I requested for Sam to come to my trailer to do my makeup.

Nora wasn't too happy about my request and eyed me with suspicion. I justified it by saying I was coming down with a cold. No one wants the lead actor to get sick. She agreed then, reminding me of the upcoming press trip to London. I was supposed to leave with some of the main cast.

"We're all going to have a meeting before you guys leave to brief you about what you can and can't say." I didn't think any of it sounded unusual; those kinds of briefings were standard procedure. I knew the network wanted us to go on a first round of interviews and show a few snippets of what we had filmed so far. Abarath had a massive audience, but we had to conquer the viewers who were not familiar with the books. We'd go on a short promo tour now and then would do a worldwide tour the next year when the show was going to air.

Having Sam alone in my trailer only made it harder for me to be good. I was the one trying to misbehave, disrupting her work, trying to steal more kisses.

"Listen," she finally said after my last attempt at delaying the process. "Whose job do you think it's going to be on the line here? You've already raised enough suspicions by calling me to your dungeon."

"Dungeon?" I asked her, fighting a smile. "I think Nora believed I was getting sick. Are you questioning my acting skills?"

"I would never," she deadpanned. She smiled at me, and then leaned down to kiss me again. "This is the last one you'll get today, so you better make it last." Her fresh, minty breath against my lips was the most delicious invitation. Her lips were made to be tugged at and bitten. I didn't know how much longer I could wait until I had her in my bed, naked. I pressed my lips against hers, and as they parted, I captured her tongue with mine, tasting her until she pulled away.

"Now, let me do my job."

"Ye better kiss me again before I leave for London tonight."

"Only if you promise to behave," she said with a grin.

"And what if I'm up to no good?" I gave her a playful look, waggling my eyebrows.

"Then you'll get nothing until you get back."

I gave her arse a squeeze, and after she swatted me on my shoulder, I promised I'd behave for the rest of the day.

We had a meeting in the afternoon before leaving the set, and that's when I got news that didn't sit well with me. Unfortunately, there was nothing I could do about it, but I wasn't sure how to break it to Sam.

After the meeting, I had the hardest time saying my lines, and I had to force the whole crew to stick around a bit longer just so I could get the scene right.

I went back to my trailer in a daze as everyone else was leaving. After a while, there was a knock on the door.

"Come in."

"It's me," Sam said as she closed the door behind her. She walked toward me with a playful smile on her face, and my heart sank. How was I going to break it to her?

I didn't want to hurt her. I never wanted to hurt her.

She started getting her things organized to clean my face, but I grabbed her by the waist and made her sit on me. I gazed into her chestnut brown eyes, trying to come up with the right words to say.

"I need to get all that grime off your face. After that, I hope I can give you a kiss or two before you leave. The drivers are already out there, waiting for you guys."

I exhaled sharply through my nose, unable to respond with anything more than a nod.

"What's up with you, grumpy pants?"

"It's nothing," I replied, forcing a smile.

She laughed softly. "I'm going to miss you, too, you know, but it's only a couple days. As much as it's going to wound your ego, I have to confess that I'll live." She smiled and placed a kiss on my cheek. I reached for her mouth and kissed her on the lips, and her eyes were hazy when she broke the kiss. "Oh, I just remembered something! I was thinking...Friday is karaoke night again," she said with a playful smile. "If you get back from London in time, you should really consider participating. We could sing a duet, so you can get over your absurd rejection of karaoke." I gave her a distraught look. I wanted to smile, but I didn't have it in me. I didn't know how I was going to tell her what I had been told in the meeting. "Only maybe we shouldn't do a love song because that would be bad."

"It would?" I asked.

"Well, yeah. If we do a love song, everyone is going to figure out we're screwing behind closed doors. Not that that has happened...yet," she added, raising both eyebrows and adding a flirty smile. I let out a low growl out of frustration. Imagining Sam naked in my bed was the last thing I needed right then.

"So, I was thinking...we could do 'Empire State of Mind' if you think you can pull off Jay Z's rap. Or...maybe we should do a Broadway duet, like 'Anything You Can Do' from *Annie Get Your Gun*. That would be a good one! Or I might have to research better duet songs that are not strictly romantic," she said, scrunching up her face.

Her hand reached for my face, and I grabbed it, kissing her palm. My nostrils flared with an exasperated breath, and she frowned.

"Hugh, what is it? I don't think I've ever seen you this pensive before."

I hummed, my nose pressed against her skin, smelling the freesia fragrance on her wrist. "I have to tell you something, Sam."

She tipped my chin up, and I looked at her. My stomach churned at the thought of hurting her.

"Is everything okay? You're worrying me."

"We had a meeting today. Nora and all the producers were there. They even phoned in someone from the network."

"Is everything okay? Are there any issues with the show?"

"No, no, but they asked specific things of some of us. Me...and Melissa, in particular."

She frowned, and then her face fell. "They want you to pretend you two are together."

"More or less."

"What does that mean?"

"I'm supposed to have off-set 'chemistry' with her in public."

"I see," she said simply. She nodded and considered

what I'd just told her. "I told you Leonia is Abarath's true love," she mumbled.

"They're telling us to remain coy. They don't want us to say we're dating, but they want us to play on our chemistry, and that means we can't be seen with anyone else in public. They were very adamant about that."

"They want people to buy into it."

"Pretty much. They think it will help the show establish its popularity." I sighed. There wasn't anything I could say at this point.

"And then what's going to happen when the fans start expecting more from you two?"

"I don't know."

"How long are you supposed to keep lying?"

"I have no idea," I replied, and I couldn't even bear to look at her eyes.

She stood up then and picked up a clean washcloth to wipe the dirt from my face. She didn't say a word the rest of the time she was in my trailer. I didn't know what I could say to make any of this better. How could I reassure her? I didn't know how I could possibly stay away from her, but I knew it wasn't right to drag her into this, to ask her to be my fling while pretending to have an ongoing affair with one of the lead actresses.

"Good luck in London," she said, placing a hand on my shoulder, giving me a forced smile. I grabbed her hand before she could remove it and I kissed it, whispering a "thank you" against her skin. She nodded, withdrew her hand, and left the trailer.

Chapter 14

SAM

The rest of the week was hell.

We were still busy, even without the main actors. We had to shoot big aerial scenes with lots of extras for some battle sequence, so all the available makeup artists had to work on hundreds of actors.

It wasn't exactly a blast, but at least being busy kept my mind off of Hugh.

Sort of.

Okay, no. It didn't.

To make things worse, in the evening, I couldn't stop staring at my phone. I kept waiting for a text, a call...something.

We had a *Casa de Sam y Cecilia* dinner party one night, and that kept me busy enough, but the thought of him was always there, in the back of my mind. Of course, it didn't help that people kept bringing up the footage from the press tour and kept discussing "how cute he and Melissa looked together."

It made me want to throw up, mostly because they were right. They did look cute together. They looked *beautiful* together.

In one of the clips I had seen, Melissa had her light brown hair down in loose waves and wore a pale pink dress that complemented her skin tone perfectly. Her eyebrows were thick and perfectly styled, and the makeup was flawless. She was as cute as a button, with delicate features and bone structure. She reminded me a bit of Lily Collins, and Hugh, sitting next to her, was the epitome of dapper. He was wearing a dark blue suit with a white button-down shirt and a skinny tie. The fabric of the tailored suit was rich and had a slight shine. His hair was styled back, a look I wasn't too fond of; I liked his hair better when it was wild and unruly.

We didn't get that far. It's not too late. I'm going to get over him, I told myself.

His blue eyes looked as if they sparkled under the bright lights of the TV studio. His scruff was perfection. His lips could have said anything, and they would have made me a believer. Yep, I was totally getting over him. Just as I thought that, one of our kisses flashed across my mind.

By the time Friday came around, I was in such a bad mood I ditched karaoke for the gym. I was desperate to get him out of my head.

I got dressed and did the only thing I knew would make me feel better.

Releasing some endorphins was the only way to find any peace of mind. I let out a deep breath as I briskly walked to the gym that had been made available for cast and crew to use. Walking always eased my mind a bit, yet I couldn't shake off the ache in my stomach and the knot in my throat.

I'd missed him, but I was afraid to face him again. Production had let us know we'd have to work that weekend to make up for the days the actors were away, so I knew I wouldn't get to sleep in. I was already mentally and physically exhausted, and by the end of the weekend, I was going to be even more of a mess.

I thought of LA, of my friends, of what we'd be doing on a Friday night like this. I'd heard it might snow in the next few days, and that made me miss the warm autumn sun even more, the hikes at Fryman Canyon Park, going out to Venice Beach for tacos. I even missed the traffic and the superficial LA conversations I would often overhear.

It was official—I was homesick again, on top of being distraught over Hugh. I felt like an idiot for even feeling that way. He shouldn't have mattered. He should have been just some guy, a rebound, maybe, yet I felt like I was lying to myself.

The hollow feeling in my stomach grew bigger, the knot in my throat tighter. Tears stung my eyes, and I wiped them away. I refused to cry.

Breaking a sweat was not necessarily my idea of a good time, but sometimes it was the only way to get out of a funk. I was going to work my ass off into oblivion, and the endorphins were going to help me get out of the pity pit I had been digging for myself.

And music. Music was going to help me weather the storm.

I reached the old store that had been transformed to house a gym, and I was glad to see Hugh's trainer was the only one there and appeared to be on his way out. I had my earbuds in already, so I waved and walked over to one of the elliptical machines in the back.

I stepped up, set the timer, and turned the music on. I closed my eyes, and everything around me started fading away.

The smooth voice of Frank Ocean felt comforting through my earbuds, reminding me of my sunny LA days from a few years back, when everything was so much easier. With my eyes closed, I could see the California palm trees. I could see myself hanging out with Amira, laughing together at something stupid. Slowly, the tension in my chest dissipated. My muscles felt less tense. The power of music was undeniable. A good song could make me feel stronger, empowered, and suddenly I felt able to sweep away most of my feelings of homesickness.

I suddenly opened my eyes wanting to grab my bottle of water and found Hugh standing right in front of me, his eyes bright and amused, a corner of his lips curled into a smile. I lost my grip and fell off the machine, almost pulling the whole thing down with me. Thankfully, his reflexes stopped the machine from tipping over, and he stretched out an arm to catch me. How long had he been there? And how long had he been staring at me?

Creep.

I gave him a sour look and straightened myself up. I grabbed my earbuds, which had fallen out of my ears and were dangling off the exercise armband in which I had stored my phone. He stood in front of me, not saying a word, his eyes still shiny with amusement, just as beautiful as they'd been on TV a couple days ago.

"What the hell are you doing here?" I growled.

"I just got back. I had a long few days and thought a workout might be in order. Apparently, great minds think alike," he said, leaning closer to me, mere inches away from my face.

I glared at him and scoffed. How could he talk to me so nonchalantly after our last conversation? He was acting as if nothing had happened. *What a fucking jerk.*

"Then what the hell are you doing staring at me? There's plenty of equipment available for your use. Didn't your mother teach you not to stare?"

"She did, but it just so happens that I cannot help myself."

I shook my head in frustration. "I can't keep up with you, Hugh. I thought you were supposed to date Melissa. I don't have time for this. I'm leaving. Thanks for ruining my workout." *And my night. And my whole weekend. And for not saying anything to make this pill less bitter to swallow.*

He grabbed my arm, and I rolled my eyes in annoyance.

"I don't want to date Melissa, you know that. I want *you.*"

My heart was lodged in my throat, beating so loudly I could feel it in my ears. Butterflies fluttered in my stomach, and I felt the impulse to run away. I wasn't in control of my emotions. I needed to get away from him.

I understood it wasn't his fault that they were asking him to keep up pretenses to please the fandom, but I was disappointed he and Melissa hadn't tried to oppose the network's request and that he hadn't suggested we see each other in secret, at least for the time being. It was clear—at least to me—that our attraction was a spark that was bound to grow into a wildfire. If we could have stopped working together, *maybe* I could have extinguished the flame, but that wasn't a possibility.

I looked up to him, and he was smiling playfully at me. I didn't understand what could be the reason for his good mood, other than him wanting to mess with me.

"What are you listening to?" he asked in a low and seductive tone.

I exhaled, frustrated with myself and with him.

"I don't even know why I'm wasting my time with this,"

I muttered, but I knew why I was doing it—because I wanted him. Part of me wanted to let go of any thoughts of him, and another part was anchored to the idea of the two of us together.

I pulled up my earbuds and placed them in his ears. His eyes were dark blue pools ready to suck me in. I let out a deep breath and looked away, unable to hold his gaze, but I could feel his eyes on me, everywhere.

He placed one of his hands on my waist and used the other to put one of the earbuds in my ear. *What is he doing?* A second later, he started swaying us together. We were dancing...in the middle of an empty gym? It was surreal. Still, I played along, and I started moving with him. Someone could have seen us, although probably everyone was at the pub. We swayed together, along with the music, and it felt so good to have him close again, his hard chest under my fingertips, his arms enveloping me. His hold on me was firm, strong—the hold of someone who wasn't ready to let go.

As I looked up to him, I noticed his eyes were brightened by that certain determination he would display on set. This was more like the Hugh I knew. It wasn't the guy who'd walked out on us a few days ago without as much as a sorry or an apology.

"I know I'm probably confusing ye," he said, his mouth just a breath away from mine.

"You can say that again."

"I don't want to stay away from you, Sam." His voice was comforting, his eyes reassuring. I knew he was telling the truth, but I didn't know how to handle this thing between us. "I like you. A lot. I haven't been able to get you off my mind all week, but I don't want to jeopardize my job...or yours. I can't be with you, not the way I'd like to...not right now, at least. Give me some time to figure things out, that's all I ask of ye."

My brows furrowed. I was confused. What was I supposed to do? Wait for him while he and Melissa paraded around together for the press?

Wait for him....for how long? I had waited for Eric to commit to me for seven years and look how that turned out. The old Sam would have nodded her head and said yes. I wanted Hugh, but something about what he said sat wrong with me. All of a sudden, my mind was made up.

I didn't want to walk away from him, but I could not accept those conditions.

"Will you do it, Sam? Will you wait for me to figure things out?"

I pressed my lips together and then looked up to him. "I'm sorry. I can't." The words left my lips and...*it felt right*. He stared at me in confusion, his eyes filled with worry, eyebrows pressed together.

"I can't wait for you. If you want me, you need to figure things out first." I took my things and left the place without ever looking back at Hugh MacLeod, who was frozen in place by my rejection.

The phone buzzed in my pocket, and I took it out to see who was writing to me.

Come to the pub, you slag.

Cece. I was mad, but she still managed to make me smile. I had told Cecilia I wasn't in the mood for karaoke night, but that was before my workout was so rudely interrupted. I didn't want to torture myself by staying at home, so I took a quick shower and then joined her, Jake, and Oliver. Maybe karaoke was going to take me out of my funk.

"Let's try something different," Cecilia announced.

"What do you mean?" I asked her.

"Since some of us have supernatural powers when it comes to karaoke—"

"Oh, bug off!" I told her, but she narrowed her eyes at me. "What about you, then? You don't seem to have any trouble whatsoever."

"Someone is learning the slang. Well played, Sam." She gave me a sly smile, deliberately ignoring my question. I rolled my eyes. "Like I was saying, since some of us are naturals at it, myself included, let's make it more fun. Each one of you write down a song on a piece of napkin—one that might be an unusual karaoke choice for another person, fold the napkin, and put it in this cup."

I let out a breath and scratched my head, regretting coming out at all. Jake elbowed me.

"Come on, it'll be fun. I don't think there's anything you can't sing, anyway."

I raised my eyebrows. "Uhhh, you'd be surprised." I wrote down the song I wanted to sing that night. There was a chance I'd pick my own entry, and I was still going to try to get my way, despite what Cecilia was planning. I loved her, but sometimes she was even more of a pain in the ass than my little sister. I made a mental note to never have them together in the same room—they would definitely end up ganging up on me.

Bitches.

"Why don't we make this a little more interesting?" Oliver said.

"How?" Cecilia asked.

"If you refuse to sing the song you end up with, you have to pay everyone's tab tonight."

"Ooohhh, yes!" Cecilia cheered.

"Oh, fuck *that.* It's on, assholes." Now I was determined to sing whatever they threw at me. I was going to show them. I was going to channel all my frustration and give a glorious performance. He wasn't at the pub, but somehow I could still smell him, still feel him. I stared into space, thinking about his words. Should I have waited for him? What was his plan, anyway? How long would I have to wait for us to be together? Why couldn't we screw behind doors? It sounded a lot simpler.

We all put our song choices in the cup, Cecilia mixed it around, and then each one of us took a piece of napkin.

I opened mine and read it, laughing. *Oh, fucking great.*

"Cecilia!" I put the piece of napkin in her face. "This was you, wasn't it? You whore!" She laughed in my face, but kept shaking her head.

"Ohmygod! That's such a good song. No, I swear it wasn't me!" She laughed as I tickled her side, thirsty for revenge.

"Then who was it? Who wrote this?" I asked Jake and Oliver, showing them the napkin.

"It was me," Jake confessed, leaning closer to me. His voice tickled my ear, and when I turned around to give him a snide look, his face was just inches away from mine. I was a little bit intoxicated, and I seriously felt like growling at him, but the smile that stretched across his face distracted me.

Damn his perfect smile.

"Of course you did. *Pelvic thruster showoff!*" I said, and everybody laughed.

Jake's song choice was Ginuwine's "Pony." *Fuckin' A.*

"What did everyone else pick?" I asked, and they all showed me their songs. Oliver got "Like A Virgin," Cecilia's entry, and Jake got Oliver's, which was "Angels" by Robbie

Williams. Cecilia got my pick, "Whenever, Wherever" by Shakira. The song was a tongue twister. I remembered trying to learn the lyrics when I was a teen, and I didn't know how many times I'd stumbled through the words. Served her right. Plus, I couldn't wait to see her shake it.

"Okay, who's going first?"

Everyone pointed at me.

"Fine! Let's get this over with...but I'm going to need some more whisky first."

"More whisky!" the guys yelled as Cecilia got up to go put in our names. When she came back, the bartender poured us some Laphroaig, a briny, smoky whisky that burned my entire mouth. I took a small sip at first, but then I made a mistake, taking too big of a drink. I coughed, and it took me a while to recover, making everyone around me laugh, bartender included. When they called my name, I grabbed a handful of Jake's shirt, twisting it in my fist. The smile of amusement that illuminated his face would have made any girl weak in the knees—well, any girl who didn't know what kind of a sly fox he was. He and the redhead had been over for weeks, and I hadn't seen him with anyone new. Still, I wasn't interested—there was too much Eric in him—but he was fun to be around and nice to look at.

"This is partly your fault, so you're coming with me."

He stifled a laugh, a twinkle of excitement in his eyes. He didn't protest. He had no idea what I was up to, but he just went along and smiled. If I didn't know how Jake operated, I could have easily fallen for his charm, especially that night. *Just use him to get over Hugh,* a voice inside me said, but I knew all too well that it would only come back to haunt me. As I walked to the karaoke area with Jake in tow, I cursed Channing Tatum under my breath. Who would have guessed that "Pony" was even a choice available in a pub in the middle of Scotland? Damn you, Channing Tatum and *Magic Mike* for making the song popular all over again. I pulled up a chair in the karaoke area and told Jake to sit on it.

He looked as excited as a puppy dog getting a treat. I sighed, thinking how much I'd rather have someone else around, someone who made my blood boil with just a word, with just a touch. No matter how sexy or charming Jake was, my body would never react to him the same way it did to just one of Hugh's dark looks. His eyes alone set my skin on fire. The song started, and some people in the back whistled.

Rupert was standing nearby, wearing just what I needed. I walked over and stole his ball cap, surprising him.

"I'm going to give it back, I promise!" I told him.

He gave me a wave of his hand and a smile, and I put on the cap on backward. As I started singing the first verse, everyone cheered again, and they did so over and over every time I moved my hips in sync with the music.

Everyone lost their collective minds when I straddled Jake. It was easier to get in the zone and focus on him rather than look at everyone's faces while I sang a song about getting it on. It was his fault I even had to sing this, so I figured we might as well be sharing the spotlight. After a while, I got lost in the music. I only had to glance at the screen a couple times to read the lyrics; I knew the song well. I must have watched that dance routine from *Magic Mike* a million times...because of the *dance routine,* obviously.

Channeling my own Channing Tatum, I danced the hell out of "Pony," all while being a dirty flirt. Jake got a little too carried away and grabbed my hips, sitting me across his lap, but I removed his hands and got up. I kept singing and swinging my hips, still occasionally flirting with him, and then I made him get up and sing the last verse with me. I got off stage and gave Rupert his hat back.

"That was something else, Sam," he said, handing me a pint.

"Glad you enjoyed it. Cecilia, you're next!" I yelled when I walked back to our table, pointing my finger at her. "Le do, lo le, lo le," I started singing, twisting my hands up in the air and shaking my hips like the blond Colombian singer. She flipped me off with a sour smile and walked toward the karaoke machine. *What a brat.*

Chapter 15

SAM

"My goodness, Jake was all over you last night after that little lap dance you gave him!" Cecilia said as we got our things ready. I grunted; I was slightly hungover from the night before. We ended up drinking too much, and then we had to come to work the next morning. Maybe having Jake on stage hadn't been the best idea. He'd followed me like a shadow for the rest of the night, occasionally thrusting his hips on me to give me *hints* about his arousal. I cringed every time he did that, but I didn't know how to tell him to stop—I had initiated the flirting, after all. Of course, he took any chance he could to whisper in my ear, asking me if I wanted to get out of there.

The expression on his face when I refused him was priceless. I knew it was hard for him to understand why I wouldn't just fuck him. Having recently come out of a relationship with a dirty sleaze ball, I wasn't looking to acquaint myself with another one. Plus, Jake liked to brag about his conquests a little too much.

After his fling with the redhead, I had seen the girl in tears, complaining to another coworker about how the dirty bastard had told everyone intimate details of their time together. I needed to steer clear of gossip at all costs, especially the type a big-mouthed guy like Jake would put out.

"He was so sad to see you go!" She laughed, and I rolled my eyes, shrugging it off. I had disappeared when he went to the restroom. Cecilia knew why I didn't want to mess with him, but she still liked to tease me about him.

It was another early morning in beautiful, chilly Scotland—and by beautiful, I meant rainy, cold, and muggy. The heater in the trailer hadn't kicked in yet, and I was rubbing my hands against each other, warming them with my breath.

"That was hardly a lap dance," I said with a shrug.

"Come on, Sam, no need to be shy. That was a very hot lap dance. I'm sure his dick was hard for the rest of the night!" she yelled just as Hugh opened the door of the trailer and stepped in.

Wonderful.

What is he doing here? Am I not supposed to go to his trailer anymore?

"Mornin'," he said with a nod of his head and a stern look on his face. I wondered how much he'd heard. Damn Cecilia and her big mouth—not that it mattered, because there was nothing going on between us. I held my head up high and gave him a slight nod, but he didn't pay any attention to me. Instead, he looked over to Cece, who said hi. His lips curled at the corners, and his eyes had a twinkle, a light that almost made them look a different shade of blue. His eyes were even more beautiful when he smiled, and I loved the way his mouth curved. It made my heart sink, because I immediately thought about not being able to kiss him anymore. My head hurt from overindulging in whisky and my stomach was queasy. I felt like I was going to get sick, but I still managed to greet him.

"Good morning. How are you today?" I asked him, but he barely acknowledged me, a deep breath flaring through his nostrils. *Great.* He was in a bad mood. Had he heard our entire conversation? He needed to get over it. There was nothing going on, and on top of that, it was none of his business. Sure, I had rejected him the night before, but we needed to keep it professional. We didn't have to be hateful to each other.

"I was just about to come to your trailer," I said in a low voice. "You... Do you want me to come over there?" A thought seemed to flash through his eyes, and he brightened up for a moment. Then, they grew dark again.

"Yes. I came here to tell you I have been waiting for you. It's Saturday, and I don't want to hold anyone up here longer than we need. We better get started," he said in a bitter tone. He said good-bye to Cecilia, turned around, and shut the door. Cecilia and I looked at each other, eyes wide and blank, shocked expressions on our faces. He had never been this rude, and we weren't running late. There was no chance he had been waiting on me. As I went over his words in my head, I started fuming. He was being rude on purpose.

Cecilia blabbered something as I gathered my things.

"Did he come out to the pub last night?" she asked

herself, tapping a finger on her chin.

My head shot up. It was possible he had a reason to be pissed.

"Did he?" I asked her.

"Hmmm, no. I don't think so. Maybe I dreamed about him?" she asked herself, lost in thought. I exhaled and shook my head. "Does he have some difficult scene to shoot today? I've noticed he's always more serious and gruff when he has a day filled with a tougher scene. He's cheerful on the days when he has fight scenes, and he's always a little nervous before a big love scene, which is the *cutest* thing," she said with an excited sigh. She was right about his nervousness—I had noticed the same pattern, too—but *cute* was the last thing I would call Hugh MacLeod right then.

Rude asshole fit the bill much better.

I flipped through the scenes we had scheduled for the day. Maybe he did have a love scene he was nervous about—not that that would excuse his behavior, but Amira complained quite often about how much she hated shooting love scenes, how hard it was to deliver your lines, your *moans* when you were butt naked in a room with thirty people capturing the moment, all their eyes on you.

I couldn't find anything notable, so I packed my shit and headed out for his trailer.

Things didn't get better as the day progressed. He was quiet all day, and every time I tried to make small talk with him, asking him about the media tour, he'd reply to each question in a rude tone. I didn't know how to handle his mood, so I stopped trying to engage him. It was hard to believe it was the same person who had always been so kind and fun. He'd told me he liked me, but he'd also said, plain and simple, that we couldn't be together right now. I understood, but he should have also respected the fact that I couldn't just wait around for him as he'd asked. This behavior wasn't like him.

Why is he being such an asshole now?

I didn't deserve it, and it only made me madder. I was fuming, counting down the hours so I could just get out of there and go get a drink.

He was giving me the cold shoulder, and it wasn't fair. It was difficult being around him like that with so many conflicting feelings bubbling up inside of me. Being close to him again reminded me of all the things I loved about him, even the good manners that seemed nowhere to be found right then. He was still the gorgeous actor I'd fallen for, the one who'd always been kind to me, who'd listened to me ramble on multiple occasions. He was still the same guy I had kissed in front of Edinburgh Castle, but now every time he looked at me, his eyes were so cold they could have reversed the melting of the glaciers in the Arctic. After making the same mistake a few times, I avoided his gaze the rest of the day.

Hugh

I was acting like an arse—I was fully aware of that. I wanted to give her a hard time, and every time her eyes met mine, they were full of fire and something else I hadn't seen before: anger. She was angry at me because I was acting like an idiot, but she'd hurt my feelings, too. She probably didn't know I had seen her the night before. Yes, I was jealous. Seeing her with Jake had made me furious, and it made me even more angry because he could give her what I couldn't. I didn't know how to handle the situation I was in. I wanted her, but I didn't want to risk my position with the network.

What they were asking wasn't fair, and Melissa and I had to come up with a plan to make them change their mind. I understood why Sam had left the night before—I wasn't promising her much. I just needed a little bit of time, and I'd never thought it would be such a big issue for her. Then, to find her rubbing against that playboy who was always buzzing around her just an hour later...it didn't sit well with me. I saw red. I had to walk out of there before she was even through with her song. I hadn't expected to find her there, looking carefree and beautiful, but there she was. God, she was gorgeous. I felt as if I had been hypnotized by her. The way her long black hair fell as her hips swung to the music drove me mad. I wanted to go back to the night she was in my house, on my couch, on top of me.

I wanted to punch Jake's face as he grabbed her hips and made her sit on top of him. What was I supposed to think? Was she already replacing me? Was her innocence just an act? Was she playing *me?* She had gotten his hands off her. She wasn't into him, was she? God, this was bollocks. I was jealous. My heart thumped loudly inside my chest, and a rush of adrenaline coursed through my body, sending a heat wave through my limbs, making the palms of my hands sweaty.

The night before, Cecilia had tried to get a rise out of me, making some comment about Sam, something about how sexy she looked. I didn't answer because there was nothing I could say without giving myself away. I knew she suspected something was up between us—we hadn't always been so subtle, and I couldn't seem to stay away from her. I craved every part of her...her smile, her laugh, her skin. I wanted her, but it was more than a purely physical attraction. She was kind and funny, smart and patient. Her shyness was like a veil protecting a beautiful soul. I could have had anyone, but she made me feel things I hadn't felt ever before.

I didn't seem to be able to stay away and, quite frankly, I didn't want to. I loved my job, and this was my opportunity to shine, but I didn't feel quite ready to sell my soul. The network would have to understand. Sam was worth the risk.

For the second time in my life, I felt like I could not give up.

I wasn't giving up on her.

SAM

My work day was almost over. I just had to keep quiet for a little bit longer, and then I would be able to walk away from him, at least for a few hours. I was so frustrated, I wanted to scream. If it hadn't been so late and already getting dark, I would have gone up on my favorite hill and screamed at the glen. I thought about it, and then I realized I couldn't even venture up there tomorrow because we had to get caught up with a scene with the main actors and wrap the episode we were shooting.

"Ouch!" Hugh yelled as I took the prosthetic off his chest. "Could you try to be more careful? I'm pretty sure you already pulled out half of my chest hair," he protested in a cold tone. I narrowed my eyes, letting out a slow breath. *Oh, please. Stop acting like a little bitch. Pretty sure you've never had to wax your balls or your anus. This is nothing.*

That was what I wanted to say. Instead, I gritted my teeth and swallowed my irritation.

"I'm sorry, okay? I've told you before, we need to make sure we shave your chest hair on this side, so it won't hurt as much. Unfortunately, that's how this prosthetic is. I forgot to do it this morning since we were in a hurry. I'm really sorry," I said apologetically, although I was growing angrier by the minute for how he had behaved all day.

I had become even more mad because after hours of fuming over his behavior, I realized the only possible explanation was that he was mad at me for saying no to him the night before.

His eyes met mine as I held the prosthetic scar in my hand, waiting for him to say something, dismissing the incident.

Something. Anything.

I cocked one eyebrow at him, waiting for some kind of apology.

But he didn't say a word. Instead, we kept staring at each other, his eyes full of fire, his chest heaving. *Oh, fuck this.*

"You know what? I'm going to step outside so you can have a moment."

What I really wanted to say instead was, *Take whatever this is and shove it up your ass.* I told myself to calm down and turned around to put the prosthetic away, shaking my head. He stood up behind me, and I froze. I could feel his warm breath on my neck, and I shivered. I glanced in the mirror in front of me, and I noticed him staring. His eyes were stormy, with a different kind of fury I hadn't seen before. I felt my heart throttle in my chest.

I needed to calm down and walk away from him. I closed my eyes and exhaled a breath. I was pissed at him, but I couldn't help but be turned on by his closeness and his musky scent. Suddenly, his hands grabbed my hips, and I gasped. *What the fuck is he doing?* My eyes shot open, and as they met his, I saw a look of pure lust in them. He pressed his body against mine, his hands roaming every inch of me over my clothes, touching my ass, my breasts, my stomach, as if he needed to caress every part of my body. *Why is he doing this right now?* I thought he couldn't be with me, thought it was implied that we needed to stay away from each other, but he was all over me.

The right reaction should have been to kick him in the nuts.

However, I couldn't bring myself to do that. Maybe it was because I had fantasized about him touching me some more since that night at his house; maybe it was because up until a couple of days ago, I still believed there was something blossoming between us. Up until a few days ago, I'd believed we had a chance.

Now that he was touching me, exploring my curves, I couldn't say no.

I wanted him. So, despite my better judgment, I let him touch me. He kissed me on the neck, right under my ear, and I closed my eyes again. I couldn't hold his gaze. It was too unsettling, too powerful. I felt heady. My breaths started coming in fast and uneven. His right hand went under my shirt, and his fingers skimmed under the fabric of my bra, giving my breast a gentle squeeze. He teased my nipple, and I shivered under his touch.

"Tell me what you're thinking, Sam," he said in a gravelly voice.

What am I thinking? I wasn't thinking—I couldn't think when I was around him like that.

I looked at him in the mirror. "You want to know what I think? I hate you," I hissed, narrowing my eyes at him. It was a lie, obviously. What I hated was how easily he could get me all worked up. What I hated was how much I wanted him.

He was a constant tease with his killer blue eyes, his flirty smiles, the way his body always brushed against mine in a more intimate way than the job required. I wasn't actually upset about that, and of course, he knew it. His hand left my breast and traveled south, right under the waistband of my yoga pants.

Fuck.

"Yeah?" he whispered in my ear. "You hate me?"

"I do," I replied with a strangled moan.

"Is that so? Then why are your knickers so wet?"

Fuck me. His fingers had found my wet center. Fuck my body for betraying me like that. He traced slow circles with his index finger on my clit, sending a wave of heat through my body. He moved his finger across my wetness, pushing a finger in and out of me. My breath became fast and ragged, and I rolled my head back, leaning against his shoulder. He adjusted his angle, stroking me with his thumb as his finger pushed inside me. His left hand teased the nipple of my right breast while the fingers of his right hand strummed me between my legs, and I let out a strangled moan. I was already so damn close. I felt his hard length as he grinded against me and increased the speed and the pressure on my clitoris. The blood rushed to my head, and I grabbed the table for support, all my nerve endings ready to erupt in fireworks. I wanted to scream and say his name, but I was too proud to do that. I hated that he turned me on so much, so easily. I didn't want to be so out of control around him, but he made me powerless. It was the very last thing we should have been doing, but it felt fucking fantastic.

"Oh, God," I mumbled, and he pressed me against him, pulling my head back, placing wet, hot kisses on my neck as he drove me closer and closer to climax.

Then he suddenly stopped.

What a fucking jerk.

Chapter 16

SAM

"You're so fucking sexy, do you know that?" he said, turning me around. He tipped my chin up so I could look at him.

No, tell me, I wanted to say, but I was speechless and out of breath. I felt lightheaded and greedy for more. I wanted more, badly.

My body was flush against his, and I could feel every hard line of his chest under my hands. His hard length was pressed against my hip, and I had to admit I couldn't wait to see it, couldn't wait to touch it. I had wanted him for too long.

"Do you know how hard you make me?"

Well, yes, I had an idea.

"Do you know how many times I've fantasized about you in the last few weeks?"

The feeling is mutual, buddy. I wanted to say it, but the

words wouldn't come out.

I was still breathing heavily. My brain was foggy and honestly a little upset that my journey to a fucking-good-orgasm had been interrupted so abruptly.

I looked into his blue eyes, so full of intent, his thick brows furrowed, a little line forming between them. He kept his grip on the back of my head with one hand and on my ass with the other. My lips parted and I said, "Show me. Show me how much you want me."

We stared at each other for one more second before his mouth crashed onto mine, and when my lips parted, our tongues wrapped together, soft and hard, fast and slow, making me want more. He brought his other hand down to my ass, and a moment later he lifted me and threw me on the table. Most of my tools fell on the floor and makeup and brushes went flying everywhere, but I was past the point of caring, unable to stop kissing him.

To hell with caution.

He placed himself between my legs as my hands started roaming the smooth planes of his chest, traveling down to his waist, to his cock. I lifted the kilt with one hand and was disappointed to find that he was wearing underwear. I groaned against his mouth, and he laughed, breaking the kiss.

"What do ye want from me, Sam? I can't go around flashing the whole crew." He laughed, a low rumble inside his chest. I had missed it. We hadn't laughed together in days. Things had been so strained between us ever since he'd left for London.

"I have been wondering for *weeks* if you went commando or not."

"Sorry to crush your dreams," he said, the corner of his mouth tipping up on one side. *There's another way you can make my dreams come true,* I thought. I grabbed his jaw, and he leaned in, eager. I kissed him with the same intensity he had kissed me with, and with my hand I freed his hard cock, beautiful and smooth under my fingers. My fingertips teased the crown, and he moaned in my mouth. It felt wonderful under my fingers. In a few months, millions of women would be fantasizing about him, about his body...and about his dick. I circled his length with my fingers and started stroking him up and down. It was big and hard, and I couldn't wait to have him inside me.

One of his hands was behind my back, holding me in place while the other made its way into my underwear again. His fingers resumed the blissful stroking that had gotten me so worked up. In no time at all, I was trying to hold back my cries of pleasure. I wanted to yell "fuck" a million times, but I knew for sure people outside the trailer would hear that. My center throbbed under his touch, needing more of it, more of him. I kept stroking him as he brought me closer and closer to climax.

"Fuck!" he mumbled, breaking the kiss. He brought his forehead closer to mine, and I moaned against his lips.

"Hugh, I'm so close," I cried, and that got him even more focused on finishing the job. He inserted two fingers and pressed my clit with his thumb, but just then, we heard a knock on the door. We both froze, wondering if we'd heard right. We weren't wrong. Someone was outside the trailer, and they knocked three more times. He backed off me instantly, fixing his underwear and his kilt, and I jumped off the table, straightening my clothes.

I looked at him to see if he was decent, and he gave me a nod.

I cleared my throat.

"Come in!" I yelled.

The door opened, and a production assistant named Simon entered the trailer.

"Sorry, Hugh, they want you back on set. Nora and Stephon said they're not done with you today."

Ugh. I wasn't done with him *either*.

Hugh's eyebrows furrowed; he was just as confused as I was.

"I don't understand...I thought I was done for the day," he said.

"What happened here?" the production assistant asked, noticing all the makeup on the floor.

"Sam tripped and landed on the table," Hugh said, without missing a beat. "I was just helping her clean up." Simon eyed me cautiously.

"Yep. That's true. I fell. Clumsy me, ha ha. You don't have to help me, Hugh. They need you on set. Just go," I said nervously. Then I realized something. "Wait...does he need to be shirtless again? I just removed the prosthetic." I could feel Hugh's death glare on me, but all I cared about was not being caught by a gossipy production assistant.

"No, he won't. He just needs the shirt he was wearing earlier today."

"Thank God," Hugh mumbled.

"There's a funky smell in here," Simon said.

Um, yeah—sex.

"It's probably one of Hugh's nasty protein-loaded meals," I joked. "I smell eggs, don't you?" I asked Simon, scrunching up my nose. That earned me another death stare from Hugh. "What?" I shrugged. "It's the fucking truth, *laddie*."

"I'll be right out," he said to the assistant in a firm tone.

Simon frowned and hurried outside. I glanced at Hugh and let out a shaky breath. He turned toward me, the look in his eyes intense and determined; it made my insides quiver. My muscles clenched, and a shiver ran through me. I was on edge. My orgasm had been interrupted twice. *Twice*. Despite everything that had happened the last few days, I wanted him. I couldn't wait. It wasn't a smart thing to do, but I couldn't wait anymore. Just as his fingers skimmed across my jaw, my back arched, my entire body begging for his touch. I instinctively licked my lips, and a moment later, I was back in his arms, his lips against mine, soft but urgent, needing more.

His tongue wrapped around mine time and time again, and I felt I could have come undone with that alone, in his arms, his hands holding my head, pressing me closer to him.

"I'm not even close to being done with you," he whispered against my mouth as he broke the kiss. I swallowed and tried to catch my breath as I heard him mutter a "fuck" under his breath. He gave me one more lust-loaded gaze as he grabbed his shirt and walked out of the trailer.

"*Ohmygod*," I let out when I was finally alone. My knees buckled, making me reach for something to hold on to. What the fuck had just happened? I took my face in my hands as I sat in his chair, still having a hard time believing what had gone down.

Weeks of sexual frustration had just exploded all over

this trailer.

I turned around and looked at the mess.

My poor makeup. In a different situation, I would have told lover boy to chill—no one throws my things around like that. Obviously, I had been too far gone to care. I looked at myself in the mirror and felt the blood rise to my cheeks. My blush was quite faint, but the expression on my face would probably give me away. My eyes were wide and dazed, my lips red and swollen. I ran a couple fingers over my lips, thinking about his kisses. He'd said he wasn't done with me, but in all honesty, I didn't know what to expect. Who knew if he was going to walk back in and act as if nothing had happened?

I looked restless, feral even, like a starving person who had been offered something to eat only to see it taken away. My hair was a mess, too. The ponytail was loose, and the hairs on top were all out of place. I fixed my hair first, and then started collecting all the things that had fallen to the floor.

I needed to stop thinking about him...his fingers inside me, his beautiful body...his cock. I needed to go home and bake. Yes, baking was going to do the trick and take my mind off his smooth cock—*stop thinking about it dammit. Think about what you could bake. Hmmm, chocolate chip cookies, sugar cookies, banana bread...* The possibilities were endless. I just needed to make sure I had all the ingredients. I thought maybe I should stop at the little supermarket in town before heading to the townhouse.

Maybe if we'd had the time to finish off, I wouldn't be feeling restless.

Fuck.

I needed to get home and let out all my pent-up frustration.

It took me a while to clean up and put everything away, and only then did I realize I should probably go to the set to see if Hugh needed a touch-up.

Damn, where is my head? Well, I knew where it had been for the last thirty minutes, but I couldn't believe I had forgotten to check on him.

I grabbed my coat and my makeup bag and headed out. Simon had said they were going to reshoot a scene they'd done earlier in the day, so I knew where to find him.

I opened the door of the trailer just as he was walking over.

I glanced around, wondering what was going on. The sun was setting, and everyone was getting ready to leave. They all seemed to be in even more of a hurry than usual since it was Saturday and we'd been there all day. Hugh walked in the trailer, shut the door, and locked it.

His eyes had the same wicked intensity they'd had earlier, and I could feel my pulse quicken. I let out a breath, walking backward, waiting for his next move.

I expected him to kiss me immediately, or better yet, I was hoping he would pin me against the wall. Instead, he walked around the trailer and turned all the lights off, even the ones on the vanity.

"What are you doing?"

"I don't want it to look like there's someone in here," he replied.

"Why?"

"Because I want them to leave us alone."

Oh. *Ohhhh.*

He planned on continuing what we'd been doing. *Well then.*

When all the lights were turned off, he walked over to me. I was still on the other side of the trailer by the door, and I was fighting an internal battle with myself. On one side, I wanted to throw my arms around his neck and wrap my legs around him. On the other, I kept thinking that what we were doing was terribly wrong.

As exciting as it was, hooking up at work was unprofessional.

If someone found out—and if this kept happening, it was only a matter of time before someone did—we were going to be the gossip of the entire staff. Then again, it's not like Cecilia and Oliver were hiding. Everyone knew they were together, and no one gave a fuck, but if people started hearing about Hugh and me, pretty soon it would get back to the network, and I didn't want him or Melissa—or the show—to be in trouble.

What to do? What was the right thing to do here? Staying away from him was impossible; my heart sank just at the thought of it.

When he reached for me, he took my hand in one of his, and his eyes grew softer, full of reverence and promise. In that moment, I decided I didn't care about anything but the two of us. He pulled me to him, holding me in his arms.

The smirk I'd grown to love appeared on his face, his eyes still soft and loving.

"I kept messing up out there. I couldn't focus. I really got on Nora's nerves. It's never happened before. I couldn't think about my lines, no matter how many times they read them out to me."

"Because of your hard-on?" I asked with a laugh, feeling his erection against me.

He chuckled. "Because of my hard-on." A smile stretched across his face, reaching his beautiful eyes, which possessed that sweetness I had grown accustomed to but were also black in the darkness of the trailer. My eyes traveled to his mouth, down to his chest. I wanted to rip that fourteenth-century-style blouse off him and feel him under my skin again.

"I'm sorry," I told him, taking one step closer to him, my eyes locked with his.

"About what?"

"Your scene."

A corner of his lips curled up. "Not your fault, Sam," he told me, letting out a loud breath. This moment was so different than the one we'd had before. I still wanted him to fuck me, but I also wanted to hug him and kiss him...so I did.

I raised myself on my tiptoes and placed a soft kiss on his lips. He stood there, motionless, looking down at me, almost as if he were waiting for my next move. I wrapped my arms around his neck and looked up to him. His gaze was burning my skin. He wasn't doing anything at all besides looking at me, and yet, I couldn't resist him.

All the tiptoeing around each other the last few weeks seemed stupid now.

I was aching for him. I wanted to get lost in him. There was no going back.

I kissed him again, and this time, his lips molded to mine. My tongue wrapped around his, and it was both familiar and new. His kisses made me heady, and when we came up for air, he said in a whispered tone, "Samhain, I can be a patient man, but I would be lying if I said I didn't want to fuck ye right now. Tell me what ye want, and I will give ye that."

"Is this one of your lines?" I joked.

He laughed. "No, it isn't. My character might be rubbing off on me a little, but I meant what I said. I'm willing to be patient, even though I am dying to have ye, right now." *Then have at it,* I wanted to say. His words made me smile, because he was willing to take his time with me.

Fortunately for him, that was not what I wanted.

"Hugh," I whispered, looking up to him, my neck craning to take in his height—six feet, three inches of rock-solid muscle. I brushed his curls to the side and took his face in my hands. He smiled nervously, waiting for me to say something. It was a sweet smile, laced with worry, but he didn't have to worry about a thing. I wasn't a little girl. I was ready for him—so damn ready. "Hugh, if there's one thing I'm not really good at, it's being patient. I need you inside of me...right now. I need you to make me come...fast and hard, soft and slow...every which way there is. I need you." He inhaled deeply through his nose, his eyes fixed on me, dark and intense from what I could see. A moment later, his lips covered mine, sucking and nipping at my bottom lip. His tongue possessed me, and he kissed me with passion and intent, his scruff scratching my skin.

He took off his shirt, and I started fumbling with the belt of his kilt. He took my hand in his and helped me to unbuckle it faster. The flesh-colored boxers he was wearing underneath were gone in a flash, as were his boots. His body was a work of beauty, and I just wanted to take my time and touch every inch of it, but first, I needed to take off all my clothes. He helped me out of my skin-tight turtleneck. My ponytail got messed up again, and I untied my hair. He gave me a once-over, his eyes falling to my breasts before looking back up to me with a predatory glint. I shivered, and he leaned down and kissed me again, running his hands in my hair.

The warmth of his body was a turn-on and a comfort. I stroked his hard length again, and his hands ran down to my sides. He unhooked my black push-up bra and when I pulled it off, he touched my breasts and teased my already hardened nipples with rough and calloused fingertips. I moaned against his mouth and sighed when he broke the kiss. He gazed at me for a moment, a look full of anticipation and need. His lips trailed kisses down my breasts, setting my skin on fire with each one. A stroke of his tongue across my nipple sent a rush of heat from my chest all the way down to my toes, and wetness pooled between my legs. His mouth left my breasts, and his fingers skimmed my belly. He knelt in front of me and kissed my navel, right above my belly button. I let out a deep breath, and I exhaled once more when his fingers hooked into my yoga pants and underwear and he pulled them down in a swift move. I was already wet, and my muscles were clenching, just waiting for him to touch me again. I shivered, and his warm hands ran over my pebbled skin. He pulled my pants all the way down to my ankles and helped me out of them. I bit my lip, looking down to him, waiting for his next move.

He glanced up for just a second, his eyes full of mischief.

He ran his hands around my hips first, massaging and

caressing my skin. I needed him so badly. I needed his hands everywhere. I touched my breasts and teased my nipples. He noticed, and that seemed to turn him on even more. The only light was coming in through the small windows of the trailer and made his face look as pale as the moon. One of his hands parted my lips, warm and soft, ready to welcome his touch. He teased my wet center, sliding two fingers in and out. My walls clenched around his fingers, and I heard his growl, his eyes the color of embers as they looked up to me.

One of his hands was pressed on my hip, and with the one between my legs, he nudged me to part my legs wider.

His face was dangerously close to my skin, and I exhaled deeply as he started placing sweet, slow kisses on the inside of my thighs. He opened my lips and started licking my sore, swollen center, circling his tongue on my clit.

I wasn't prepared for the low, guttural moan that came out of my mouth. It felt so fucking good. Encouraged by my sounds, he kept licking, applying the sweetest pressure on my trembling clit as his fingers worked in and out of me.

"Ohmygod," I moaned. My knees became wobbly. As he moved his tongue faster, I could barely hold myself together. He noticed and stopped.

He lifted one of my legs and placed it on his shoulder, and then he did the same with the other, spreading them wide, making sure I was hooked in place.

Motherfucker.

What was he doing? This was some *Cirque du Soleil* shit.

He placed his face right there between my legs and

started licking again.

"Oh, fuck," I moaned. "Oh, fuck. Ohmygod." I was squirmy, but somehow he kept my hips in place with his arms. It felt so fucking wonderful, it was like unlocking a whole different level of orgasmic experience I'd never reached in my life.

He worked me relentlessly with his tongue, circling, pressing, swiping on my swollen clit, teasing my entrance with the tip of his tongue.

I was breathing heavily, preparing for the best to come. My muscles tightened under his touch. I was so, so close.

And then my ass was up in the air and my head bumped against the ceiling of the trailer.

"Ouch!" I mumbled, and I heard a muffled "sorry" come from between my legs.

Then I got ticklish, because the motherfucker was laughing right against my skin.

"Oh my gosh, stop laughing! You're tickling me. I'm going to fall!"

He stopped then, and I crouched just slightly so I wouldn't bump against the ceiling again. He secured the hold on my legs and looked up to me.

"I'm not going to let you fall. I'm going to make you come," he said in a muffled voice laced with determination. He walked us over to the couch in the corner, and then he lowered me down slowly, so sure of his movements, I wondered if he had a habit of eating women's vaginas standing up.

He placed me on top of the couch. With almost a foot under my feet, we were face to face.

"Hi," I said, kissing his face, tasting myself on his lips.

"Hi," he replied, his voice hoarse.

"That was some Tarzan-level move," I joked.

"Tarzan, aye? I can role play, if ye want me to," he said, cocking an eyebrow. His erection pressed against me, and I got another idea.

"No," I replied, kissing him again. "Sit." I stepped off the couch as he sat down. He took my hand, thinking I wanted to straddle him, but I shook my head and gave him a languid smile. I knelt between his knees, his erection hard and straight in front of me. It was so long, large, and smooth. It was beautiful, a really good-looking cock, and I had seen a couple of ugly ones in my life. I touched the top with my fingers and gave him a flirty look. I could still see him up close, but for the most part, we were two figures clothed in darkness. As I circled his tip, his eyebrows furrowed, and he let out a strangled moan that was so damn sexy.

It was going to be even more sexy to see him come. I caressed his legs and his lickable abs, teasing his shaft with my breasts. Then I took it in one hand and started licking the tip, circling over and over. A low growl escaped his lips. I licked all along the side of his beautiful cock, looking up to him briefly before taking it all in my mouth as far as I could take it. His low, strangled moans were music to my ears, and when I opened my eyes, one of his hands was fisted in his hair, the other digging into the fabric of the couch. I took it and placed it on my breast. He looked at me with furrowed brows, a mix of lust and reverence. I pulled his cock out of my mouth and licked all the way from his balls to the tip. He hissed a breath and gave my breast a squeeze.

"Fuck, Sam. You're going to make me come and I don't

want to. Stop."

I sucked him again and then let him go with a pop, and when my eyes met his, I gave him the most innocent glance a good girl like me could give him. He smirked, pulled me up on his lap, and took my hands in his.

"I need to be inside of ye. I need to fuck you. Isn't that what ye wanted?"

"Yes," I said almost shyly with a nod of my head, but then my hips rocked against his erection.

"I swear you're going to be the death of me. You're so damn sexy." He took my breast with one hand, and he ran his other one across my stomach, all the way to my vagina. I moaned and closed my eyes when his hand touched me there. I had almost come twice in the last two hours, but I had never actually finished. I was a bundle of nerves, eager to get some relief. "You make me so fucking hard. I need to be inside you," he said again.

"And I need you to be inside me, but I don't have a condom, so what are we going to do?"

"The pocket on my belt."

"Huh?"

"There's a pocket on my belt. I stole some condoms from Frank's trailer."

I giggled to myself. I got up and went looking for his belt in the dark. I found what Hugh was talking about and took the condoms in my hand. When I walked back to the couch, he had his hands behind his neck and was smiling at me, as if he were enjoying a private show.

His smirk was back. I could see it even in the partial darkness.

"See something you like?" I teased.

"As a matter of fact, I do," he said, his accent heavier on the last word. "Your *bahookie*."

"My what?"

"Your *arse*. Your ass. It's been taunting me for weeks."

"Has it now?" I smiled.

"Aye. You're beautiful. Every part of ye is, but your arse is the eighth wonder."

I laughed.

I was butt naked in front of him, and for some reason, I wasn't embarrassed in the slightest—maybe because it was dark or maybe because he made me feel comfortable. He made me feel beautiful. I'd always had quite the complex when it came to my ass, even after big butts had become as popular as big breasts.

I turned around and pushed my butt in his direction so he could have his way with me. He caressed my skin, and I felt wetness drip between my legs again. He made me gasp when he bit the skin of my backside, and I moaned when he pushed my butt cheeks apart and stroked me with his tongue. I could only take so much more of all this teasing. I needed his cock inside me like yesterday.

"Hugh...fuck me. Please," I begged, my pussy throbbing under his tongue.

He sat me down on his legs, and I heard him rip the foil packet of a condom. I turned my head and stared, transfixed at him as he rolled the condom down his shaft.

Fuck, what a vision he was. I licked my lips, and he caught me, giving me another one of his malicious grins. He pulled me to him and caressed my breasts, my head reclined on his shoulder. He placed wet kisses on my neck and ran his nose along my jaw as his hand teased my wetness.

"One of these nights, I will take ye like this...reverse cowgirl," he said, his length pressed against my back. "But tonight, I want to look at ye, see you when you come." His words were erotic and intoxicating, and combined with how he was warming me up once again, it was driving me crazy. He suddenly swatted me across my butt, and I gasped.

"Get up," he ordered in a low but firm voice as he turned me around. My nipples were hard, my whole body so attuned to him already. It was a strange feeling, to feel so comfortable with someone I had never been intimate with.

He told me to sit across his lap, and I did, my butt slightly up to grant him access. He placed a soft kiss on my lips first, but then it grew into a wet, passionate one that did nothing for my self-control. He placed the tip of his hard, smooth length at my opening, and I adjusted myself so he could enter me.

He thrust his hips up, and I let out a moan, his cock stretching and filling me. I was no virgin, but no one had been inside there for months, and his cock could certainly not be compared to my vibrator. The feel of him inside me was spectacular. As my walls stretched and accommodated him, he started lifting his hips and I started rocking mine. I bit my lip, trying to stop a smile of ecstasy from stretching across my face. It was glorious. I could feel his eyes on me, and a moment later, his mouth was latched on my nipple, sucking and biting while his hand played with the other.

I felt like there had been way too much foreplay this evening, and now that this was finally happening, I was so worked up, I wasn't going to last long at all. In fact, I didn't want it to last. I wanted to come—as soon as possible. It had been too long since I'd had an orgasm with a real cock inside of me.

"Harder, Hugh. Faster," I said as I started lifting my own hips up and down his length, holding myself on the cushions of the couch. I was so wet, I felt my juices dripping down his length. Low moans escaped my mouth, and they amplified as we both increased speed. I opened my eyes to stare at him, and his focused look reminded me of the expression he often had when he was shooting a fight scene. He placed his hands on my sides, right under my breasts, and he slammed me up and down, moving in sync with me. Even his low grunts turned me on. He thrust hard into me one more time, pushing himself all the way in, bringing me over the edge.

I let out a loud cry as the orgasm erupted through me, sending a shot of adrenaline through my body. Blinding fireworks danced across my eyes as I rocked my head backward, my arms latched around his neck. Hugh came a second later with one more deep thrust. I let out a deep breath, and when I glanced back at him, he had a spent but satisfied look on his face. I leaned down and kissed him, and he let out a guttural growl as I wrapped my tongue around his. Sexiest thing ever.

He rested his forehead against mine, and we stayed like that for a few seconds while we both tried to catch our breath. I had wanted this for so long. Though a small part of me was still worried about the implications of sleeping with the star of the show, the other part didn't give a fuck. The latter was, in fact, hoping this was just the beginning of many nights of blissful pleasure, many nights of pure, unadulterated fucking.

I tried to get up, but he held me close, cradling the back

of my head, looking at my face as if he were seeing it for the first time all over again. He kissed me with such devotion in that moment, I realized maybe, just maybe, this wasn't just about fucking. Maybe this wasn't just a sexual attraction neither of us could escape. Maybe it was more. I caressed his face as he looked into my eyes.

My heart felt as if it were beating faster now than earlier, and even though I had been naked for a while, it was just in that moment that I felt exposed. He caressed my back, drawing small circles on my skin, and I shivered under his touch.

"Samhain," he said, pronouncing my name the Scottish way, his eyes fixed on mine. "I fear ye have me ruined for every other woman." I smiled softly just as he kissed my lips again. I closed my eyes then, trying to memorize how perfect this moment was. No matter what was going to happen between us in the future, I wanted to remember that instant always.

Chapter 17

SAM

By the time we got dressed and headed out of the trailer, it was pitch black outside.

The wind had picked up, and the clouds covered the moon and the stars.

"It looks like it's going to start raining. We better hurry up," Hugh said.

It was only eight thirty, but it looked like it was the middle of the night. A gust of cold wind blew through me, and I shivered. Hugh noticed and hugged me to him, almost shielding me from the cold with his body. Having him so close felt nice, and it made me feel even more inebriated. My body was still riding the sex high.

I felt satisfied, and yet at the same time, I needed more.

We didn't speak. The wind filled our silence at first, and a few minutes later, the rain took its place. It started pouring out of nowhere, as it often did in Scotland, and although we were both wearing waterproof jackets, it was hard to see and walk in the dark.

There was a road between our set and the village where we stayed that wasn't lit, and it felt like walking right into a black hole. The only things that made me not feel scared were Hugh's hand holding mine and the certainty that I was safe with him.

The rain subsided slightly, which made it easier for us to reach our condos. I wasn't wet underneath my jacket, but my face was freezing, and my legs were definitely soaked. We reached my place first, and our little street was deserted. I figured most people were probably huddled inside with a glass of whisky. I gave Hugh's hand a squeeze and said good night, but he pulled me back into his arms and kissed me—first a peck, and then two deeper, longer kisses.

"I would invite you over if I didn't have to learn my lines," he said against my mouth, his warm breath washing over me.

I caressed his face and nodded, trying to hold back a smile. "We have another long day tomorrow, and I really hate when the guy I have to work with acts like a little bitch." He smiled at me, biting his bottom lip. After a few seconds, he finally let go of me. He stepped back and bowed slightly, just as he would have done during a scene on set. I picked up my imaginary gown and curtsied.

I giggled as he walked away and kept laughing because he turned every so often to look back at me. I stood on my porch watching him until I could barely see him down the little road.

I went inside the house and found Cecilia curled up on the couch with a cup of tea and her kindle in her lap, which surprised me—she was rarely alone these days.

"What? No Oliver tonight?" I asked.

"Good heavens! You're soaked! What were you doing out there? Are you bloody insane, Sam? Why are you just now getting home anyway?"

"I had to stay after you left because Hugh had reshoots...and then I went for a walk. He was in a really pissy mood today. I had to get it out of my system. I was fine until it started raining." I felt bad lying to Cecilia, but it wasn't a complete fabrication; he *had* been in a terrible mood all day.

"Do you know why he was in such a bad mood?" she asked.

"Maybe he was just tired. I honestly have no idea." Things had gotten so out of hand, I had completely forgotten to ask him why he'd been so cranky.

"Jake came looking for you," she said with a smile, raising her eyebrows.

"Huh, really?" Jake was persistent. Had he not gotten the gist after I'd left without even a good-bye? Besides, it's not like there had been anything going on between us, ever. We flirted the first week, but after I turned him down and he moved on to the redhead, we only hung out in groups. We had seen each other in social settings, but I didn't think I had been friendly to the point that he'd think it would be okay to stop by...until the night before. We had hung out, I had sort of given him a lap dance, he'd put the moves on me, but I had shut him down and left. Why was it so hard to get the message?

"I wonder what that's about." I hung my jacket and started taking my wet shoes and clothes off by the door.

"Um, I know what that's about," she said, cupping her hands in front of her breasts to mimic the size of mine. I shook my head.

"There's plenty of *this* to go around here. He could be hitting up just about anyone else," I replied.

"Oh, but he wants you. I saw how he looked at you last night. He's really attractive, although way too much of a flirt. I'm sure he'd be perfect to just fuck here and there…if that's what you want…which you don't." I laughed at her ramblings. "Then again, it's obvious why you couldn't care less—why bother with Jake when you can have McHottie?"

I flinched. "McHottie? What do you mean?"

"Oh, come on, Sam. Do you really think I'm blind? Hugh, of course! You two have been dancing around each other for weeks. It didn't sound like you were alone on the porch. You were with him, weren't you? Are you guys going to have sex any time soon or not? The sexual tension around you two is unbearable. Sometimes I feel like I can't breathe," she said, fanning herself.

I took a deep breath and told myself to put into practice what Amira had taught me about acting. "What? Did you not see him being a complete asshole to me this morning? Yes, he walked me home, but nothing happened." *Hopefully, she missed the kissing…*

She frowned, deep in thought, as if trying to figure something out. "Ha! I remember now! He was at the pub last night, briefly. He saw you and Jake during your 'Pony' performance. You should have seen his face when you were singing and giving Jake a lap dance. I almost felt sorry for the bloke."

"Okay, maybe I was teasing Jake—it was his song choice after all—but I wasn't trying to lead him on."

"I know, but come on—Jake was totally into it, and Hugh looked *pissed*. He stormed out of there a few minutes after. I mean, the guy is usually a joy to be around, and he was livid. You should have seen him."

"Well, now I am pissed. I still don't believe he was jealous, but even if he were, he had no right to treat me so coldly. He was a total jerk all day," I said, feigning exasperation, hoping Cecilia would believe me. I did feel bad for not telling her the truth, but Hugh and I had been hot and cold so many damned times in the last couple of weeks, I honestly didn't know what was in store for us the next day.

"But you made up, right? Did he apologize for being an ass?" she asked.

"Y-yes," I lied, realizing he hadn't actually apologized for *anything*. The dude owed me.

Hugh

I just realized you never apologized to me for being an ass. That's pretty shitty.

The screen flashed with a text from Sam. She was right. I unlocked the home screen and typed a response.

You're right. I'm sorry. I was a total ass. Come here now and I will apologize a million times. :-)

No way, man. You will never learn your lines if I come over there.

I sighed, disappointed. She was right.

You're right. You can't come over. I would end up devouring you all night. I would never learn my lines, and tomorrow I'd suck so bad I would just make everyone waste a bunch of time.

If you're good to me tomorrow, I'll come over in the evening.

I'll be looking forward to that all day.

SAM

As weeks went by, I hoped I would start feeling more at home. I wasn't as homesick as I had been in the beginning, and my evenings weren't quite as lonely anymore. Hugh and I didn't have much time to spend together after work, but we tried to make it count. He wanted to tell Nora so we wouldn't have to hide as much, but I convinced him to sit tight for a couple of reasons. The first was that after their media campaign, we'd have reporters show up for interviews and photo shoots from time to time, and I didn't really want to deal with all that.

The second—and most important—reason was that Nora knew about me. She knew what had happened back in LA. If Hugh wanted to tell Nora, it meant I would have to tell him the truth, and although I wanted to get the weight off my chest, I was afraid of his reaction. I was scared of what he'd think of me. I wasn't used to having to hide anything, and sometimes I worried he could see on my face that something was wrong. I needed to tell him the truth, but I wasn't ready.

Despite lack of time together, things were going great between us. On our days off, we'd meet up on the hill where we met the first time and go for a hike. It was nice to be able to hold hands and kiss him out in the open, even though we still tried to be careful. A couple times, we met in Edinburgh and went to visit Margaret in the hospital. Her baby had to stay in the incubator for a few weeks, and the new parents had momentarily relocated to Scotland. Margaret was staying in Edinburgh, and her husband came up on the weekends. Posy Lake was growing and doing well, and Margaret looked happy despite the stress of not being able to go home with her newborn yet.

For the first time in a long time, I felt happy, but I still couldn't say I had gotten used to the climate. In fact, I liked to joke that Scotland and I were in a love/hate relationship. As much as I was falling in love with Scotland's amazing scenery and the warm and infectious people, the weather never ceased to be a thorn in my side—and not for lack of trying. I observed my colleagues at work, and I did everything they did. I dressed like them, using the same type of gear, yet it wasn't enough. When we had outdoor scenes, my teeth would not stop chattering. I didn't complain, but on more than one occasion, I felt I was the weak link of the crew.

I didn't want to fail, especially with all that had happened back home with Eric. I needed this to work out. However, on those trying days, everyone could read the struggle on my face, Hugh more than anyone else. After a particularly long and cold day, he asked me if I was doing okay.

"I thought Scotland and I had an understanding, a deal of some sort," I grumbled, frustrated. He broke into a rich, deep laugh, which made me feel even sillier about the whole thing.

"You don't strike a deal with Scotland," he replied, trying to rein in his laugh. "Scotland is like a maddening woman you can't get enough of. You're supposed to give in and accept everything, the good and the bad," he said with a gleam in his eyes, his expression a mix of amusement and mischief. I scoffed, taken aback by his words. He leaned down to kiss me on the lips, and his were warm, soft, and inviting, but I didn't reciprocate the kiss. He stopped and met my glare.

"Am I the maddening woman in this scenario?"

"Maybe," he joked as he leaned down to kiss me again. I almost wanted to give in, but then I pulled back.

"I would watch what you say, Mr. Actor, unless you want your chest *accidentally* waxed again."

"Ouch. No." He patted his chest with his hand, his face scrunched up in a pout, remembering how bad it had hurt the last time. The frown turned into a dangerous-looking smile when his eyes met mine. He reached for me, this time lifting my chin and kissing me again. He possessed my mouth in every possible way, leaving me breathless before too long.

He broke the kiss and pulled me to the couch, motioning for me to straddle him. As I leaned closer to him, I was ready to crash my lips against his, but he had other ideas. His thumb traced the contour of my bottom lip as we both panted for air, and just like that, my body was awoken again. His eyes seemed to capture every detail of my face, as if he hadn't memorized it yet. Then, as if suddenly coming out of a haze, he started taking my clothes off urgently, making me feel as though he couldn't get me naked fast enough. I enjoyed his excitement and loved the high that came from feeling wanted. I didn't know what turned me on more: the way his breath came in fast and ragged, the concentrated look in his eyes, or his hands covering every inch of my body as clothes were shed. My throat went dry, aching for him, needing to feel him everywhere. His blue, steely eyes were searing as a blaze when they met mine. How could I resist him when he looked at me so ardently? How could I ever be indifferent to him now that I knew the way it felt to be touched by him? He slowed down again, placing a kiss on my lips and then letting go. I stroked his erection above his clothes, and the strangled moan that escaped his mouth caused my belly to tighten with a delicious ache. His thumb caressed my top lip then went down my chin, tracing my skin from my neck to my clavicle, all the way down to the swell of my breast, down to my erect nipple. He took it between his thumb and forefinger, teasing it, and gave me a burning look before dipping his head to suck on it. I arched my back against him, a low, guttural moan escaping my lips as I rocked my hips against his. His lips left my nipple, and he placed soft kisses between my breasts as his warm breath washed over me.

"You're not maddening, Sam. What's maddening is how much I want ye all the time."

Chapter 18

SAM

"You know, we've slept together, but I've never been to your place." He said it in a low, hushed tone, but I still glared at him. I was working on him, applying touch-ups between scenes, and we were outside, surrounded by the crew. I gave him a horrified glance.

"Would you shush? Do you want someone to overhear that?"

"I haven't even been invited to one of your parties...*yet*." He gave me a cheeky grin, one that was so stupidly irresistible it made me break into a fit of giggles. I shook my head in disbelief, trying to stop myself from smiling.

"I thought we agreed it was best to stay away from each other in public," I whispered as soon as I regained some composure, looking around to make sure no one was paying attention.

"What happens at these house parties everyone talks

about anyway?" His eyes sparkled with a wicked gleam, and butterflies fluttered in my stomach.

I laughed. "What do you think happens? There aren't any spin-the-bottle type of games if that's what you're asking."

"You guys don't play spin the bottle, aye?" he teased.

"No, it's more a game of *empty the bottle*," I joked, thinking about the many empty bottles of wine I'd thrown away a couple weeks before.

His eyes were full of mischief, and when he combined the smolder with a heart-stopping smile, I had no choice but to give in. "Fine. Why don't you come over tonight? Bring a few actors with you so it won't look suspicious."

"He really likes you," Melissa said to me later that evening as we cleaned up the kitchen. I had made a crockpot pot roast with potatoes. Dinner at our place had become such a hit, people had started bringing food over to accommodate the growing number of people attending. Hugh came over with a couple of actors, and we kept our distance, as torturous as it was. We only allowed ourselves to talk a little bit and have a seemingly normal conversation, trying not to gaze into each other's eyes for too long. It was hard to pull back and keep my hands to myself, especially with the way he always looked at me, all brooding and longing. The smolder was on at all times, even though he didn't need to charm me any more than he already did. I was constantly starving for his touch and his kisses.

"I don't know what you mean," I said to Melissa, trying to act surprised, but she reassured me right away.

"Don't. He told me about you two." *Well, that would have been nice to know.* "Oh, don't look so worried, Sam. It's just that we have so many scenes together, I noticed the shift in his mood. You make him really happy."

"Um, thanks?" I frowned. I had no idea where this

conversation was going. She was the one who was supposed to be his potential girlfriend in public.

"You don't need to worry about me. I don't have any intention of following through with the network's request. To be honest, I think it would be a disaster."

I gave her a quizzical look.

"Look at all the TV and movie couples who've been asked to 'act it up' for the media. I mean, this isn't a reality show. This is my job. I love it, but that doesn't mean I want it to take over my entire life."

"I understand." I did, but I was also a little surprised by Melissa's comment. As a rising star herself, I thought she'd jump at the opportunity to fake a relationship to create more buzz about the show and establish her status in Hollywood.

"Of course, it wouldn't be hard to pretend to be attracted to Hugh...if he was my cup of tea, that is." I laughed at that, because it was hard for me to conceive that other people might not find him sexy or interesting. The man had charm in spades, and it wasn't just his pretty face that got me all hot and bothered. He was also goofy and funny, a natural storyteller. I loved his self-deprecating humor, and he was kind, attentive, and generous—Margaret had told me he'd let her stay at his apartment so she wouldn't have to stress about finding a place while she was in Edinburgh for the baby.

"So, who's your type, Melissa?" I asked her, curious to find out if there was any other guy whom she found sexier.

"Please, call me Issa." I had heard some people address her that way on set, but we hadn't worked together at all, even before Margaret left for maternity leave, so I didn't want to be presumptuous. "I hate my name. It's so...generic." I laughed at that, because all my childhood I had wished for a name as generic as Melissa.

She suddenly looked serious. She briefly looked around, and when her eyes were on me again, she said, "I hope you can keep this to yourself, Sam. I am not ready for everyone to know...yet." I stared at her in confusion. "My type is more...feminine. I like women. I'm gay."

Oh.

I looked at her a bit surprised, because I'd had no idea whatsoever.

"I see," I said with a smile.

"My sexual orientation is another reason I don't want to agree to this charade. If we go along with it, even for a little bit, we'll be trapped for years. People will expect it from us, they'll want to see us together, and if we decided to stop acting away from the set, they will lose their goddamned mind. Don't get me wrong—Hugh is a fantastic actor and a beautiful person, and I hope we can be friends for years to come, but I have no intention of pretending for the cameras. I'm honestly a bit disappointed they even asked us to do that. They should know better than that. Fake relationships always backfire anyway."

"Thank you for being honest with me, Mel—*ahem*, Issa. I appreciate that."

She gave me a sweet smile. "I'm rooting for you two, Sam. You guys make a good couple. Things will get better in the next few months, I promise, and then you won't have to keep each other at arm's length in public. The longing looks between you two alone are killing me."

"Ohmygod!" I covered my face with my hands. "And I thought we were being *subtle*."

She stifled a laugh. "Hugh is a great actor, but it's obvious he can't help himself around you."

"Now I'm worried everyone sees what you see," I said with a sigh.

"Nahhh, they have no clue," she said reassuringly. "It's

just that I'm good at figuring people out. I think it's because of my *gaydar*," she added with a cheeky smile and a wink.

Hugh

"Can I ask why you're so crabby today?" I opened my eyes to find Sam staring at me, eyebrows raised in question. Her brown eyes were as sweet as ever, but felt a little disconnected.

"Am I?" I lied, my voice colored with a mix of surprise and confusion.

"Um, yes, you have been. I have been trying to talk to you all morning, but you've hardly listened to anything I said. What's going on?" She smiled at me, but her smile fell when she saw the distraught look in my eyes. Her lips pressed into a straight line, and she frowned. I didn't want to alarm her, but I had been distracted; I had a lot on my mind. Between filming, the exorbitant requests coming from the network about upcoming TV appearances with Melissa, and my secret relationship with Sam, I felt a bit stressed.

On top of that, I'd had a conversation with my brother Declan about Sam the night before. When I mentioned her sister Mira, he said something about a scandal they were both involved in some time ago. He couldn't remember exactly what it had been about and hadn't elaborated, so we'd moved on to a different subject—my growing ego (his words), to be exact. After I hung up the phone with him, I couldn't stop thinking about what he'd said about Sam and Mira. I had never been curious about her past, and I hadn't asked her any questions about her ex-boyfriend or why she'd decided to come work in Scotland. I wanted to get to know her, but I wanted her to tell me about her life in her own time, on her terms. Even so, after the chat with my brother, curiosity got the best of me.

I did something I hadn't done until then: I looked her up.

What I had read about her recent love history troubled me, but it wasn't because of what had happened. Well...yes, it was in part because of what she'd done. Admittedly, I was a bit surprised by what I'd discovered, but more than that, I was perplexed as to why she hadn't said a word about it.

Why was she trying to hide it from me? She didn't strike me as a liar, but I could have been wrong. I looked up to her and finally managed to answer.

"Dinna worry, Sam. I just couldn't sleep very well last night. You should never have left my bed," I told her softly.

"You know I did it only because I had to," she whispered softly.

"If we talked to Nora about it, maybe I could have you stay the night without having to be paranoid all the time."

"You would be okay with everyone knowing about us on set? How are you supposed to make people believe you and Melissa have something going on if you're seen around with me?"

"I know." I hesitated, and then I decided to change the subject. "Are ye going to the Halloween party? The one the guys from the crew are throwing?"

"I am. Cecilia is *making* me go. She said that since it's my birthday and we have a day off the next day, I can't say no."

"Your birthday is on Halloween?" I asked, stifling a

laugh.

She closed her eyes and nodded slowly, looking bashful.

"You mean not only is your name Samhain, but you were born on the night of Samhain? I'm starting to think it wasn't much of a coincidence your mother gave you this name, Sam."

She let out a loud sigh and rolled her eyes. "Tell me about it, man."

"Are you sure you're not a witch?" I asked her with a smirk.

"Don't even go there," she replied with a gleam in her eyes and a half-smile.

SAM

"What is this?" I asked Cecilia, looking at the garment she'd handed me in horror.

"Don't be so bloody difficult, Sam! This is what you're wearing tonight." The tone of her voice was defiant, and she rolled her eyes at me.

"Good grief, Cece! You really drive me crazy sometimes." She looked at me quizzically, and I let out a loud breath. "Let me rephrase and make myself clear: you're *bloody* crazy if you think I'm going out there wearing this."

"Why the hell not? You'll look amazing in it!"

"My boobs are going to spill out of this."

"You're mental. Your *curves* are going to look ahhh-mazing in that outfit," she corrected me. "Come on! I have been excited about this since I bought the bloody costume." I shook my head, shutting down her request. Her pleas were not going to get her anywhere.

There was no way I was going to the Halloween party dressed as Wonder Woman. It wasn't that the costume was bad—it looked well made, and it resembled the latest version of the Wonder Woman uniform, the one worn by Gal Gadot in the upcoming Wonder Woman movie—it was just too much, or perhaps more accurately, not quite enough.

"I could never wear this. It's too...skimpy. I might as well go out in my underwear."

"That is exactly the point. Go out there in the sexiest outfit ever and show Hugh what he's missing." I had remained mum about Hugh with Cecilia, but she didn't believe there was nothing going on between us. We tried to keep our flirting to a minimum in front of other people, but there was only so much we could hide. She teased me regularly about him, and I would just repeat over and over that it wasn't true.

I hated lying to her, but it was for the best. Plus, arguing with her was good practice in case someone else asked me what was going on.

"Hugh's not into me."

Laughter erupted from her, the sound echoing in our living room. She was having fun at my expense, pointing at my face. I rolled my eyes and waved dismissively. When she finally stopped cackling, she said, "I'm not blind, Sam. He fancies you. It's impossible to miss."

"He does not fancy me. We're friends," I said with a shrug.

She laughed. "Pffff! Sure, because friends always undress each other with their eyes. You're going to bloody deny it? There's so much electricity between the two of you, sometimes I think I might get electrocuted just from standing nearby."

"You're ridiculous."

"I'm not and you know it," she said, adjusting her red wig. My roommate looked badass dressed as Black Widow, and she hadn't bought her costume in a store. She had somehow gotten someone from the costume department to help her with the task, and it looked beautiful. She made a great Natasha Romanoff. The jumpsuit hugged her curves, but she was way more covered than I was.

"You look amazing, by the way," I told her.

"Don't try to butter me up, Sam. It's not going to work. You *will* walk out of here dressed as Wonder Woman," she said in an angry tone.

"It's not fair that you're going to wear more fabric than I am. Why do you need to be Black Widow? Why can't you be Wonder Woman?"

"Duh. Number one, I don't have the boobs to fill that," she said, pointing at the costume in my hands, "and two, Oliver is dressing up as The Hulk."

"Oh, really? Sounds like things are getting serious between the two of you."

A bright smile stretched across her face, and she gave me a shy nod, but just a second later she glared in my direction. "Don't try to distract me. Wear that costume. Seriously. You'll look beautiful. Besides, it's your birthday. Don't you want to look good?" She started muttering 50 Cent's "In Da Club" while swinging her hips and throwing her arms up in the air.

I sighed. "It's just that my take on Halloween leans more toward scary and less toward sexy kitten."

"Are you sure you're from LA?"

I laughed and rolled my eyes. "Yeah, I am pretty sure," I joked. "Why?"

"Because you're nothing like the other LA girls I've worked with. You're so...shy and buttoned up. Are you against wearing skimpy Halloween outfits?"

I glared at her. “First off, I am not shy and buttoned up. Second, I am not against skimpy Halloween outfits. I wore them—about a decade ago—and outgrew them.”

“Do you want to go as a scary witch? Is that what you really want to do? How are you going to make your man’s jaw drop?”

“I was thinking more sexy witch, not scary witch...and I’m not trying to win anyone over—”

“You’re impossible. Hurry up and get dressed,” she said, tapping her wrist as if she were tapping a watch, even though she wasn’t wearing one.

“Oh, gosh, you’re such a pain. By the way, did you check the weather? The last thing I want to do is go out in this *thing*.”

“I swear, sometimes you are such a pussy. Wear the damn thing! If not for you, do it for me!” she insisted.

I suddenly felt like giving up. I knew I wasn’t going to win this round—Cecilia could be incredibly persistent.

I had spent the last few weeks in thermal clothes, boots, and heavy socks. Despite loving makeup, my morning routine was simple. I had no desire to wake up earlier than I had to just to apply a bunch of stuff on my skin. Usually I would shower, wash my face, apply some hydrating cream, some foundation and concealer, and a couple coats of mascara. Getting ready for the party took me back to the life I’d had in LA for a second.

It felt like years ago; my days were so different now. It was hard to believe just three months before I had been hanging poolside at my sister’s house. I applied some gold eye shadow, eyeliner, mascara, and fake eyelashes. I put some bronzer on my cheeks. I admired myself in the mirror; I looked mysterious and badass. I put on what I had been given and sighed, thinking about the fact that most likely I wasn’t going to see the man who made me all hot and bothered. He had decided it would be best not to show up to the party, even though he'd been invited. Hugh said he knew he was going to have a hard time staying away from me, and we couldn't afford to get caught, not before we talked to Nora and tried to get her on our side. Every time I heard him talk about that, I grimaced. If we talked to Nora, I'd have to tell him the truth. It was getting hard to harbor my secret, but I wasn't ready for our bubble to burst. I wanted to live in it a little bit longer.

The time we had together was never enough.

As I looked at myself in the mirror, I realized how much I wanted to see him...how much I wanted him to see *me*. All I could think about was the way his fingers touched me. I fantasized about the two of us, tangled up in the darkness, unable to get enough of each other. Each time I looked at him, I could only see longing, not regret. I knew he was trying to behave, but I was tired of having to hide the way he made me feel.

I told myself to stop thinking about him and think about channeling Diana Prince.

As much as I hated to admit it, I made a pretty good Wonder Woman. I applied some shimmery body lotion on my chest, shoulders, and arms, and it gave my skin a certain superhero glow. My boobs fit—*barely*—and magically, there was no spillage elsewhere. Still, it was a very look-at-me outfit, and I was so not that girl. My strengths lay in sexy understated outfits that still left some room for mystery.

For my own sake, I sucked it up, and Cecilia's face beamed with joy as I came down the stairs.

"At least let me take a picture of you, silly American girl. You can show your mum how gorgeous you look!" She snapped a few shots of me with my phone and then placed it in her handbag—my tiny clutch wasn't made to hold a big-ass cellphone.

When we got to Jake's place, the party was in full swing. He and Kirk (Jake's roommate) had moved all the furniture, and everyone was dancing in the living room. There were far more people than I'd expected. Cecilia and I drank from her flask as soon as we got there, but decided to just dance instead of getting drunk. We didn't need a massive hangover to recover from. The living area of the boys' townhouse was semi-dark with just a few lampshades lighting the room. The dark ambiance was nice. Some guy I had never seen before was spinning records, and I wondered if Jake and Kirk had hired a DJ.

The party was far better than I'd thought it would be, and it was definitely better than hanging out at the pub as we had originally planned. People were dancing, and as Little Mix's "Black Magic" came on, Cecilia pulled me to dance with her. Whoever was spinning the records knew what he was doing. He had the perfect mix of pop-dance songs alternated with less famous, edgy ones. I recognized a Banks song I loved, as well as a vintage Jennifer Lopez tune. We were dancing with a group of people we knew, but at some point, I lost track of Cecilia, who had gone to get something to drink with her Hulk. I kept dancing on my own, and surprisingly, no one bothered me—for a while, at least. Then, I felt someone brushing against my body, and when I opened my eyes, I saw a guy dressed in a Kylo Ren costume standing in front of me.

If I hadn't known the way his aftershave smelled, I might have not recognized him. If I hadn't known the way his knuckles felt under my fingers, I could have mistaken him for someone else, but as soon as he held my hand, I knew it was him.

What was he doing there? He had told me it wasn't safe for him to be out, but now here he was. After staring for a good thirty seconds, I was able to catch a glimpse of his blue steel eyes through the netting of the mask. Even if I hadn't recognized him by his hand or been able to see his eyes, I would have known it was him by the way he held me while we danced. We moved together just as we had in the gym. He placed his left hand on my waist, his fingers skimming the bodice of the Wonder Woman costume. I was dying to see the reaction on his face, but it was also intriguing to have him that close to me without anyone knowing who it was. He leaned down and lifted the helmet just barely so he could whisper in my ear.

"Are you trying to kill me, Sam?" he asked, digging his fingers into my hip.

"Obviously not—I didn't even know you'd be here. In fact, you said you wouldn't be coming. Why did you come?" I whispered in the direction of his ear.

"I wanted to wish you a happy birthday," he murmured against my ear.

Oh. "Thank you." I ran my hands down his broad shoulders and his strong arms, and when I reached his ass, I pressed him closer to me. I was wearing very little, and it felt like he was as well. Did he even have any pants on? It looked like he just had on the tunic of his costume. I could feel his hard cock pressing against my hip, and I rubbed myself against him even more. If this was what he wanted, I was going to drive him crazy until he begged for mercy.

"And I came because of your picture," he said.

At least I thought that was what he'd said. *My picture? What picture?* The music had gotten a bit louder, and people were talking around us on top of that. I figured I must have misheard.

"Samhain, you're torturing me," he said in a strangled voice that I could barely hear. He had lifted the mask slightly again, and I could see his lips mumbling something, but I couldn't make out what it was.

"I could say the same about you," I told him, hoping he could hear me.

I wanted to kiss him right there in front of everyone. I wanted to make out and not care about the consequences, but he readjusted the mask on his face, and I dismissed the thought. It couldn't happen. *Not here, not now.*

Why had he shown up? Why did he want to tempt me like this? A man in a Deadpool costume made his way through the crowd and brushed against us, pushing Hugh closer to me. I grasped his arms, straightening myself. Hugh took something out of his belt, took my hand, and placed the object in the center of my palm.

A key.

I glanced up to him, trying to see his eyes. He tipped his mask up slightly again.

"Come," he said in a low growl.

Oh, I'm planning on it.

Chapter 19

SAM

I didn't follow him.

I waited. I didn't want him to know just how much I craved his company. I kept his key secure in the tiny wristlet clutch I had on me.

I danced with Cecilia, Blair, and Kirk. Jake was somewhere putting the moves on another girl. We drank whisky and toasted to my birthday. I was having fun, but I couldn't stop thinking about getting a certain man out of his costume.

"Who was the guy you were dancing with a while ago? Where'd he go?" Cecilia asked, cocking one eyebrow. She looked around the room, and when she couldn't find him in the crowd, she looked at me with a sly grin.

"I have no idea. He was wearing a mask. He never told me his name," I lied.

"Really?" The corners of her lips tipped up; she didn't look convinced.

It was time to make my exit—I had made my mystery

man wait long enough.

"I'm going home," I lied to Cecilia. "Can I have my phone?"

"You're lying! You're so lying," she said with conviction.

I frowned. "No, I'm not. I'm tired, and I want to go home."

"Your phone has been buzzing for a while. You're not fooling me, Sam. Here." She handed over my phone and gave me a coy smile.

Even though it was locked, she could still see all the texts from Hugh. *Dammit.* His name was saved as "H", but still, bad move. I should have assigned him a different name. I unlocked the screen and read his messages. Then, I scrolled up and noticed a picture of me dressed as Wonder Woman in the message history along with a cheeky text. I hadn't sent that.

"Cece, *what* did you do?"

"What you bloody fool should have done. He *needed* to see what he was missing. That was him, wasn't it? Earlier?"

"It was," I finally conceded. It was pointless trying to hide anything from my sneaky roommate. She'd basically set me up. She smiled with an air of satisfaction on her face, and I hugged her despite how smug she looked.

"I owe you one...I think. I should go. I've kept him waiting long enough. Don't tell anyone or I might have to kill you." We exchanged a look, and I left the boys' townhouse after grabbing my coat.

I couldn't walk fast enough in my high heels. Luckily, Hugh's place wasn't far away. I rang the bell and unzipped my coat hastily, feeling even colder, my nipples pebbling under the fabric of the Wonder Woman onesie. It was only then that I remembered the key he had given me. We hadn't had sex in a few days, and it was pointless to try to say I hadn't thought about it every single day. My hands trembled like those of an addict who's gone too many days without a fix. I didn't want to feel that way, but I couldn't help it. I wanted him.

Before remembering the key, I'd had a different plan.

I had thought he would open the door and I would drag him straight to the bedroom. Since he didn't answer, I fished the key out of my tiny clutch and opened the door.

I certainly hadn't been expecting a handsome man wearing a Kylo Ren costume and an apron around his waist. Was he cooking dinner?

What the what?

Now that I could actually see him, I approved even more of this costume—his ass looked spectacular. I shut the door, and he finally turned around, a bright smile stretching across his face.

"It's about time you showed up, *mo chridhe,"* he said in a low rumble, his eyes unreadable. I thought I might be in trouble for a minute, but then he smiled. I ditched my coat and as our eyes met, he gave me a once-over. He let go of the knife and whatever it was he'd been chopping. The look in his eyes had my heart kick-drumming against my chest, my throat went dry, and I licked my lips as he walked over to me. I looked up to him and saw that his usually bright blue eyes were brooding with desire.

Yes. Come to mama.

I reached for him, taking his face in my hands just as his arms went around me and pulled me tightly against him. He gave me a grin that made my stomach fill with butterflies, my skin burn with need, and my knees buckle under the weight of anticipation. I couldn't wait any longer. I kissed him, letting my tongue do the talking, telling him how much I had missed his lips, his mouth, his body—*everything*. I missed everything about him, and we'd been flush against each other just a while ago.

He moaned in my mouth, and the sound of it did nothing but fuel the frenzy I was already succumbing to. I had to have him. *Right here, right now*. I reached around his waist, trying to untie his apron and get him out of his getup.

He had other ideas.

He stopped my hands. Whatever he was cooking had gotten his attention, and he stopped the kiss, leaving me thirsty for more.

"Wait a second, Sam," he said, holding up a finger, trying to regain his composure. He kissed me softy on the lips. "Your costume is really sexy, by the way. Your picture nearly gave me a heart attack." There it was again—that damn irresistible smirk on his lips.

I followed him to the kitchen.

He was mixing something that smelled like a whisky-based sauce, and he had what looked like heavy cream in a bowl and fresh prawns in another.

"Yeah, about that...I didn't send that picture," I said, leaning against the counter, facing him.

"Ye didn't? Then who did?" he asked in a curious tone as he lifted his head from the pan he was holding.

"Cece did." His eyes widened for a second, and he took a deep breath through his nose. He gave me a careful look then nodded.

"I'm sorry. I didn't tell her anything, she figured it out on her own. I didn't mean for this to happen," I said, trying to excuse myself. "But..."

"But?"

"If you didn't want people to know, maybe you shouldn't have showed up at the party. I guarantee you everyone is going to wonder who I was dancing with. There's not much to do up here. People are *starved* for gossip."

"Sam," he said in a low voice. When I looked up, he smiled at me reassuringly. His eyes didn't look worried, but there was a different type of emotion I couldn't place. "I am not going to worry about that, and neither should you. We're going to try to keep things on the down low, but if our cover is blown, we'll handle it. I don't..." He paused for a second, as if he were thinking about the possibility of staying away from each other. "I don't want to stay away from you. I don't think I can," he said, almost as if he were talking to himself. He frowned, and I wanted to reach for him, to smooth the frown over, but he was the one who stepped in closer, still keeping an eye on the sauce. He leaned in and took my chin in his hand.

"As long as you want me, I want to be with you." He kissed me softly, and then whispered, "Happy Birthday" against my lips.

Being there with him felt like a dream I didn't want to wake up from. Everything was new and exciting, but I had no clue what the future held for us.

Still, I knew he was sincere about his intentions. For some reason, I felt I could trust Hugh MacLeod, even though I had been burned badly. His breath was warm, and his voice felt like an embrace, but he let go of me again and I sighed. When I opened my eyes, he was staring at me, a cheeky grin plastered on his face.

I looked down and bit my lip, a bit embarrassed by the fact that just a touch from him set my skin ablaze. He poured a glass of white wine for me and one for him, and then he toasted to me. I smiled nervously and exhaled a deep breath.

I hadn't felt this cherished in a long time.

"Do you need any help?" I asked him.

"No. I just need you here by me," he replied, interlacing

the fingers of his left hand with mine.

"Thank you for making dinner. No one's ever cooked for me before."

He looked surprised by my revelation, and then he frowned, his eyebrows pulled together. He gave an imperceptible shake of his head, and then his lips curled at the corners. "You deserve this and much more, Sam," he said in a low voice. When he glanced back at me, the soft, loving look in his eyes made my heart flutter like Tinker Bell's wings.

I loved the way he said my name. His accent seemed to be more pronounced on the most random words, and he was completely owning me. "You're kind and sweet and take care of everyone around you. If people don't see it, it's their loss. They're the fools." I was touched by his words, but I couldn't help but feel a hint of guilt inside of me. Was I really such a good girl? I had done some pretty bad things recently, and a lot of people had gotten hurt as a consequence. I didn't feel like my conscience was so sparkling clean. I let out a deep breath, and he frowned.

"Did I say something wrong?" he asked.

I exhaled loudly and decided to change the subject. "I was just trying to remember how you say fool in Scottish. I swear I just learned that the other day."

"Dafty," he said with a charming smile. *"Dobber* is another good one...or *dunderhead,* my personal favorite."

"You have a favorite word for fool?" I laughed.

"Aye, I do." I could have stared forever at the wrinkle that formed on his cheek when he smiled; I loved it so much. His easy charm was hard to resist, and I was completely captivated by him.

"Come on, let me help. I don't know what to do with myself in the kitchen if I'm not cooking."

"Fine. You can set the table. The prawns are almost

done, and there's a scallop and asparagus salad in the fridge. I also have a regular salad, if you ken how to dress it up."

"I do ken how to dress up a salad, sir."

"Sir, aye?" he repeated with a wicked gleam.

"Aye," I said in a playful tone as I gathered the ingredients for an orange vinaigrette.

"Hey, Sam."

"What is it?" I turned in his direction, only to have my cheek covered with a dollop of cream. I stared at him in shock as an ornery smile stretched across his face. "What did you do that for?" I asked him, the tone of my voice higher than normal.

"So that I can do this," he said before leaning down and licking my cheek. He cleaned my skin and placed soft, feather-like kisses on my cheek and neck. Our lips clashed a moment later, our tongues dancing together, hungry and needy. He pressed me against the counter, rolling his hips against mine, letting me feel how hard and ready he was for me.

I tugged the hair on the back of his neck gently and kissed him fast and hard. I pulled his hair with a little more force so he would stop and look at me.

"Stop teasing me. Let's eat and be done with it so you can fuck me."

His voice was gruff, heavy with lust. "Your wish is my command."

Chapter 20

Hugh

The Saturday after the party, I found a way for the two of us to go to the cottage down in the valley. The guys wanted to go on a hike on a mountain an hour away from St. Martin, but I lied and said I felt a bit under the weather. I needed to talk to Sam about what I had found out, but I didn't want to do it there. The night before, someone had come over and knocked on my door while she was there. We were upstairs, and I pretended I wasn't home. After a while, I got several messages from Mick and Marcus saying I needed to join them at Frank's house, where they were all partying together.

I needed to talk to her in a place where we wouldn't be interrupted.

I needed to know the whole story, and I wanted to hear it from *her*.

We left early on Saturday morning before the sun was even out. It would have taken us a couple of hours to get to the cottage on foot, but it only took about forty minutes by car. A few weeks after we'd spotted the cottage, I had gone there by myself. The place was deserted, and a sign by the door with the owner's name and phone number told me it was a rental property. Through the windows, I could tell the place was furnished. At the back of the house, there was plenty of wood stacked up, and the cottage even had solar panels nearby. Curious to see how it looked inside, I managed to get in and was pleased to discover it was even cozier than I had imagined. The view from the top floor was astounding—you could see the ocean from one of the bedrooms.

In that moment, I knew Sam was going to love it.

I couldn't wait to see her reaction.

I had to admit, a small part of me had reservations about her because of what I had found out. Even so, I knew I had to hear her side of the story before casting judgment.

We got to the cottage when it was still dark out.

I had told her I was taking her there, but she didn't know it was a rental or that we'd be spending the night.

The first thing I did when we got there was turn the thermostat on—I wished the owner of the place had done so himself already because it was a bit chilly. It was the first weekend of November, and although a temperature of five degrees Celsius was average to me, I knew it felt like the dead of winter to Sam.

I grabbed some wood from a basket near the fireplace and lit a fire then glanced at her moving around the place, taking in every little detail.

"Are we sleeping here tonight?" she asked excitedly.

"We are."

"Do you want me to make some coffee...or, um, tea?"

"Coffee, please."

I exhaled, thinking we should probably talk about what I'd found out sooner rather than later. My chest tightened at the thought of bringing up the subject. As much as I needed to know the whole truth, I didn't want to upset her.

As soon as I got the fire going, I stood up and walked to the kitchen.

She'd already started the coffee and was opening the cabinets looking for mugs.

"Aha! Found them."

"Sam, I need to tell you something," I said hesitantly.

"What is it?" she asked, turning my way for a second, her face brightened by a sweet smile. She grabbed one mug and set it on the counter, and then picked another one that said *Best Maw Ever* in pink. She laughed.

"I know what happened in LA...with you and Eric." She looked at me with a shocked expression. Her grasp on the mug loosened, and we watched it fall to the floor and shatter into a million pieces.

"God, I'm sorry. I'm so sorry," she said, kneeling down on the floor to pick up the pieces.

"It's just a silly mug," I told her.

"Yeah, but I'm pretty sure the first rule when renting a place is to not break anything."

"Sam," I said, grabbing her wrist. "I don't give a damn about the mug." She looked down and nodded, her eyes heavy with remorse. We finished picking up the pieces in silence, and then I wiped the floor down with a paper towel, trying to collect all the small ceramic shards. I glanced at her out of the corner of my eye as she picked another mug, placed it on the counter, and poured the black coffee.

"Is this why you brought me here? To tell me you knew about me?" She wasn't looking at me, but I knew from the choked sound of her voice that she was trying to hold back the tears.

I placed a hand on the small of her back. "That's not the reason why. I wanted to be here with you...but I also needed to talk to you," I said, trying to sound as reassuring as I could.

She turned around to face me, eyes glossy and lips trembling.

"I wanted to tell you, I really did."

"Why didn't you then?"

"It's just...things have been finally going right between us, and I wanted to enjoy it a little bit longer." She let out a deep breath and looked down, and then her eyes met mine again. This time, there was no trace of remorse or sadness in them, only resignation. "Look, I understand if you want to take me home right now. I should have been honest with you since the first time we kissed, if not earlier. I know I'm no good for you, especially not right now when your career is about to take off."

"Sam, what the bloody hell are you even talking about?"

"You brought me here to break up with me, didn't you?"

Her words hit me like a wave, the shock causing my blood to rush to my head. The palms of my hands were sweaty, and I suddenly felt anxious—I thought I was in danger of losing her.

SAM

He was breathing heavily, staring at me through stormy eyes, looking as if he'd been trying to collect his thoughts. Did he know everything? Did he hate me?

"I will admit I have been worried about...what I found out. I've been wanting to talk to you about it, but I took some time to reflect."

"And?" I asked with a frown.

"I don't think what you did is going to make me like you less, but I need to know the *whole* story, Sam, and I need to hear it from *you*."

I nodded. "I wanted to tell you so many times, actually. I don't know why, but I always felt the need to let you know, even before—" I said as I looked at him sheepishly. It was the truth; even before we'd kissed, I had always felt the overwhelming urge to open up to him, as though something in my blood told me he wouldn't judge me for what I had done and how impulsive I had been.

"I do have to say, I'm kind of surprised no one on set has mentioned it so far—not even when it came out that Mira was my sister. I'm shocked no one has put two and two together. It was in the press, on the Internet, social media...it was everywhere. What I've done was *everywhere*." I glanced up to him, and for the first time ever, I felt *guilty*. I didn't feel guilty for what I had done, but I did feel guilty for not telling him the truth.

He was going to break up with me, I just knew it.

I took a deep breath. "I told you how Eric was cheating on me with my boss...well, I didn't just find out...I found out the night the show we worked on won a Golden Globe. It was *during* the ceremony. I left the ballroom to meet him and congratulate him. I thought it was going to be a special night for us..."

He took my hands in his and brushed his thumbs across my knuckles, nudging me to go on. "And? What happened?"

"I saw them kissing...Eric and Quinn, I mean. They

were co-writers and co-creators. I-I was devastated. In a moment, I saw my relationship go up in smoke. I don't think I've ever been more heartbroken. It was...awful. What he—what they did to me was awful." I gave him a sheepish, remorseful look, and I almost smiled when I saw that the expression on his face was leaning toward understanding instead of judging.

"Did you confront him that night?" he asked in a deep, gravelly tone. His voice sounded so calm and reassuring, but I couldn't afford to keep my hopes up.

"I couldn't. It wasn't a good time. I told him I felt sick and went home."

"So, when did you let him know you knew? It must have been terrible for you to swallow that. You two had been together a long time, right?"

"Seven years."

"That's longer than a lot of marriages," he reflected, raising one eyebrow.

"I never told Eric I had seen him that night, Hugh. I didn't confront him right away. I stayed with him."

"You stayed with him?"

"Yes. For months. For four months, I collected evidence," I muttered, absorbed in my memories. "Lots of evidence." My mind went back to the beginning of the year, and as my head was flooded with memories, I told Hugh the whole story.

I slept with the enemy for months. For roughly sixteen weeks, I acted like the devoted girlfriend I had always been. I laughed at his jokes, I bought him his favorite beer, I picked up after him, and I found his shit when he couldn't. I never put up a fight, never raised a red flag. I had a mission to accomplish, and I could only do that if I kept up the charade. I had sex with him even when I didn't want to. Sometimes I would come, despite not wanting to enjoy it. I went down on him any time he hinted at a blow job. I never questioned his excuses or late nights.

In a way, it was almost funny. Men can be so fucking unobservant. I basically ran the whole sting under Eric's nose, and he never suspected anything.

Not once.

In fact, he seemed even happier than before. He'd just won a Golden Globe, and both his girlfriend and his mistress were happy. Ratings were still not that good, but the future was looking somewhat bright.

As was my revenge plan.

Operation D&H—Douchebag and Harlot, as I affectionately dubbed them—was going great. I had enlisted my mother's help and got some...equipment from one of her friends. I hid it everywhere—his office, her office, his car—and I started piling up the material. The downside of it was that I had to go through all the recordings—audio and video—of the two bastards. I had to listen to flirty words, seduction games, and the fucking moans. The kitten-like moans were the worst. Quinn sounded like one of those porn actresses. There was absolutely no need to moan like that, ever; any woman with half a brain would tell you so. I was thoroughly disappointed because up until I'd found her rubbing up against my boyfriend, I had been kind of fond of her.

One night I told Eric I was going to spend the weekend with Amira, and instead I stayed at my sister's house while she was away on a local shoot to go through all the material I had accumulated. My mother started questioning my sanity because I kept collecting and collecting evidence while still living with Eric and acting as if nothing had happened. In reality, I couldn't stop thinking about how and when to drop the bomb.

My life was a fucking mess, and it sucked. My revenge plan was the only thing going according to plan. I wanted it to be executed perfectly.

It had to be epic.

I knew I should have felt devastated—depressed, unmotivated. I should have just left Eric and gone to live at my sister's, but I didn't want to give up on my plan. Even though part of me was thoroughly heartbroken, the part thirsting for revenge was stronger, pulling me forward.

At work, we lived in a euphoric state for a couple of months, but not even the two awards the show had won did much to boost our ratings. We thought we'd still get lucky, but nothing was for certain. These days, networks cancelled even moderately successful shows if they weren't pulling the ratings they expected.

Bottom line: the future of the show was still up in the air.

I kept debating when and how I should let Eric, Quinn, and the rest of the world know about their cheating ways, but I couldn't decide.

There were so many different ways I could administer the blow, but still, none of them sounded right. Then, at the end of April, Beyoncé dropped her surprise concept album, "Lemonade." I had always been a fan of hers, but after watching the HBO special I felt...electrified. She was speaking my language, one betrayed, humiliated woman to another. "Lemonade" definitely put a spin on my revenge.

I called Amira, and she had her stylist get us in touch with a talented seamstress that could recreate the Roberto

Cavalli dress from the "Hold Up" video. Initially, Amira tried to get me the real thing, but it proved nearly impossible even for her stylist since it was fresh off the runway and had become a hot commodity.

When I tried on the dress the seamstress made for me, I could hardly contain myself. I had been walked all over, and I was ready to release all my frustration, pain, and heartbreak. I was ready to make my lemonade.

"I need to be there," Amira said.

"What? Hell, no. You can't be involved in this."

"No, I need to see this happening. I'll video it. Pleeeease?" she asked. "We can make our own version of 'Hold Up.' I'll come with you."

"You can't be there, Amira. You have too much to lose. Your publicist and agent will be furious. You cannot be involved in this."

"Fine then, I'll have Bucky take a video for me so I can witness your triumph. I won't be there, but at least let me help you get ready."

It all went down on a Friday at noon. I went to work early that day and brought the dress and a basket full of evidence.

During my lunch break, I pulled out my laptop and uploaded the incriminating video/audio mix I had made to YouTube. Then, I sent it to everyone on our email list. A few minutes later, I hid in a dressing room and put on the dress. I came out looking almost as fierce as Sasha Fierce herself, and I held a basket full of USBs in my hands.

That's right.

Instead of going around the show's offices smashing things with a baseball bat, I walked around throwing USBs loaded with the revealing video on everyone's desks.

Everyone was getting back from the lunch break, and from the looks on their faces, I could tell they were thinking something was wrong with me. Some gave me compliments on my dress while others just gave me weird looks.

Bucky was videoing the whole thing, smiling like a fool.

Someone in production asked if we were shooting a spoof of Beyoncé's 'Lemonade.'

Not quite.

I left the building with Bucky, middle fingers up in the air as my phone started buzzing incessantly with messages and calls from Eric—and pretty much everyone else I knew in Hollywood.

The entire time I had been planning my revenge, I'd wanted to hurt Eric and Quinn. I'd wanted to hurt their reputation. What I hadn't thought about was that the network would use it as an opportunity to cancel the show.

And I certainly hadn't thought Eric would try to make me pay.

I was called by Eric's attorney to come in that weekend for a formal meeting with his and Quinn's legal representative, and my mother contacted her lawyer since I didn't have one. To my surprise, when I went to the meeting, the bitch wasn't there. She either didn't have the courage to face me or was too busy licking her wounds after being exposed to the world.

Eric wanted me to hand over the original files, but at that point, it was out of my control since I'd made at least three hundred copies and distributed them to everyone I knew—I had even sent one to TMZ. Anyone could have uploaded the video, even after mine got taken off YouTube. As my attorney explained this, the face of the man I used to love turned the ugliest shade of purple, and I saw a side of him I'd never seen before.

"You fucking bitch! You're done! I promise you will not work in this city ever again!" Eric yelled at me. For the very first time, I felt happy we were over. I froze as he made a spectacle of himself. His attorney had to restrain him, and after a while, I left with mine, wondering if I'd really get slapped with a defamation lawsuit as Eric's attorney had said I would.

The scandal was all over the place that weekend, and even though Eric and Quinn were minor players in the Hollywood game, it didn't take the gossip sites very long to find out he'd had a girlfriend who just happened to be Mira Farouk's sister. In fact, some of the headlines were: "Mira Farouk's sister delivers epic Lemonade-style revenge to her cheating boyfriend".

I wasn't mad about it. I'd accomplished what I had been focusing on for months, but I wasn't sure what to do next. I hadn't thought about what would happen afterward, and I hadn't thought about the fact that my plan would end up hurting other people.

A couple weeks after my Lemonade-inspired diss, the show got cancelled. The network blamed the poor ratings as well as the scandal, calling the show's cost "damaging," a "loss" for the channel. I had known my stint would create a stir, but I hadn't thought it would go in that direction. Many of my friends lost their jobs.

A lot of people blamed me.

In the end, my revenge plan backfired.

For weeks, I couldn't find another gig. I didn't really need to start working right away, but in order to start over, I needed to move out of my sister's house. Plus, now that I had a lot of free time, I didn't know what to do with myself. I had been working ever since I had gotten out of school. Amira suggested I sit tight and wait for her to have a break in her schedule so we could travel together to all those places she had always had to go but never really had the time to visit. It was a great plan.

Unfortunately, I felt restless, and after a couple months of looking for a new job, it became clear from the many rejections I had gotten that no one wanted me on their set.

I was a liability.

I was deemed a hassle, someone who'd cause unnecessary drama.

Me—dramatic.

I had been a good girl all my life, a patient, loving girlfriend waiting for her boyfriend to commit when, in the meantime, he was screwing his coworker.

And now, no one in LA wanted to work with me. It made me angry.

I was the one who had been betrayed, but now I was seen as the dangerous one.

"The reality is, when I set all of it in motion, I had no idea how it would play out. Of course, I had no intention of damaging the show; I just wanted to tarnish *their* reputation. I wanted *them* to suffer, not anyone else. I hadn't realized what kind of repercussions there would be for knocking down the first domino."

I looked into his eyes, trying to decipher what he was thinking. What did he think of me? Did he consider me shallow and vindictive? Was he going to cast me away as others had done?

"How long have you known?" I asked him.

"A few days." He exhaled deeply through his nose. His face looked serious, but not severe. He looked pensive, and my eyes fell on his lips, which were slightly curled up at the corners, even when his face was serene and expressionless.

"Why didn't you ask me about it sooner?"

"I have been trying to find the right time."

I frowned and narrowed my eyes at him, needing more of an explanation.

He noticed my confusion, and with a loud exhale of breath, he said, "My brother told me about you. He remembered reading some headline. I looked it up and read some stuff after that. I wanted to talk to you about it, but I knew we needed to be alone, and I didn't want to do it last night. I didn't want to ruin your birthday."

He didn't want to ruin my *birthday?*

"Aren't you mad? Don't you think I'm *mental?*" I asked, using Cecilia's favorite word for crazy.

He shrugged, and that alone shocked me.

"I have been trying to understand how I feel about it for days. On one hand, I can't fault you for what ye've done. I mean, the bastard deserved it all. I am not sure I could have ever lived through being with a person who's cheating on me. It's awful. It must have been awful, Sam."

"It was," I said in agreement, still shocked by his calm and understanding demeanor. Hugh MacLeod couldn't be real. He was too good, too perfect.

He exhaled, and in that moment, I feared I might be in trouble.

"On the other hand, you did publicly scorn them. I am not sure I completely agree with the way ye handled it, but I am in no position to judge you. I have never been through something like that. Who knows what I'd do if I found myself in the same situation? I don't think it would be fair for me to point fingers." I had been holding my breath. The air trapped in my chest came out all at once, accompanied by an overwhelming feeling of relief at hearing his comforting words. He didn't hate me, but still...what did this mean for us?

"So...you're not mad at me?" He shook his head no. "You don't hate me?" Another shake of his head. "You don't think I'm a crazy troublemaker? A bad person?"

"No," he said, and after he let out another breath, his lips curled up in a dazzling smile. Suddenly, the light in the room began to change. I turned around to see the sun coming up behind me through the kitchen window, and it looked like a giant red ball flaming around the edges. It was rising above the sea, transforming the water into a golden mirror. I turned around to look at him and found him smiling at me. The sun shone in his eyes, turning them a light shade of orange, his whole face a light gold. The sunlight made his hair look a fiery red, and I felt stupid because I couldn't stop staring at him. His eyes were fixed on my face, full of...*love?*

Strange. I had been dreading him finding out the truth, and he'd just had the opposite reaction of what I would have predicted. He still wanted me after I'd just told him plain and simple that I was bad news for his career.

"I didn't want to talk about what happened in LA for selfish reasons," he said. "We'll have to be careful and keep it quiet until we can manage to make the network reconsider their stupid strategy, but I am not letting you go." He took my face in his hands and placed a kiss on my lips. "Sam," he said in a low growl, his breath a sweet caress against my skin, his voice charged with need. "I want you. If you're a bad person, I want to be bad with you."

Chapter 21

Hugh

Our naked bodies together looked like caramel and milk. I could never get enough of burying myself in her, her legs wrapped around me, taking me home again and again. I could never get enough of touching her soft curves, the swell of her breasts, her glorious arse. When we were together, there was one word I repeated over and over in my head.

Mine, mine, mine.

I wanted all of her. She was mine, and I could never let her go. Going back to a life without Sam wasn't a possibility. She'd asked over and over if I was going to be okay with what I'd found out, if I could forgive her, but the problem was that I didn't seem to have a choice when it came to her. My weakness should have worried me, but instead I felt empowered admitting to myself how much I cared for her. I was falling in love with Sam, and it was the most amazing and inebriating feeling, comparable only to the excitement and euphoria I experienced when performing.

We hadn't gotten a lot of sleep the night before, so after our talk, we had come to bed and fallen asleep after getting lost in each other.

I woke up after a while, partly because it was a bit too bright in the bedroom. When I lifted my head from the pillow and turned in her direction, I was once again bewitched by the woman in my bed, a dark beauty against the white bedding, her black hair framing her stunning face, so peaceful in her sleep. I lifted the comforter slightly to admire her body. Her full breasts showed her tan lines, as did her lower belly. In both places, her skin was just a lighter shade of brown. The slight, natural curve of her belly drove me insane. She was a Venus. She looked like a goddess, soft curves in all the right places, and that little triangular patch of black hair was the gateway to the most blissful heaven. She stirred, and I covered her again, not wanting to disturb her, but her hand moved and her eyelids fluttered. She frowned for just a second, taking in her surroundings. She smiled sleepily at me, stretching out an arm to touch my face.

"I didn't mean to wake you," I told her.

"It's okay," she whispered. "I don't want to be sleeping all day. I want to be with you."

I laughed. "You are with me."

"I want to be *awake* with you." She ran her hand through my hair, playing with my locks. My hand caressed her skin from her waist, to her hip, to her arse. She arched her body in response, and a low hum escaped her lips. She wrapped her leg around my waist, pulling me closer to her. I chuckled.

"Do you want to go for a walk by the beach?" I asked her.

She chewed on her lip and gave me a sultry look.

"What is it?"

"I would love to, but—"

"But?"

"We need to do something about your hard-on first," she said with a serious look. I laughed heartily, and she wrapped an arm around my neck then pulled me on top of her.

"Make love to me, Hugh MacLeod," she said, her voice full of need. Her eyes burned with desire as I lowered myself on top of her. I trailed kisses down her chest, pinching one of her nipples with my fingers. I moved down to her stomach, her body shivering under my lips as I kissed her right above her belly button. I licked the skin below her navel before I brought my mouth down to the small patch of hair at her pussy. I kissed her right there and she squirmed under my touch, her legs trembling on my sides, her hands fisting the sheets in anticipation. I parted her lips and flicked my tongue against her swollen, trembling clit, wrapping my arm around one of her legs, pinning her down. I increased the speed, and her hips buckled, asking for more.

"Ohhh, fuck me," she moaned as her fingers twisted in my hair. I laughed against her skin, and she squirmed under my breath, her hips arching against my mouth. I inserted two fingers into her warm wetness as my tongue licked and sucked on her clit until she stiffened under my touch and came, crying out my name. It was ecstasy hearing her moan my name as I brought her to the brink of pleasure over and over. I could never, ever get tired of that. I sat up, and she looked at me sheepishly, her cheeks colored in a faint shade of red, her eyes bright but feral.

"I need you inside of me—now," she said in a raspy tone, pulling herself up on her elbows. I reached for a rubber on the nightstand and handed it to her. She tore the foil with her teeth and leaned closer to put it on me, but first she licked the tip of my cock and sucked it slowly. A growl escaped my mouth, and I tried to think about several things that would distract me from coming too soon, namely sport injuries. Sport injuries were such a buzzkill, and I could always count on them to keep me from premature ejaculation. Sam rolled the condom on my cock and looked up to me with hooded eyes. I placed myself between her legs and brushed my cock against her sensitive clit and wet pussy. She lifted her hips and I held on to them, sliding inside her. An "Oh, fuck" escaped my mouth as I stilled for a moment. Being inside her was too good, too much all at once.

She opened her eyes, alarmed, but I reassured her with one long, slow thrust.

Her mouth opened, forming an O, but no sound came out.

"Do ye know how fucking good you feel?" I asked her as I thrust into her deeper.

She licked her lips and cleared her throat. "As good as you do, I imagine."

"I can't get enough of you, Sam," I told her as I thrust into her faster, her legs wrapped around my hips, her body moving in sync with me, meeting each one of my thrusts. "I'm afraid this hunger will never stop."

She smiled, her face in ecstasy as I moved frantically inside of her.

"Don't stop. Don't ever stop," she said right before I started teasing her throbbing clit with my thumb. Then she came, squeezing her walls around my cock, her body shuddering. I came a moment after her, the orgasm rushing through me like a river, white, blinding fireworks exploding behind my eyelids. I collapsed on top of her, breathing heavily as her own heart slowed down to a steadier beat.

She ran her fingers through my hair.

"Want to know something?" she asked.

"Aye," I muttered, still trying to regain my breath. I kissed the skin of her belly.

"I will never stop being hungry for this either."

SAM

The Monday after my birthday and our secret getaway, we were on a bus to go work on a different location. I had been in a daze all morning after having two full days with Hugh at the cottage. We alternated romantic walks on the beach with toe-curling sex by the fireplace. We cooked together, and after we got lost in each other for the millionth time, we told each other stories of when we were kids. It was the best weekend I'd had in a while, and it put me in a lust/love-induced daze.

I was falling for him, but it was too early to talk about love. All I knew and cared about was that when we were together, the hunger in his eyes matched mine.

We had gotten back late the night before in an attempt to avoid meeting anyone, and after I got back to my place, I had a hard time going back to sleep. We had to get up early the next morning, so we were all quiet and sleepy—except Cecilia, who was chipper in an almost obnoxious way. She hadn't been home when I'd gotten back, so she hadn't had time to quiz me about where I had been all weekend. She was listening to some music, and by the sound of it, it was Madonna again. She had been on a Madonna kick, listening to the entire discography on her phone every day, and apparently, she hadn't gotten sick of having the same songs on repeat.

"I should have dressed up as Madonna in the 'Express Yourself' video instead," she whispered, leaning toward me. "And I could have dressed you in one of those suits with a corset underneath. Your boobs would have looked great. You even look like one of her vocalists from the early '90s."

I rolled my eyes and laughed. It was such an odd Cecilia thing to say.

"Um, thanks?" There was no point in arguing. It was too early, and she always seemed to win every time we had a discussion. *Pesky little thing*. She looked at me, waiting to hear my opinion on the matter.

"You have nothing to say?"

I shrugged. "It sounds like a fun idea, but we did just fine with the Wonder Woman costume."

"*We,* huh?" She winked.

"Yes, it was a lovely suggestion," I said coyly, pressing my lips together; I'd said too much.

"*Lovely*, hey?" She looked around, and when she saw that everyone else around us had dozed off, she whispered, "So, what did he do? Did he give you a big strong *hand* and lift you to higher ground?" she asked with a lewd gesture.

"Oh, my God! Stop that!" I whisper-shouted, looking around us, but thankfully everyone was asleep. Alas, she didn't stop there.

"Did he make you feel like a queen on a throne? Did he make love to you 'til you couldn't come down?" she asked, paraphrasing the lyrics of the song.

I closed my eyes and covered my face with my hands. A moment later, I peeked through my fingers and gave her a small nod.

"I knew it," she said with an air of satisfaction. "That should teach you, Sam."

"Teach me what?"

"To never ever go against me."

"Stop smirking like that," I told Hugh in a hushed tone. He looked down at me through his eyelashes as I stroked my brush across his cheek, splattering fake blood across his face. "Someone will notice if you don't stop." I took another chunk of makeup and applied it to his skin. His lips pressed into a line, and then he bit his bottom lip, the look in his eyes sending a rush of color to my cheeks.

"Did you have a good weekend, Sam?" he asked, impenitent, with a James McAvoy-esque grin that made him look stupidly handsome.

"It was wonderful," I whispered, smiling but refusing to meet his eyes. He let out a low chuckle, and I didn't have to look at his face to know what he looked like when he did that. I *loved* that he was so happy this morning, but there were at least fifteen people around us setting up for the next scene. Although his behavior was endearing in some ways, it was also irritating. I didn't understand why he wasn't trying to be more careful. He didn't seem to care, but I did. It was hard enough to focus after the two days we'd had together, but he seemed to be determined to make me lose all my concentration.

He made a face as I brought my brush to his cheek again. "Why is this blood so much darker than what I usually have all over me?"

"This is dragon blood. We agreed that fake dragon blood should look different than fake human blood."

"I see. Why is it so much thicker? What did you put in there to make it like that?"

"I could tell you, but then I'd have to kill you."

"Is it animal blood? I swear it smells."

"Please. Do you think we could afford to have PETA on our ass like that?"

"I suppose not."

"We just added red and blue food coloring and cocoa powder to give it more texture."

"Hmmm." He gave me another steely gaze, and I shook my head. There was a giant contraption shaped like a tower covered in the same material of green screens. During post-production, the automated boxy thing would become a dragon. There was a tube sticking out of it that was connected to a spray gun and a tank filled with twenty pounds of fake blood. At some point during the scene, it was supposed to spray blood all over Hugh. Slashing the belly of a dragon would have such consequences.

He reached for the opening in my hoodie and squeezed one of my breasts. I waved his hand away, narrowing my eyes at him. I looked around and made sure it was safe to talk. "You're being impossible today. How am I supposed to do my job?"

"My hands are cold," he said with a shrug and a smug grin.

"My boobs are not hand warmers."

He laughed. "I disagree. They're so...warm, and inviting. They make excellent pillows, too," he said in a deep voice, clicking his tongue playfully.

Images of our weekend together flashed before my eyes, and I looked down, unable to hold back my smile. I fiddled with my brush and the dish holding the blood.

"Are you done with touch-ups, Sam? I need to fix his hair," the hairstylist asked.

"Y-yeah, Serena. He's all yours."

As I walked away to let the hairstylist do her job, I realized just how much I was falling for him. I had to hold back a stupid smile from spreading across my face. It was the best and the worst to be surrounded by him and his presence every day. I knew each one of his movements, each one of his expressions. I recognized his presence by the sound of his steps. I knew the rustling of his boots when he walked in the trailer. He was a vision in his regular clothes, but he was absolutely breathtaking in costume.

I knew his face so well, I had every line memorized. It wasn't just his body or his touch I craved. When he wasn't with me, I longed for his voice, the way he talked to me, low and unhurried. I craved the sound of it, sexy and reassuring at the same time. His voice had the power to turn me on like no other with the way the words sounded coming out of his mouth, his accent making every syllable new and interesting.

Days later, when I turned my phone on during a break, I found a text from my sister.

Call me as soon as you can. I have news.

When Amira said that, she usually meant *Oh, I was nominated for so and so award* or *I'm going to be on the cover of Vogue next month*, so, when I called her, I didn't expect that she meant our Christmas plans had been disrupted.

"I mean, who schedules reshoots around Christmas? It sounds suicidal, if you ask me."

"I know, I know, and I'm so sorry, but it's in this remote part of Thailand and they got the permits and everything, and the director is a perfectionist..."

"Huh, I have yet to meet a director who's not a perfectionist." Perfectionist was a nice way of saying that the director was a pain in the ass. I had worked with a couple of *perfectionists* myself.

"So, is everyone coming?"

"Yes, even Robert."

"What about his girlfriend?"

"Which one?"

"The nerdy-looking one."

"Oh, that's been over for weeks. How is Scotland by the way?"

Magical. Fantastic. Astonishing. Those words coming to my mind *might* have had something to do with Hugh suddenly appearing in the trailer, fully clothed in a new costume I hadn't seen before, but who knows...

"Scotland is...gorgeous," I said into the phone, never taking my eyes off him. "I have to go, so I'll call you tomorrow...but wait—what's the plan exactly?"

"I'll send you an email with my schedule and then a group email so we can coordinate with the rest of the family."

"Sounds good. Love you, Mira."

"Love you, too, Sam. Say hi to the Scotsman for me."

"Will do," I said, trying to imitate Hugh's accent.

He cocked one eyebrow at me, and I appraised him some more as he took a seat in his chair.

"What's new with Mira?" he asked.

"Looks like she's making me go to Thailand for Christmas," I said, feigning annoyance.

"Beaches, crystal-clear water, and sun? Sounds miserable," he joked.

"I know, right?" I replied with a smile.

Chapter 22

SAM

"So, you're going to miss out on the beauty of Scotland at Christmas. There might even be snow on the peaks, and you're not going to see it," he said with a smile. November had gone by in a flash, half of December had already passed, and there we were talking about our Christmas plans. I dreaded being away from him, even for just a few days, but I was impatient to be reunited with my family. I almost wished I had the guts to ask him to come with me, but it was too early in our relationship. Plus, I doubted anyone would be happy with me if I brought back our fair-skinned Scottish hero with a tropical tan.

His words sent a warm rush through my body.

"Is that a nice way of saying you're going to miss me?"

"Perhaps." He smiled and then kissed me on the lips.

"Where are you going to be? Edinburgh?"

"Oxford."

"Then why are you trying to lure me with all your

snowy peaks talk?"

"Because, ultimately, that's where I would like to spend Christmas." He kissed me again, and I melted under his touch. "In Scotland. With you," he added, his accent more pronounced on the last syllable. His hand moved between my legs and started teasing my sweet spot, which seemed to be always so wet and ready for him.

"Keep going," I moaned, and he did as I asked. "Why Oxford?"

"That's where my family lives."

"What?"

"Did I never tell you that?"

"No, you failed to mention it—completely."

"My bad," he said with a half-smile.

"No, now I want to hear the whole thing," I pressed.

"What do you want to know?" he asked, suddenly coy. I tickled his side, and he laughed.

"I thought you'd lived your whole life in Edinburgh. You said you grew up there, right?"

"I did, but then we moved to London when I was...thirteen, maybe? I wasn't too happy about it. I loved Edinburgh."

"Why did your parents have to move?"

"My father got a job. He's a professor. He teaches Celtic languages."

"No way! Not only were you born in Scotland, but your father teaches Gaelic. You had a leg up on this role the entire time!" I teased him, and he laughed.

"I did not! I mean, yes, I could have had my father help me, but I had no interest in learning Gaelic—not until I got this role anyway."

"You so cheated. This whole thing was rigged!"

"Come here, you *Sassenach*. I'll show you rigged," he said, shutting me up with a kiss. My lips parted, and his tongue captured mine, moving in slow circles around it as his hands wrapped around my waist and dragged me on top of him so I was straddling him. He made me raise my arms and took my shirt off. My breasts were at eye level with his face, and his fingers skimmed under my lacy bra, giving them a gentle squeeze. I grinded my hips on his, and I could already feel his hard-on. He started placing kisses on my chest and took the straps of my bra down, exposing more skin.

He took a deep breath, and the look on his face set my skin on fire, my chest burning with rabid flames. He pulled the cups down and sucked on my nipple, twirling his tongue around it, sending a wave of pleasure through my body. He unhooked my bra and removed it, giving me a sensuous, lusty look.

He caressed and squeezed my breasts, sucking on the other nipple this time. His scruff teased me in the most delicious way. I moaned, the tension between my legs becoming unbearable. I needed him to touch me right there. I needed him inside me. I ran my hands through his curls, holding the back of his head. He bit my nipple and then reached for me, searching for my mouth. I lowered my face to his and kissed him until I was breathless. Making out with Hugh was easily my favorite pastime. I could have spent a solid hour on that couch just kissing him...if I didn't know any better.

But I did.

And I needed him out of his clothes as soon as possible.

Almost as if he were reading my thoughts, he broke the kiss and said, "Take off your pants now." His voice was almost a growl, his eyes possessive, but still lined with a trace of playfulness.

I smiled seductively and bit my lip as I stood up to remove every item of clothing I still had on. I did so slowly, staring at him as his eyes drank me in, his gorgeous lips parted, his breathing fast and ragged. As my pants hit the floor along with my underwear, his arms circled my legs just below my ass. He started trailing kisses right below my belly button, going lower. I exhaled nervously, tensing with anticipation. A moment later, my ass was up in the air as he lifted me onto his shoulder and stood from the couch.

"What are you doing? Put me down!" I cried.

"I need to have you...in bed. We never seem to make it upstairs." He was right. We always had so little time, it seemed we could never make it to the bedroom.

"It's your fault," I joked. "You're the one who wants to *talk*. Next time, just take me straight to your bed." When he got to his bedroom, he put me down on the mattress and exhaled a breath, giving me a cautious look. He narrowed his eyes at me.

"Don't fault me for wanting to get to know you."

My hands pointed at my naked self. "You can get to know me in bed, too."

"I want to get to know all of you," he said, moving in closer, his warm breath washing over me.

"Ask me anything. I don't have any other secrets," I teased him, and he responded with a playful look. I wanted to get to know him better, too, but we never had enough time to be together, and I craved his body all the time. It was already hard enough pretending to be indifferent to him in front of other people. He couldn't possibly ask me to keep my hands off him when we were alone. The one or two hours we could get every other night was my happy place, and I wanted every minute to count.

He leaned in to kiss me, but I pulled back.

"It's your turn now. Take it *all* off," I commanded him. I sat on the bed as I watched him giving me a show.

Good grief. His body was a testament to how hard he

worked to achieve it. It made me sad that I hadn't studied anatomy because there were far too many muscles on his body that I didn't have a name for. He was already barefoot, and he took his jeans off in a hurry. When he dropped his pants, his eyes met mine. He proceeded to take off his underwear without taking his eyes off me. I swallowed, looking at his naked body in all its glory as his erection sprang free. He gave me a piercing look and came to sit on the bed next to me.

He pushed me down on the mattress and kissed me, soft and rough, alternating the rhythm while one of his warm hands rested on my cheek and the other one explored my body, making my skin tingly with excitement.

I frowned, suddenly remembering something important. I broke the kiss.

"Stop, there's something I have to tell you."

He suddenly looked worried. "What is it?"

"I think Jake is onto us." It was true—Jake had noticed. He'd noticed that Hugh and I were usually missing from get-togethers and that we always maintained a certain distance if we happened to be in the same room. Even when he and other actors would come over to my and Cecilia's place, we avoided being close to one another. I was always afraid one of us would let our guard down and touch the other as we did in private. Still, it wasn't easy to be immune to his charm. In fact, it had become increasingly harder to ignore him. He could smile at me from across the room and butterflies would release in my stomach. I tried to be subtle, but I couldn't prevent the dreamy look in my eyes, and in the end, Jake had noticed—and had confronted me about it.

I'd denied it over and over. He wouldn't stop questioning me, and eventually, I had to tell him quite rudely to knock it off. He'd finally dropped the subject, but what had surprised me the most was that he had a few words of warning about Hugh. He'd told me he understood if I had a crush, but that I should not trust him.

"How?" Hugh asked. "We have been extra careful—to the point of paranoia, if you ask me. You know what I think we should do—we should just tell everyone and be done with it. We should tell Nora first, of course. Why do you think Jake knows?"

"He was warning me about you."

"Huh?"

"It's actually kind of funny. He asked me why I kept rejecting him, blah, blah, blah—"

"That guy doesn't know how to take no for an answer, does he?" he growled, and I could see that his mood was already changing, his eyes growing darker.

"Wait, wait...I told him I like him as a friend, but that I'm not into him, and when he asked if I fancied you instead—those were the words he used—he told me not to fall for you, because...wait for it...he thinks you're a womanizer," I said, clapping my hands excitedly. Hugh narrowed his eyes, giving me a puzzled look.

"Me?"

"Yep, that's right...*he* thinks *you* are the womanizer. He said that every night you have a different girl showing up at your door—" I stifled a laugh, but Hugh looked still worried.

"Sam, you know there's no one else. I've only been spending time with y—" I stopped him, covering his lips with mine.

"I know, and here's the best part: he thinks you're hiring escorts," I said, breaking into a laugh.

"What?"

"He mentioned he saw a redhead and a blonde." I gave him a wink, and the worried expression on his face turned into a more relaxed one as a bright smile stretched across his face.

"I told ye those wigs were a bad idea," he said, cocking one eyebrow.

"Oh, really?" I said with a fake British accent. "You didn't seem to mind the other night when I wore that short blond bob. I liked it—I felt like Julia Roberts in *Pretty Woman*." I smiled, and he gave me a look that was a mix of desire and adoration. He made me feel like I was the center of his universe.

"It was not because of the *Pretty Woman* wig," he said, running a finger down my chest and making my skin break into goose bumps. "It was because you showed up wearing nothing but a trench coat. You're a bad girl, Sam," he teased in a husky tone, his accent heavier on the last sentence.

"I never claimed to be good," I whispered as his hands skimmed my body, my center heavy with anticipation.

"I'll take any part of you, good or bad." His hands started teasing me again, and I grabbed his cock, hard and smooth under my fingertips.

"Excellent answer, *mo gràdh*," I said against his lips.

Chapter 23

SAM

December brought a lot of news. Amira had been nominated for a Golden Globe for her latest release, and the network was sending Hugh and Melissa to LA. They were going to be presenters at the Globes and would also be doing another small media tour.

Hugh and Amira were impatient to meet each other in person, and one night we managed to FaceTime while I was staying at his place.

“Your sister is amazing at everything she does, but she really kills it every time we have a karaoke night,” he told Amira through the screen, and I felt myself blush. I was sitting on his knees while he spoke to my sister, and I couldn’t help but grin like an idiot.

“I know!” Amira laughed and pointed her finger at me. “She’s my Beyoncé. She’s shy, but when she gets to sing, she becomes all Sasha Fierce. It’s like seeing her transform into a completely different person.”

"I just like karaoke," I said, but neither one of them was listening to me.

"She's a brilliant girl, and she does a mean Freddie Mercury."

"Amen to that! Make her sing a Lady Gaga song next time. She gets all theatrical when she sings 'Bad Romance,'" my sister said.

"Can you guys stop? I'm right here!" I asked in a pleading tone.

Hugh squeezed his arms around me and kissed me on the cheek.

"Why? Can't I talk to your sister about falling for you?" he asked, his nose trailing down my neck. *Bam.* If I hadn't been on fire before, I definitely was after that.

"What's the deal, sweet cheeks?" my sister called from her end. "It's not like we're talking shit about you."

Hugh laughed, and suddenly I felt as if my skin was on fire. Between the jokes, the comments about my singing, and the fact that he'd said he was *falling for me*, I didn't know what embarrassed me the most.

Oh, who am I kidding? As embarrassed as I was at witnessing them talk about me, it also felt nice. Seeing Hugh talk to my sister made me realize once and for all that this thing between us was real. The last few weeks I had been riding a high, and now that he knew everything, my secret no longer weighed on my chest. Being up there made me feel different, too. It wasn't just the drop-dead-gorgeous scenery Scotland had to offer; it was that my life in St. Martin was so different from the one I'd led in LA and not just because of the setting. After weeks and weeks of being there, spending every day with the cast and crew, I felt completely removed from everything Hollywood.

For the first time in a long time, I didn't feel homesick.

In fact, I didn't miss it at all.

The screen of my phone lit up, distracting me from my view. The snow had been falling incessantly, turning Heathrow into a mess of biblical proportions.

I miss you.

I sighed and then smiled. We had barely been apart a couple of days, but I missed Hugh, too. I adjusted myself in the uncomfortable chair for the millionth time. My entire body was a bundle of strained muscles. Traveling during the holidays sucked, and I had already told Amira this was the last time I flew across the globe for her at Christmas.

I let out a deep breath, looking at my reflection in the airport's glass windows. Around me, there were dozens of stranded travelers, some sitting in the airport chairs, some lying on the floor, trying to either rest or kill time. Our blank stares said it all. I had been in the airport for eighteen hours, and there was no way to know how much longer I would have to wait for the chance to board a flight. A heavy snowstorm had struck London and had brought the city to its knees. I hadn't even known it could snow like that there. The buses stopped running, the trains were delayed, and so were most of the flights. The departures monitor was nothing but a slew of *delayed* and *cancelled*. I debated how to reply to Hugh without sounding like I was at the end of my wits.

I miss you, too.

Are you in Thailand yet? Wait...why are you

replying to my text? It should be nighttime on that side of the world.

I'm stuck at Heathrow. My flight got cancelled because of the snow.

When is your flight?

Undetermined.

Sam, you're not spending Christmas at the airport.

I don't have much of a choice.

Yes, you do.

I could just picture his serious, concentrated expression as he typed that.

I'm not going to let you spend Christmas in the airport. I'm coming to get you.

That's really sweet, but not necessary. I'll be okay.

My phone started buzzing in my hand. He was so bossy sometimes, and I secretly liked it.

"Samhain," he said in his super serious, almost intimidating tone, pronouncing my name not the Scottish way, but the way my mother believed it should be pronounced. I loved when he said my full name. It sounded beautiful, even if it wasn't the correct pronunciation, and I loved when he used that tone, particularly in the bedroom.

I almost squirmed hearing his voice over the phone. "There's no way in hell I'm letting you sit in an airport at Christmas."

"It's not that bad." I sighed. Admittedly, it was pretty bad, but it wasn't anything I couldn't deal with—at least for a few more hours. I stared at the clock on the airline kiosk at the gate. By midnight, I was probably going to lose it and start banging my head on the wall.

"It is." I could hear his beautiful accent through the phone, and for a moment, I didn't feel so tired and alone anymore. I needed to have his voice with me at all times; it was so soothing, so calming. The man needed to narrate some audiobooks. He needed to read me things; I could have listened to him read the phone book. Every word was more interesting coming out of his beautiful mouth.

"Sam, I understand you're trying not to make a big deal out of it, but no one should ever be stuck in an airport on Christmas Eve unless you know for sure you're going to get on a plane soon."

True. But then I remembered why I needed to stay put.

"Hugh, I can't leave. I'm on a waitlist. What if they call my name and I'm not here?"

"Samhain, this is not up for discussion. We'll figure it out. In fact, I'm already on my way." I could hear the *pling* sound of a car unlocking. Good grief, the dude was hardheaded. *Stubborn Scot.*

"Hugh, you can't do that! I mean...it's not that I don't appreciate the gesture, but it's really not necessary."

"Sam, I'm not going to let you stay there. What kind of man would I be if I let my girlfriend sit in an airport on Christmas Eve?"

Girlfriend.

I loved when he said that. My brain and heart high-fived and did a happy dance. I smiled to myself, and my chest filled with a new hope. Maybe my holidays weren't going to be so shitty after all.

"Okay. If you insist," I replied.

"I do." There it was again—the accent that awakened parts of me that should have been too tired to even care. "It's probably going to take me longer than usual with the traffic and the snow. I will call you when I'm getting closer."

"Please be safe. I'll talk to you later." *I love you* almost slipped past my lips, but I stopped myself just in time. I was going to spend Christmas Day with my boyfriend.

And his family.

His mother, father, four brothers, niece, and nephew—and I looked like...someone who had been sitting in an airport for eighteen hours had ingested way too much Starbucks and probably had potato chips crumbs on her shirt—yeah, I wasn't kidding about that last part. I brushed the crumbs off my shirt and realized I needed a quick makeover.

Thankfully, everything I needed was available to me with the swipe of a card.

First stop: Boots. Then, Harrods.

I ended up staying with the MacLeods on Christmas Eve and Christmas Day. I met his parents, all his brothers, his niece, and nephew.

When I say I spent Christmas with the MacLeods, I actually meant I spent it with little Claire MacLeod, Declan's daughter. Claire and I were instant BFFs, and she monopolized my time as soon as I crossed the threshold of the MacLeods' home. We spent most of our time together braiding each other's hair—okay, it was mostly me doing the braiding—reading Christmas stories by the fireplace, and on Christmas Day, she had her favorite uncle (Hugh) put together most of her toys so we could play with them.

She had the blondest hair I had ever seen, and it fell to her shoulders in wild waves mixed with strands that were completely straight. The thickness and wildness of her hair reminded me a little bit of Hugh's hair. She was eight and was very well-mannered for a little girl her age—then again, my interactions with children were mostly limited to movie sets, and those kids were always brattier. She was as curious as they come. She had a million questions for me, starting with why my hair and skin were so dark and why I spoke differently.

Her brother, Rory, was six. Unlike his sister, he had straight, short red hair, and his eyes were a crystal blue. He was shy and soft-spoken compared to his sassy sibling.

Declan and his baby-mama had separated a few years before, and Hugh had briefly told me about the divorce—the first in his very Catholic family, which caused quite a stir. Then, his mother talked about it more in detail as I tried helping her out in the kitchen.

Declan and his wife had met while working for British Airways; he was a pilot and she was a flight attendant. They were young and in love for years before they got hitched right after they found out they were pregnant with little Claire.

"They were happy for a few years," she said, her voice laced with a certain melancholy. "Or at least, they seemed happy. Carissa, my daughter-in-law—well, I guess *ex*-daughter-in-law now—was crumbling under the pressure of juggling a career and a family. They had Rory soon after. She and Declan were on different shifts so one of them could always be with the kids. We tried to help as much as we could, but in the end, they grew apart. She was unhappy and wanted a divorce. Declan even quit his job and started working as a private pilot to have a more flexible schedule, but it still didn't work." She let out a deep sigh. "They share custody of the kids. They should have been with their mum tomorrow, but she went on a trip. She's…enjoying the single life, I guess."

"I'm sorry to hear that. It must have been hard on all of you, especially the kids."

She gave me a silent nod. "Are your parents still together?"

"They divorced when I was eighteen. I was no child, and it was still traumatic. I don't wish it on any family. Sometimes I still wish they could have stayed together, but I understand there was no way around it." I left it at that, deciding not to bring my mother's sexuality into the conversation.

"Let's talk about something happier," Fiona MacLeod said with a warm smile. "Hugh tells me you're a great cook." I smiled, slightly embarrassed, but mostly delighted. I had no clue his family even knew about me.

"I'm okay, I guess."

"Ah, and she's modest! You like baking, aye?"

"I do." I heard footsteps and smiled. Suddenly, a pair of arms wrapped around my waist.

"She's an amazing baker," he said, his voice tickling my ear.

I bit my lip to stop the grin forming on my face. Happy didn't come close to covering it; he made me euphoric. Claire waltzed into the kitchen and asked her grandma for help.

The two of them left the room, and as soon as we were alone, he started nuzzling my neck. I turned around to face him. "You told your mother about me?"

"Aye, of course I did. I had to," he said. "She read it on

my face as soon as I got here. She said something was different with me. She's right—I'm falling for a beautiful, kind, smart woman," he said, brushing away a strand of hair. He kissed me softly on the lips, and as much as I was enjoying getting to know his family, for a moment, I wished we were alone.

"Ewwww!" Rory exclaimed from the kitchen doorway, pointing at us, his face an expression of sheer disgust. He ran away after he'd successfully broken us apart.

Hugh gave me a pensive look and then frowned.

"What is it? Worried about your nephew exposing us?"

He laughed. "No. I was thinking...don't you talk to your family about me?"

I pressed my lips together, not wanting to give anything away. The amount of girl talk I'd had about him with my mother and sister was embarrassing. I certainly didn't want to flaunt how much I was constantly swooning over him.

"Sometimes," I said coyly, trying to resume the Christmas Eve preparations.

He tickled me around my waist, knowing I couldn't stand to be tickled in that spot without squirming.

"*Just* sometimes?" he asked, feigning horror.

"Okay, okay. Stop!" I cried. "I talk about you all the time, okay? With Amira...and my mom."

"What about your father?"

"It hasn't come up yet." He cocked one eyebrow.

"I haven't told him because I know he'd say it's too soon to get into another relationship—" *And look how the last one turned out,* he'd say to me.

"What about your mom?" he asked in a serious tone.

"She just wants me to be happy."

He nodded and gave me a dark, mischievous look. "Good, because I plan to make you *verra* happy." He kissed me again, and then kissed my forehead. He wrapped his strong arms around me, and I let out a sigh. I pressed my head against his chest, and as I listened to his steady heartbeat, I hoped he was being serious and would keep making good on his promise.

Hugh's brothers were the rowdy bunch people write romance series about. They were all tall and handsome, but each one was also very different from the other, both in personality and looks.

Declan, the divorced pilot with two beautiful kids, was the oldest and resembled his father the most.

Hugh was the second born. Although I already knew a lot about him, I had only recently found out he was the spitting image of his mother. The shape and shade of their eyes were identical. Fiona's hair was a light red these days, but I learned from an old family photo that she used to have brown hair as well. Hugh's chin, however, resembled his father's.

Fergus was the third child in the MacLeod family. He was twenty-eight and a marine biologist with the Finnish Institute of Marine Research. Apparently, he was the brainiac of the family.

Tamhas was twenty-six and an elementary school teacher in London. Ewan was the youngest, the surprise child as his mother called him. Based on the comments from Mr. MacLeod—or Lewis, as he asked me to call him—I gathered Ewan was the most rebellious and biggest troublemaker of the five of them. When Ewan was a teenager, he got involved with some bad kids and almost dropped out of school. He had somehow turned his life around and was now attending Oxford—something told me his father had probably interceded for him—and the next year he'd be spending a semester studying in the US. Much to the dismay of his mother, he loved motorcycles. At dinner, he told me he wanted to travel across America on Route 66 on a motorcycle one day, possibly his own. From the corner of my eyes, I saw Fiona frown.

"Declan will take you to Thailand. Turns out, he's had a cancellation and is free for the next few days. It's already settled."

"A private pilot who's free during the holidays? Do you think I was born yesterday? How much did you give him?"

"Aye, let's just say he got an offer he couldn't refuse."

"Hugh, you can't do that. I can't accept that."

"He did have a cancellation because of the snowstorm, so I didn't force his hand there. He can take you. It will be far better than going through Heathrow again."

"I don't mind it. I can't have your brother take me all the way over there. It's not like giving me a lift from Oxford to London."

"To be completely honest with you, he offered. I secretly think he has a huge crush on your sister. He jumped at the opportunity as soon as I said she was going to be there." He winked, and I shook my head while giving him a tight-lipped smile.

"Declan better be careful—my sister is a charmer and a player."

"Well, sounds like he'd get a taste of his own medicine. It's settled then. My brother will fly you to Thailand."

"God, when you say it like that, it sounds even crazier,"

I said, grabbing his face with my hands.

"It isn't. I'm only sorry about one thing: that I can't come with you."

My shoulders sank. "Why not? I was already fantasizing about it. You and me, sandy beaches, crystal-clear water..."

"Have you forgotten what you told me a couple days ago?"

"Gahhh, how could I be so stupid? I can't believe I almost asked you to Thailand with me!" He couldn't tan. I told him that even if he went skiing, I was going to kill him. For the purpose of continuity, we couldn't have him showing up with a mountain or tropical tan; there was very little chance for his character to get a whole lot of sunshine in the highlands.

"What if you stay indoors like Edward Cullen?"

"Edward who?"

"Never mind," I replied, biting my lip.

Chapter 24

SAM

As much as I missed my Scot, my family and I had a blast in Thailand. Amira was able to hang out with us for a couple days before she started shooting again, and my parents (and their spouses) had rented a big place able to accommodate at least fifteen people, so Declan stayed with us for a few days. It felt a bit like camp.

Turned out, Declan really did have a monster crush on my sister, and she didn't seem immune to his charm. Declan was almost as tall as Hugh, with short brown hair, blue eyes, and a reddish beard. He was funny and had the same easygoing personality as his brother. Amira seemed quite captivated. My sister was undoubtedly a looker; the older she got, the more she reminded me of Aishwarya Rai, the Indian actress. The only differences were that Amira's eyes were blue and her hair was a very light brown. These days, she colored it a warm shade of blond, because she said that any time she went through casting for a new movie, they asked her to change her hair color.

Although I liked her natural color, the blond highlighted her features even more.

On the last night Declan stayed with us, he and my sister disappeared somewhere while we were all out at a club. We didn't see them for the rest of the night, and the day after, Amira left to shoot on location.

I decided to stay out of it. I missed Hugh, and even though we texted a lot, it was a travesty that I got to spend more time with his brother than with him.

Declan left a day after Amira did.

He was supposed to pick up some clients in Phuket and go back to the UK. As he got ready to leave, he had the proudest smirk on his face, one that looked entirely too familiar.

"Do you think he and Amira got it on last night?" my brother Robert asked that afternoon while we sunbathed on the beach.

"I believe so," I said with a sigh.

"Do you think he'll kiss and tell?" my brother asked in a worried tone.

"Declan? Please. Scottish men are men of honor, or at least the MacLeods are."

"Are they now? You seem pretty taken with your boyfriend," he said with a smirk.

"I am," I replied with a brilliant smile. "What about you? What happened with that cute girl with glasses? You seemed so into her!"

He gave me an embarrassed look and opened his mouth, but struggled to find the words.

"You won't like what I have to say."

"Robert, you didn't! How could you do that to the poor girl? You know what I went through with Eric."

"Sam, I'm sorry. It was a colossal mistake. I behaved

like an asshole, and I realized it too late. I didn't deserve her." We both let out a deep sigh at the same time then looked out at the ocean. While Amira was busy shooting on a private island nearby, my extended family and I visited all the cool spots. We canoed to Khao Phing Kan, which was also known as 007 Island because it was where they'd filmed *The Man With The Golden Gun*. We also went to Leo's beach from *The Beach*, and we even went north of Bangkok to visit the Buddhist temples in Ayuttaya. My mother, the religious flip-flopper, claimed she was going to start studying Buddhism and attend the temple by her house when she returned to California. Even her wife snickered at that behind her back.

Hugh and I missed each other when I went back to Scotland; he and Melissa had just left to attend the Golden Globes and do some press beforehand.

He kept sending me snaps of the two of them in California, and I started growing restless by the hour. Since we'd gotten together, we hadn't been apart for this long, and being away from him was killing me. I longed for the day when we could finally be together out in the open, and I knew he did, too. In fact, a few days later, he sent me a message that filled my heart with hope.

Melissa and I told the network we're not up for their games. Soon we won't have to hide anymore.

I can't believe you guys did that! What did they say?

Not much. They didn't look thrilled, that's for sure. Nora made them understand we were not happy with how they wanted to handle publicity. Melissa told them she's gay and refuses to be

trapped.

We could be with each other out in the open. We wouldn't have to hide anymore around our coworkers. We could finally be *us*.

I am glad you two talked to them, but I am worried about you, Hugh. Your career...

I'm still going to have a career, Sam. I won't have a life, ever, if I allow them to bend me like this.

I knew he was right. Another message popped up on my screen.

We can finally be together. Out in the open. I told them about us.

My chest tightened. Was this a good idea? They had already pissed off the network by telling them they didn't agree with their marketing campaign. I didn't reply right away; I didn't know what to say. I was worried. For some reason, I didn't have a good feeling about this. Network executives were usually dicks. They weren't the dreamers who wrote shows and movies or the people who brought them to life. What they mostly cared about was making their money back and then some. Hugh sent me another text.

You're not going to say anything? I thought you'd be happy.

I am, just worried. I hope they're not going to be hard on you guys. I miss you. I can't wait for

you to be back.

I miss you, too, mo gràdh. We'll be back in St. Martin on Friday night.

Friday night, aye? Want to finally say yes to that duet?

Over my dad body.

What? Dad body? I laughed to myself. He most certainly *did not* have a dad bod.

What?

Err, over my dead body. Damn autocorrect.

I love you. I wanted to tell him how I felt, but it seemed an awful thing to do over text messaging. I did love him, and I knew he felt just as strongly as I did, otherwise he wouldn't have gone up against the network executives like that. If he didn't love me, he would have played the game they asked him to play to safeguard his career.

I can't wait for you to be back.

It was true. I enjoyed working with other people while he was away, but I missed our routine. I had become so attuned to him. He was my colleague, my friend, my lover. One of these days I'd be able to say he was my *boyfriend* out loud. My heart was lodged in my throat at the thought of having a "normal" relationship. I couldn't wait.

The next couple days were a blur. I knew Hugh, Melissa, and Nora were coming back on a private plane to

Edinburgh, and they'd be in town sometime during the evening. I was counting the hours, but we had been crazy busy shooting other scenes that didn't require the presence of the lead actors.

By the time Friday morning came around, I was exhausted, but I was excited to hug my Scot again.

Unfortunately, the day started in a rather unpleasant way.

A couple hours after I got to work, I was asked to go to one of the offices for an impromptu meeting. I thought it was something regarding the entire makeup and hair department, but I soon found out I was the only one who'd been summoned.

I had a bad feeling about it.

When I got to the production office, I was met by a few people in suits, UK representatives of the network. I wondered, for a second, if Hugh and Nora knew about this, and then I realized how perfectly they'd timed the meeting. Hugh and Nora were up in the air, and I wasn't going to be able to reach them for hours. The suits had all the time in the world to get rid of me. I knew it was happening even before they unceremoniously explained to me that I was being terminated.

I was getting fired, and I knew just the reason why.

Hugh's name, however, was never mentioned. Instead, I was accused of underperforming and not being qualified or experienced enough for the position I had been covering for the last several months. According to them, my performance was not on par with the levels of quality they intended to achieve on this production. This, of course, was news to me. Never had I been told I wasn't doing a good job the entire time I had been there. I took my job seriously, and I knew this was not why these people were getting rid of me.

This was payback for Hugh and Melissa sticking it to

the network. This recrimination was exactly what I had been afraid of.

"Ms. Farouk, we are sad to see you go, but as you can see, it's necessary. We are just aiming at something better."

"Mr..."

"Ellis."

"Mr. Ellis, you obviously cannot expect me to agree with your statements. I have been an outstanding employee the whole time I have been here. I've been a team player and took the place of Margaret Lovett when she had her baby early. I haven't received any complaints, so excuse me if I am a bit peeved by all the accusations you are throwing at me."

"No, no, no one is accusing you of anything, Ms. Farouk. We're just looking for something different. Something *you*, unfortunately, can't give us."

They were telling me, plain and simple, that I wasn't good enough at what I did. I knew it was pointless to argue any further, so as soon as they were done with their explanation, I left the office and went to get the few things I had on set.

Walking off a set in broad daylight is not something that can be done easily. Everyone asked me where I was going, and when I told them I had been sacked, they couldn't wrap their heads around it, couldn't let it go.

Cecilia and Blair insisted I needed to stay put until Nora and Hugh came back, but I knew there was no use. Nothing would change the execs' decision.

Also, getting fired on a set in a faraway location was much different than being let go in Los Angeles. I had to pack.

I went home and did just that, but my flight wasn't until the next day. The corporate fuckers had gotten me a ticket in business class, at least—probably because it was too late to find an economy seat. I wanted to keep my shit together, but my eyes filled with tears as soon as I pulled out my suitcase and started organizing my stuff. I cried for a good while, my heart breaking at the thought of leaving the man I loved and all of *this* behind. I was going to miss everyone. I was going to miss Scotland.

Later that night, after I had packed all my stuff, I met my ex-coworkers at our favorite spot.

"This is a sob-fest. You guys suck. Some farewell party." Cecilia, Oliver, Jake, Blair, and Rupert stared somberly at their drinks on the table. I thought my joke would wake them from their shock-induced stupor, but I was wrong.

I looked around at my stone-faced colleagues, who still couldn't comprehend why I had been fired. Not everyone knew about Hugh and me, and at this point, it didn't even matter. It was better for them if they didn't get involved. Plus, talking about us felt like a desecration. The memories we shared were so special to me, and I didn't want to tarnish them.

"Nora is not going to be happy," Oliver said. "She hates when the network butts in like this. Do you think she knew about it?"

I shook my head. "Nora wouldn't do that to me. She's my sister's friend, and although we are not overly close, I know she respects my work. She wouldn't do this."

"Do you think Hugh had a problem with you?" Rupert asked, oblivious.

"No, I'm sure he didn't have a problem with Sam," Jake said in a snide tone. I could see from one look at him that he hadn't believed me when I'd told him there was nothing going on between me and the Scot. I pressed my lips together and gave Jake a look, then I answered Rupert's question. "Hugh and I get along great."

"We never even sang a duet together," Cecilia pouted.

"Shit. That's right. How's that possible?"

"Because you're a bloody competitive cow, Sam," she said in a sad tone. She smiled somberly, and I put my arm around her.

"Takes one to know one, my dear friend."

"Well, it's no use mourning the time wasted. Let's do a duet now!"

I wasn't in the mood to sing, but I didn't want to say no to her. Besides, I thought maybe karaoke would get me out of the funk I was in. *Wishful thinking.* I couldn't bear the thought of how or when Hugh would find out. I had no idea when he would exactly get into town. I was hoping I'd get to see him one last time.

"Why this song?" I asked when she pointed out a title for us to sing.

"Because it's fun, and it's just what we need to get out of our funk."

I nodded and went along with it.

She wasn't wrong.

A smile stretched across my face as soon as we started singing Little Mix's "Black Magic." The rhythm was infectious, the lyrics were fun, and as everyone around us clapped and cheered, Cecilia and I celebrated our friendship in one of the best ways we knew. Toward the end of the song, as I danced along to the music with my fun, sassy roommate, my eyes scanned the crowd. I wanted to remember these people. They would forever hold a special place in my heart. I was sad to leave, but I knew I would never forget them, and maybe one day, I'd get to see and work with some of them again.

Suddenly, I found a familiar pair of eyes watching me. The stern look on his face told me he knew, and my chest tightened once again at the thought of having to say good-bye to him. I wanted to see him smile. I wanted to see his lips curl into that irresistible grin one more time.

I did the only thing I could think of: I sang the last two choruses to him, pointing at him in the crowd, no longer caring who knew or what everyone thought of it. He was the only thing that mattered. I needed to let him know how much he meant to me.

I hugged Cecilia as soon as the song was over, and we kissed on each cheek. I turned around to find Hugh in front of me, dangerous and delicious looking.

I had missed him terribly, and now I had to say good-bye. He leaned down and captured my mouth in front of everyone, kissing me with the urgency of lovers who aren't ready to part ways. His tongue circled mine over and over, possessing me in every way possible as the whole pub erupted in cheers and whistles. I was barely paying attention to the people around us, because in that moment, Hugh lifted my legs and wrapped them around his waist. Only then he did break the kiss, guiding us through the crowd, and I gasped for air as everyone waved good-bye.

Hugh

"You need to put me down," she said, laughing as I kissed her neck and tickled her skin with my stubble.

"Not a chance."

"Hugh, you can't carry me all the way to your place."

"Watch me," I muttered. I was going to carry her if it was the last thing I did. Besides, I needed to feel her; it was the only thing preventing me from losing my mind. As soon as we'd landed, we'd gotten wind of what had happened. To say I was furious was an understatement. If we hadn't been so far into production and if I didn't fear a lawsuit, I would have almost considered quitting the show altogether. But, as much as I hated what they'd done to Sam, I couldn't quit.

"Seriously, Hugh, put me down!"

"The lady doth protest too much. As a matter of fact..." I grabbed her legs and put her down, just briefly. I took a deep breath and stared into her eyes for a moment.

I needed her. I wanted her. I wasn't ready to say goodbye.

She adjusted her clothes and exhaled a deep breath through her nose. Her lips pressed into a line, and I noticed her eyes fill up with tears. I couldn't bear the thought of my Sam crying.

"Thank y—" I didn't let her finish, instead grabbing her by her legs and throwing her over my shoulder, impatient to get home.

"You insufferable Scottish caveman!" she yelled. "Put me down!" Her colorful, playful insults kept coming, but I could barely hear her over the sound of my own laughter.

SAM

I had been counting down the hours to when I would see him again. I was ready for one last night together. What I didn't want or expect was to spend part of our precious time arguing about the future.

"I don't want you to leave," he said with conviction.

"I know. I don't want to leave either, but I have to."

"You don't have to. You could stay here with me."

"Come on, Hugh. Be serious. That's not a realistic plan." He gave me a piercing look, turning the smolder on. *Damn him.* It was like getting hypnotized. I put a hand between us and guarded my eyes so I wouldn't fall for it. "Nope, nope, nope. You're not doing this to me. I can't stay here—it would only create more tension and more problems."

"You should get to stay," he said, the tone of his voice sounding lighter. "Drop the hand, Sam. I need to look at you. I haven't seen you in days. I missed you so much." A certain familiar warmness radiated from my chest throughout my body upon hearing his words.

"I missed you, too," I told him. I was happy for a whopping ten seconds, gazing into his eyes. Then sadness took over again. How was I supposed to say good-bye to him?

"You could stay in Edinburgh. The apartment has been empty for weeks." Margaret had left the apartment in November, since little Posy was finally able to leave the hospital. As much as I appreciated that he was trying to find a way for me to stay nearby, I knew it wasn't the right thing to do.

He glanced at me, raising one eyebrow, waiting for an answer.

I shook my head and looked down. He sighed, sounding exasperated, and when I looked up again, he was running his hands through his hair, making it stick up in every possible direction.

I smiled and reached for him. We needed this night to be the best one yet. I was ready to stop holding back my words and tell him how I felt. I wrapped my arms around his narrow waist and pressed my body against his.

"Listen to me, Hugh." That got his attention. He looked down at me, his eyes wild, dancing between my eyes and my lips. "I love you. I love you, and it's breaking my heart that I have to leave. As much as I would like to stay, both you and I know it would end up in disaster. You are way too busy and have too much at stake right now to worry about me. Having to go back to LA sucks, but there's no other solution."

He stared at me for a few seconds, his eyes searching mine, narrowing deep in thought, as if there had to be another viable solution.

"What about us?"

"We'll just have to wait and see."

"You love me?" he asked, as if he wanted to make sure he'd heard me right.

"Very much. So much that I can't breathe if I think about having to say good-bye to you."

"I love you, too. You know that, right?"

I nodded. "I know. Otherwise, you wouldn't have stood up for us."

"It's all my fault, isn't it? I caused this. I should have kept my mouth shut."

"It's not," I reassured him, caressing his jaw, my eyes memorizing every line.

"I just didn't want to keep playing their game."

"I know." I swallowed past the knot in my throat and blinked away my tears. There was no solution, at least for the time being. Come morning, we'd have to part.

"Take me to bed, *mo gràdh,"* I said with a smile. "You better give me one hell of a good-bye."

That night, when we were in bed, I traced every line of the planes of his chest. We'd drunk some whisky, and after we'd lost ourselves in each other time and time again, I started muttering the lyrics of the song Cecilia and I had sung earlier that night.

"I should have known," he said, staring at the ceiling.

"What?"

"You're a witch. A black witch. Having me fall for you like this," he said, half-asleep, his fingers combing through my hair. "How am I supposed to go back to life before you?

I am a dead man, Sam. You ruined me."

"So did you," I said simply, not adding anything more. I doubted there would ever be another man like Hugh MacLeod in my life. I tightened my arm around his waist, listening to his breathing slow down until he fell asleep, his lips slightly parted, his expression peaceful. I allowed myself a couple of tears then rested my head on his chest and slept one last night with him.

The next morning, I paced the room, waiting for my car to show up and take me to the airport. His eyes looked slightly resentful, and I was the reason why.

I had told him we shouldn't keep in touch, at least for the time being. I had tried to explain how hard it was going to be for me to go back home and start over—again, for the second time in less than a year. I tried telling him that waiting for his texts and calls would only make the separation harder.

He had seemed to agree and understand at first, but now he was fighting against it, begging me to reconsider.

I was in his arms, my head pressed to his chest, listening to the turmoil going on inside him. His hand caressed my back, and his beautiful voice echoed through his ribcage. He was listing all the reasons why we shouldn't say good-bye to each other.

Suddenly, he pulled back. With his hands holding on to my arms, he searched my eyes. "You know I would never do what Eric did to you, right?"

"I know," I said simply. I believed him. I knew he would never do such a shady thing.

"Then why are you doing this to me? Why are you the

one letting me go?"

I'm doing it for your own good.

"Listen. You have two more months of shooting ahead of you, and then it's going to be a whirlwind of press tours. I don't want you to be the one worrying about his girlfriend on the other side of the world."

"What if I want to worry about my girlfriend?" he asked with a smirk. "Why are you making this decision for the both of us?" He looked hurt, and it broke my heart.

I wanted him to understand why I was doing this. He had too much at risk, too much to lose. The network had obviously come after me after he and Melissa put their foot down. What else would they do to make their point? He deserved to get the success he had been working so hard for.

"I'm making it for you, but I'm making it for me, too. I love you, but I don't think I can survive a long-distance relationship right now."

His nostrils flared, and he chewed on his bottom lip. "How can you stand in front of me, telling me you love me and still walk away?" he said, his voice booming with anger.

"I have to," I replied calmly, hoping he'd understand.

"Well, I can't accept this. I'm not going to stand here and watch you leave. I'm sorry, Sam." He gave me one last glance, his eyes a mixture of anger and sadness. He put a jacket on and stormed out of his own house.

Some good-bye.

You did the right thing, I told myself as the knot in my throat turned into a sob, and the tears I had been holding back all night spilled across my cheeks.

Chapter 25

SAM

The only positive thing about being back in LA was seeing my family again. Even so, as the days went by, the uneasy feeling in my chest grew bigger and bigger, making it hard for me to breathe. My dad and I hung out a couple weeks after I got back, and when I looked at him, he reminded me of the comic Cheech Marin from the Cheech and Chong comedic duo, particularly the '70s version of Cheech. His hair was still mostly black, with only some silver strands here and there, and his mustache was full, not that different from the one he had rocked when we were kids, although these days it was even longer. We went for a hike in Runyon Canyon Park where we'd gone together many times before, but that day something was off.

The air was wrong, and the scenery didn't strike me the same way it usually did. The dust bothered me. There were too many people.

I finally realized it was *me*. I was off. I let out a low growl in frustration. Scotland had ruined me.

"You're different, Samhain. What's wrong?"

"Nothing." I let out a deep breath.

"You'll see, soon you'll find another job." I cocked my eyebrow. For the first time, I wasn't worried about that. I was worried about why I felt so uneasy in a place I used to love.

"It's not that, Dad."

"Then what is it, my dear?"

"I don't know. It's so strange. You have no idea how many times I wished I could be back here...and now..."

"Now?"

I was at a loss for words. Actually, the words were trapped in my throat, itching to come out. *All I want is to go back to where I was.* I didn't dare say that out loud, worried I'd hurt my father's feelings. How could I tell him that, after just a few months, LA didn't feel like home anymore?

"I was only gone five months, but I feel like I've lost my place in the world. I don't know where I belong anymore, Daddy."

He laughed, rocking his head back and that irritated me. I glared at him.

"It's not funny, Dad. I'm really confused about this, and you're not helping."

"My dear, no one understands you more than I do, trust me. I had a home before this home, but it didn't feel right. Don't get me wrong, I am very grateful my family was able to move to England. I would have never had the same opportunities in Pakistan, not in a million years," he said with a light shake of his head. "I have been lucky, very lucky to grow up where I did, but if there's one thing I understood when I got here, it's that you decide where your home is. When I came here, California looked like the most beautiful place in the world. It looked exactly like the place I had dreamed of growing up. It looked like it did in the movies. I'm not saying it was easy, my child. This was a different world, and the late seventies were a messy, confusing time, but there was still that excitement, that electricity in the air. The American dream wasn't dead back then."

He glanced my way and gave me a reassuring smile.

"Am I rambling yet?" he asked, cocking one eyebrow. We kids teased him a lot about getting off topic.

"Not yet. Keep going," I told him, interested by what he had to say.

"This is your hometown, but that doesn't necessarily mean this is where you belong. You decide where your home is. If this place doesn't feel like home anymore, no one should be forcing you to stay. Your heart will tell you where you belong."

I nodded. My dad was right. If only it were so simple.

I had been longing to come back for weeks, but things had changed. I had changed, and now I felt different. Was LA not home anymore? Was that the reason I couldn't resume my life as I'd known it?

The Oscars were slated for March, and Amira wanted me to go with her. To distract me from my Scotland fiasco, she asked me to help her choose a look for her along with her stylist. She told me that since I was unemployed, she wanted me to be her personal assistant so she could give her own a break. I wasn't thrilled about the prospect of babysitting my sister, but I had done it all my life—for free—so I didn't think it would be so bad. Unfortunately, I had forgotten how many freaking parties and interviews there are leading up to Oscar week. I had to admit, however, that going through rows and rows of gorgeous dresses that had just come off the runway was a dream come true.

"Do you know if he's going to be there?" I asked tentatively, my stomach flipping just at the thought of him. I had been trying to get used to the idea of Hugh possibly being at the Oscars, and I was both terrified and excited at the thought of seeing him again. Despite my attempt at cutting off all contacts, we ended up exchanging a few texts. They were always pretty generic and "neutral." It was as if both of us couldn't afford to tell each other how painful it was to be apart.

I missed him a lot and had been tempted to tell him many times just how hard it was to be without him but I didn't want to distract him. I appreciated his efforts to keep us together. He'd done what he thought best. I wiped a tear away. Just the thought of him made me beyond emotional, twisting both my stomach and throat in knots.

Amira tried putting me into a gorgeous gold dress, but besides not wanting to look like the female version of an Oscar, I was afraid the fabric was far too delicate. I had no experience whatsoever in wearing dresses that were worth thousands of dollars. In the end, we found an Elie Saab one that was a bit easier to wear and absolutely stunning. The color was an emerald green, and as soon as I saw the fabric of the dress slipping out of the garment bag, I fell in love. The bodice was covered in an intricate beading, but the skirt was wide and comfortable. The color reminded me so much of the place that had been my home for the last few months and that I missed so badly. It reminded me of the man I hadn't seen in weeks, but that I was still very much in love with. It had a deep V-neck in the front, but it was still demure enough to secure the ta-tas. It was cinched at the waist, and I still liked it when I found out I would have to wear a small corset underneath. Unlike the gold dress, the green one was easy to move around in, and it felt incredibly comfortable. Plus, the fabric of the dress was draped at the back of my shoulders, making it look like the dress had wings. I felt like a goddess. I felt like one of the heroines from Abarath.

"Sam, you look beautiful."

"You do, too, Mira," I said, glancing at her slender figure in an Armani Privé silver gown.

My stomach was in knots on the ride over to the Dolby Theater, and my palms got sweaty as we stepped out of the limo. A few days before the Oscars, I had read a headline that said he was going to be there with a costar. I knew crossing paths with him was a possibility. What I didn't expect was to have him and Melissa right behind us, making their way through the line of reporters, talking about the show. There was a lot of noise on the red carpet, and I was trying my hardest not to look like a spaz while my sister was being interviewed by Michael Ausiello from *TV Line*. Still, my ears were so attuned to his voice, I could isolate it from everything else. I couldn't really make out what he was saying, and I was thankful I hadn't completely zoned out when Michael Ausiello asked me if this was my first time at the Oscars.

"It is. I'm really excited my sister chose me over anyone else in the family!" I looked at the camera, sending Rob a message. He had wanted to come so bad so he could get exposure for an app he was fixing to launch. *Selfish brat.*

"My sister is my best friend and has been one of my biggest supporters since I started out. She used to drive me to auditions before I was old enough to drive. It seems only fair that she gets to share this night with me."

"Have a wonderful time, ladies," Michael Ausiello said, bidding us good-bye.

There were at least fifteen people separating me from Hugh MacLeod, including assistants, publicists, and journalists. I briefly turned around, and as I searched for him, our eyes locked. He was standing just a few feet away from me, looking stunning in a perfectly tailored tuxedo, his hair a little longer and falling across his forehead. The intense stare he gave me took my breath away as his lips curled into a small smile, and he nodded a silent hello. I did the same, unable to hold back the smile from stretching across my face. His eyes darted back to the interviewer who was having microphone issues and had thankfully missed our exchange. I grabbed a handful of my gown and followed my sister to the next interview.

When we reached the spot for the interview with *E!*, Amira cut through the crowd for her interview with Giuliana Rancic and I waited nearby, trying not to look too lost in the sea of people.

"Sam." His voice made the hair on the back of my neck stand up. I closed my eyes for a second, thinking I had imagined it, but then he called my name again. When I turned around, he smiled brightly at me. Something inside my chest tightened, and the knot in my throat grew bigger. I had never known a smile could make you ache so bad. No matter the lies I had been telling myself, I had missed him like crazy.

"Hey," I said softly, forcing myself to smile.

"You look beautiful." There it was again—that sexy voice that had stolen my heart.

The smile on my face grew wider. "Thank you. You look very handsome."

Melissa rounded him and threw her arms around me excitedly. I smiled brightly, looking at Hugh as I hugged Melissa back.

"Sam! You look gorgeous! This gown is such a beautiful shade of green," she said, taking my dress in. Hugh's brows furrowed, and his eyes grew darker for a moment.

"I chose it because it reminded me of Scotland," I told them both. *It reminded me of you,* I wanted to tell him. His eyebrows shot up, and his eyes met mine once again, ardent with desire, full of the words we wanted to say to each other.

I loved him. Maybe there was a chance he still felt the same.

My confession seemed to render him speechless. Melissa, however, was being a chatty Cathy.

"Sam, we miss you so much! The set is not the same without you."

"I miss you guys, too! And I miss Scotland," I added as I saw Hugh's eyes grow wide with alarm. "I had no idea I would end up loving it so much." He nodded and gave me a warm smile. Melissa was suddenly quiet, witnessing the silent exchange between Hugh and me. An assistant called them to tell them they were next. Melissa gave me another hug, and Hugh gave my hand a squeeze. I almost threw myself into his arms—old habits die hard.

"I'm sorry, Sam. We have to go." His voice was heavy, loaded with a certain regret. I felt my heart sink, and I nodded, looking down, trying to hold back the tears. He leaned closer to me, but I still couldn't look at him.

"I will find you...later," he whispered in my ear, causing my heart to resurrect like a phoenix from the ashes. It started fluttering inside my chest like the wings of a hummingbird. I locked eyes with him, and he gave me a small nod right before he and Melissa turned around and started climbing up the stairs.

Amira was coming down just as they were going up, and they briefly exchanged pleasantries for the camera, acting as if they hardly knew each other.

I *loved* award shows. I loved that moment right before the winning name is called, the anticipation in the air, the sudden quiet in the room that lasts a few tense seconds before the winner is announced.

One of the things I loved the most about this business was seeing the underdog win. There's nothing as exciting as seeing raw, fresh talent get recognized. I loved seeing the vulnerability of the actor on stage, and I especially enjoyed when they were able to deliver a message in the most chaotic and surreal five minutes of their life—bonus points if they made a speech without looking at notes. My mother, especially, hated that shit. She always said, "If you're an actor and you're used to learning your lines, how come you can't learn a thank-you speech?" She talked about it so much that Amira eventually got in the habit of memorizing a few lines and names whenever she was nominated for an award. Even so, one time she'd forgotten to thank her director. I could only imagine how confusing and overwhelming that moment can be, especially when you are new to the game and you don't expect to be taken into consideration.

Most people hated awards shows, but I loved that part of my job.

After what had gone down with Eric, I'd thought about changing careers. At the time, I had had enough of fake people and terrible attitudes. For a while, I felt disillusioned and considered taking a different path, but I realized that I really loved my job. I couldn't think about doing anything other than what I had been doing for almost a decade. I loved the creative process, the work, the hours that went into it. I loved watching the actors bring a story to life. I loved being part of the small village it takes to make a story a finished product.

The ceremony was long, but fun, and Hugh Jackman once again did a great job as host. Now that we were at the Vanity Fair party, I was trying to hide from Eric and Quinn, who were now *engaged*—barf. I had seen them earlier from a distance, and I really wanted to avoid an awkward encounter. I was also hiding from Hugh. I had no idea what he'd meant with his *I will find you later*. It had been hard to pull myself together after our brief talk, and I wasn't ready to bump into him again, mainly because I couldn't pretend any longer. I couldn't hide how much I wanted him.

I wanted to believe he still cared for me, but I had no real idea how he felt about us, especially since I was the one who had wanted to cut ties. In other words, I was chickening out. I picked up a glass of champagne from a waiter's tray and took a big sip.

To hell with everything. I was determined to spend all evening trying to avoid all three of them. Unfortunately, being Amira's wing-girl meant we had everyone coming up to us to congratulate her on her nomination, lying to her face telling her she should have won—she shouldn't have, not this year at least—and talking to her about that certain script they had sent her way.

I swore almost every conversation in Hollywood went the same way*: how are you, what are you working on, did you have a chance to read what I sent you?* And so on. These were the times I was glad to be part of Hollywood's "working class."

The music stopped and the lead guitarist of the band took to the microphone, presumably to announce the next song. I was briefly distracted by the conversation my sister and I were having with Ellie Kemper about the upcoming season of *The Unbreakable Kimmy Schmidt*, and for a moment, I didn't realize what was going on.

"Ladies and gents, may I have your attention, please? I know this is a party, but we have an emergency. This young man here asked me if I could help him win back the heart of the girl he loves. This is Hollywood, and we all love happy endings, right?" the guitarist asked the audience, and everyone cheered. The three of us stopped talking and looked curiously toward the stage.

Then, I saw a very tall man—a man who looked very much like a certain Scot I knew—take the microphone as the guitarist introduced him.

"Sam, ohmygod!" My sister reached for my hand and gave it a squeeze as she pulled me closer to her to see what was going on.

It was definitely Hugh, and he looked like he was about to sing.

What. The. Hell.

I let out a breath of surprise.

"Did you have any idea he was going to sing?" Amira asked me, and I shook my head in disbelief, my eyes focused on him as if I were hypnotized. Just then, his beautiful voice came over the speakers. His accent felt warm and familiar.

"I swore I'd never sing in public because I'm a terrible singer, but I know this is the only way to win back the woman I love, so…please go easy on me."

People cheered. He turned to the band, letting them know he was ready to start. The drummer hit the drumsticks together and yelled "One, two, three, four!" as everyone in the ballroom seemed to switch their attention toward the stage.

As the notes of Van Morrison's "Brown Eyed Girl" filled the ballroom, everyone cheered again.

"I would appreciate it if you could clap along," he said in a deep voice that boomed through the sound system. As Hugh started singing the first couple lines—he wasn't that bad of a singer at all—a lot of people stopped talking, curious to see where this was going. I had to admit, I was curious as well. Had he really just said "the woman I love" or had I just dreamed it? Was he singing *me* a song?

From where I was standing, I could see his eyes scanning the crowd. He was looking for me, but he couldn't see me because I was way in the back, and I had to raise myself on my tiptoes to see *him*. He closed his eyes for a moment and the smile that stretched across his face stole my heart once again. Damn him, he was so beautiful, and he was singing me a song, despite his reluctance to sing in public.

"What are you waiting for? Go!" Amira yelled, placing a hand on my back and pushing me toward the stage. I almost lost my balance, but I recovered and started walking toward him, asking people to let me through, getting side-eye here and there.

At last, he spotted me, and he pointed his finger at me.

"This is for you, Sam."

As everyone realized he was talking to me, they started making room, leaving me in the middle of the ballroom. It was like the parting of the Red Sea.

I lifted my eyes to meet Hugh's and noticed that despite his initial hesitation, he seemed to be enjoying it. He didn't seem nearly as uncomfortable as I'd expected or maybe he was just that good of an actor. He winked at me when he sang about making love in the green grass, and I covered my face with my hands for a second, but then I quickly removed them—I couldn't stop looking at him and grinning like a fool. I was aware of a few flashes and phones pointed at me, but I was past the point of caring. In fact, I was singing along with the lines I remembered, and he smiled wider as he noticed me swinging my shoulders and hips to the rhythm of the music.

Everyone around us clapped along and cheered, and the cheers got louder as Hugh stepped off the stage at the end of the song. In that moment, I couldn't hear any other sound because my heart was thumping loudly in my chest, overpowering everything else. I wanted to walk toward him, but my legs wouldn't move.

It didn't matter anyway. He was in front of me in just a few seconds, my hands trembling with excitement and anticipation.

He took my face in his hands.

"I love you, Sam. I need you in my life. I know you did it for my own good, but I refuse to be apart any longer." He didn't wait for me to respond. Instead, he covered my lips with his in an urgent, passionate kiss that had everyone cheering and whistling. I had *almost* forgotten about everyone else.

The band started playing a slow-tempo song, and I wrapped my arms around his neck as we swayed along with the music, his kisses alternating between slow and maddening, deep and rough. I was aware that people were snapping pictures, but I didn't care. He pressed his forehead against mine, and I sighed, pressing my body closer to him.

"So? You heard what I said...I don't want to be apart anymore." His voice was unsteady, his breaths coming fast and ragged.

"You need me?" I asked him, cocking one eyebrow.

"I do need you. Everything went to shit after you left Scotland."

I laughed. "Ha! Not possible. I don't believe it."

"It's true. It was so *gloomy* without you," he said in that beautiful accent of his.

"I remember you saying to me before that Scotland was never, ever gloomy."

"I know, but that's how I've felt since you've been gone. I have missed you so much, Sam." The honest look in his eyes was enough to make my eyes well up with tears. I believed him; of course I did—it was exactly how I'd felt, too.

Everything had been gloomy for me since I'd left Scotland. I constantly felt as if something were missing, because I had been missing *him*.

The knot in my throat made it impossible for me to say anything. I lowered my eyes, the tears threatening to spill out. He tipped my chin up, and what he saw was enough to wash away his hesitation. He kissed me again, his lips soft and careful against mine for just a second before becoming a turmoil of passion. His tongue wrapped around mine, devouring me. Suddenly, I felt so elated that I cried into his mouth, and a tear ran down my cheek. His strong arms wrapped around me just like they had before, my body flush against his. Just like before, I felt safe in his arms, the peaceful feeling spreading through my chest, washing away every fear.

Almost every fear.

"Hugh, I love you, and I want to be with you."

He nodded, looking relieved, and a small smile

brightened his expression.

“But...what about the show, what about the network? They’re not going to be happy about this.”

“What’s done is done,” he said with a coy smile. “There are hundreds of people in this room. I saw the flashes. I wouldn’t be surprised if our picture is already online. Maybe one of the headlines will say ‘Abarath actor serenades his girlfriend at the Vanity Fair party.’ What do ye say, Sam?”

I blushed. “Had you planned this all along?”

“Maybe. I have been trying to think of a way to fix this ever since they made you leave. Melissa and I came to the conclusion that a public confession of my feelings for you was the only way.” He kissed me on the lips, and when he pulled back, he had the most ecstatic smile on his face.

“And that song! You’re not a bad singer, you know that, right?”

“Aye, ye might be biased. I’m certainly not as good as you.”

“One of these days, I’ll get you to sing with me.”

“There she goes again,” he said, laughing to himself. I leaned against his shoulder as we kept dancing slowly. His cheek rested against my head, and my heart was swimming in a sea of warm, fuzzy feelings, heightened even more by the twinkly lights in the ballroom that provided the perfect setting. My brain, however, wouldn’t stop asking questions. Yes, he loved me and I loved him, but was this the best thing for him?

“What is it?” he asked before I could open my mouth.

“Are you sure this is what you want? Now that your life is about to change and become more crazy and complicated?”

“Too late now,” he joked.

“Not helping. Are you sure this is a good move? What about the uber-passionate fans?”

"I don't care," he replied. "Plus, shouldn't this *stunt* earn me some points and establish my status as a romantic hero?" I laughed. "All I know is I'll go crazy if I can't have you by my side. Do you love me?" he asked, as if he didn't know the answer.

"You know I do. I have been in love with you for a while, Hugh MacLeod." His eyes softened at my words, and as I caressed his face, he took my hand and kissed it.

"I meant what I said, Sam. I *need* you in my life. What do you say?" he asked. The raw emotion in his eyes was enough to make me want to tear up.

"I can't wait for you to take me home," I said with a smile, trying to steady my voice. He narrowed his eyes, confused by my words. "To Scotland," I added. The grin that stretched across his face was blinding and infectious. I smiled, too, but soon his lips were on mine again, sealing our confessions with one more kiss.

People say life is stranger than fiction. I had been in the make-believe business for a while, and I had forgotten that sometimes life can be better than the greatest love stories of the silver screen. Life sometimes beats any scripted show, any movie, any choreographed romantic scene.

I couldn't wait to see where life with Hugh would take me next.

Epilogue

SAM

When I had arrived in Scotland the first time, I'd felt like a fish out of water. I was undoubtedly lost. The second time, even though I didn't know what surprises awaited me, I didn't feel so lost anymore.

However, I had to admit, I had expected a warmer welcome.

It had been months since I had left on that cold, rainy day in January. I thought my friends would show their faces and welcome me back with open arms.

When I got to St. Martin, I realized I hadn't been given the same townhouse as before. Cecilia and Oliver were getting married, and they had somehow managed to get a place together. I wasn't too upset about it, because I was hoping Hugh and I could do the same, but when I looked at the papers I had gotten from production, I discovered I had a reservation at the local hotel and that surprised me. Why had they gotten me a reservation for a hotel? Where would

I stay permanently, and more importantly, where was my boyfriend?

It had been a few weeks since I'd seen him, and I missed him. We had been meeting across the globe for most of the year. I tried calling him, but he didn't answer the phone.

Men.

He could have at least come to the airport to pick me up. *He used to be so attentive...guess the fame has gone to his head,* I joked to myself.

In reality, it couldn't have been further from the truth. Despite being unreachable that day—my man had decided to be a producer on the show this season and told me he had a meeting he couldn't miss—Hugh and I met any time we had the chance. After the Oscars, I got a call from an old friend to go work on his new movie in New York, and Hugh made sure to come visit me there whenever he could in between promos.

Reviews and ratings for season one had been great, so much so that *Entertainment Weekly* called *Abarath* "The Must-Watch Show of the Summer." Hugh, Melissa, and the rest of the cast also earned rave reviews for their performances, so much so that a lot of TV bloggers were talking about Golden Globe nominations for the next year.

After my movie wrapped, I took a few more jobs around LA, music videos and commercials, mostly. I didn't know if I had been "forgiven" by my peers or if my new relationship had elevated my status—probably both.

I had the chance to choose between going back to work on *Abarath* or being a key makeup artist on the set of a historical drama set around the American revolution.

I was tempted to accept the position in the States...for a total of five minutes. I missed my Scot, but I also missed Scotland. I longed to see my favorite valley covered in heather again. I was even prepared to deal with the bloody dreadful weather.

A month before coming back to Scotland, I had joined Hugh for a couple stops in Asia while he and Melissa promoted the show. Alyssa had been busy on Broadway, filling in for the lead actress playing Angelica Schuyler in *Hamilton*.

Our Hong Kong and Tokyo trip had been a blast, and we even met Amira, who was in Japan to secure the rights to a comic book she wanted to turn into a movie or maybe a miniseries. One of my favorite memories was of all of us trying to fit into a tiny sushi place near Tokyo's fish market. It was, hands down, the best and freshest sushi I had ever tasted.

As I checked into the hotel, an employee at the front desk gave me an envelope that was addressed to me. *Strange*. Maybe Hugh had left me a note. I opened the envelope while the clerk completed the check-in process, and I found a key with a piece of paper.

The man was certainly fond of keys. What was this one for? I didn't think it was the one for his hotel room, and it looked much different than the ones we'd had for the townhouses last year.

I went up to my room and tried his number again. Nothing.

I took out a change of clothes, put my luggage away, and opened the piece of paper in the envelope. It was a charming, albeit badly drawn map of a place I knew well.

I smiled, and then sighed, because now I knew where to find my boyfriend.

I took a quick shower and tried to make myself presentable before leaving the hotel. I walked past the street of townhouses where I'd stayed the previous year. A million different memories flooded my head, and suddenly my chest filled with that certain mix of anxiety and anticipation I felt any time I was going to see Hugh again.

A year had passed, and he still gave me butterflies.

It seemed like the feeling was mutual, because whenever we were together, he couldn't get enough of me.

I called an Uber—a rare commodity in St. Martin—and gave instructions to the driver for how to get to my destination. My favorite spot in all of Scotland looked a bit different than I remembered. The heather was just now starting to bloom, and the splashes of lilac color were few and far between. Something else was different, too—it was sunny, exceptionally sunny. The weather was gorgeous, a perfect summer day by Scotland's standards. The few clouds in the sky were white and fluffy. It was picture-perfect scenery, and I was even more in love with it than I had been the first time. By the time I reached the X-marked spot on my map, my heart was in my throat, and I felt a bead of sweat trickle down my spine.

Smoke was coming out of the chimney, which I found odd, because it wasn't a cold day, but I was happy for the smoke signals, because at least I could be sure he was there. I imagined he'd come out and greet me, but he didn't. I said good-bye to the driver and walked up the small path leading to the front door. I reached for the handle, but it was locked. I took out the key he had left for me and opened the door.

I smiled as my eyes took him in. He was standing in the middle of the empty living room, right in front of the fireplace, and he was facing me. All the old furniture the place had had when we'd rented it was gone. I frowned for a moment, but when his face broke into a smile, my nervousness and tiredness vanished.

His hair fell across his forehead in that unruly way I loved, and I couldn't wait to run my fingers through it again. He was wearing a dark blue sweater that hugged his biceps and highlighted his pecs with dark blue jeans that made him look taller, towering even, in the cozy living room.

I walked hurriedly to him, wrapping my hands around his neck a moment later, my lips pressed against his, our bodies flushed.

We didn't speak.

There was a lot of kissing at first, as well as hands in all kinds of places. It had been a month; it simply couldn't be helped. My thirst for him was unquenchable, and only after a while did I come back to my senses and remember to ask him why we were meeting here. We didn't have to hide, not anymore. I stopped kissing him. He suddenly pulled back and gave me a curious look that soon turned into a grin.

"God, I missed ye."

"I missed you, *mo chridhe,*" I said while caressing his smooth jaw, and his smile widened. He stole one more kiss, but then I stopped him. Questions, I had so many questions; kissing would have to wait.

"Wait...first off, what's with the treasure map?" I asked him as I pulled out the paper. He just looked at me, a tight-lipped smile in place. "Which reminds me, here's your key." I handed it over to him.

"It's yours," he answered, biting his bottom lip, almost as if he were trying to fight back a smile.

"Huh? What do you mean?" I frowned and let out a breath, more out of frustration than anything else. The tiredness from my trip was catching up with me all of a sudden and I was confused...about everything.

He handed me an envelope. *What is up with him?*

"Boy, you're all mystery and mischief today. First the map and the key, now this. I feel like I'm a contestant on The Amazing Race. Where to next?" I asked rhetorically as I gave him a pointed look. He said nothing, just kept smiling, the corners of his lips curling in the most delicious way. I wanted to kiss him *right there.*

"Just open the envelope, Sam."

"Okay, okay." This envelope was much thicker than the other one, and as I opened it, I pulled out several papers that were folded together.

My eyes scanned through it—it was a bill of sale, transferring the property, *this* property, to me...and Hugh. It wasn't signed and thereby not fully executed, but it was an official document. My mouth went dry, and my heart started drumming inside my chest so loudly, I felt it in my ears. I swallowed, and then I looked up at him with a certain curiosity, as if it were the first time I'd seen him up close.

I let out a fast breath, and then the words came rushing out of my mouth, unable to contain them any longer.

"You bought me a house?"

"It's merely a cottage," he said with an irresistible smile and a shrug of his shoulders.

I shook my head and narrowed my eyes. "Don't you dare belittle my house."

"You like it?"

I gave him a coy look. "You know I don't just *like* it. I *love* it," I replied, and the smile on his face got even bigger, his blue eyes glistening with delight.

"You'll have to share it. You're not the only owner."

"I know," I whispered, trying to fight back a smile, euphoria taking over my entire body. I tried to press my lips into a line to avoid grinning, but I couldn't help it. It wasn't that I didn't want to let him know just *how much* I loved it; I was simply afraid I was going to make a big fool out of myself.

"Are we going to stay here this year?" I asked him. Now that I wasn't as distracted as I had been earlier, I noticed a few things as I looked around. It was hardly the same cottage we'd stayed at the year before. The walls had been painted, and the floors had been refinished.

"This year...next year," he said evasively, looking at me, his eyes playful.

I frowned, fighting to keep my attention on him now that I was distracted by the place. He had redone the whole place. When? How? How long had he been planning this? The drumming in my chest didn't stop. Suddenly, he took my hand and guided me to the kitchen, which was no longer the charming but outdated one we had seen the last time. This kitchen had brand-spanking-new white cabinets with state of the art appliances and a luxurious blue Viking stove that took my breath away. It was too much. The floor in the kitchen had been redone with stone and connected the kitchen to the side door, which was now the door of the mudroom. I couldn't wait to see the rest of the place, but I was sure of one thing already: I loved it, and I loved the man who had orchestrated all of it.

"I love you," I told him, my eyes filled with wonder.

"You love me or the cottage?" he asked with a smirk.

"Both. Equally," I said in a serious, dazed tone, and he laughed.

He took my hand and led me to the staircase.

"After you," he said. I started climbing the stairs, but I couldn't take my eyes off him. I was surprised, amazed...confused. When had he set all this in motion? Fixing up the cottage had to take months. I stopped on the last step and turned around.

"When? When did you start the renovations?"

He leaned against the wall and relaxed. He broke eye contact for a moment, staring into space. His lips pressed in a tight line.

"Soon after you left Scotland." He let out a sigh, and that combined with the expression on his face hurt like a blade slicing my skin. I hadn't realized how sad he'd been when we were apart. "I always thought things would eventually get back to how they were. Somehow, I knew you belonged here with me," he said quietly, but then his eyes widened as if he'd suddenly said too much. He guided us to an empty room I assumed was the master bedroom, although the floor plan on the upper floor was drastically different from how I remembered it.

The old floor plan had had one bedroom on each side of the cottage, each with a different view. On our first visit, I had joked that it would have been hard to choose between the heather flowers on one side and the sea on the other.

The new room featured both views: purple blooms on one side, blue waves on the other. I looked up to him, and I tried to open my mouth to say something, anything, but I was speechless.

"Now you'll never have to choose," he said in a low voice. He smiled, his lips pulled up on one side, carefully studying my reaction.

"You... I-I can't believe this." I was hardly making sense. I felt heady, unable to put together all the things I wanted to tell him. I felt overwhelmed, in a good way.

I couldn't contain the rush of excitement spreading through my body. So many different emotions erupted inside me, warming my chest, making me smile like a child staring at Fourth of July fireworks. The feelings that bubbled up inside me came out with a deep breath. I couldn't take my eyes off him. I loved him, and he needed to know how much. He was everything.

Finally, I felt confident enough to say what I was thinking, but just then, his lips parted and he said, "I'm glad you like the house, but it comes with another condition."

"Be my husband," I blurted out at the same time, taking one of his hands between mine.

A smile stretched across his face, reaching his eyes, so

luminous and bright on this exceptionally sunny day.

Hugh

"Be my husband," she said again, with even more conviction this time. "I know this is not how it's supposed to happen, but it's the only thing that makes sense to me right now. I love you." Her eyes were glossy, filled with tears, searching mine for an answer. It was hard not to smile, even though things had taken an unexpected turn.

"You stole my line," I told her.

Realization set in her eyes, and she suddenly looked elated and astoundingly happy. She bit her bottom lip, fighting a smile. "I stole your line? What do you mean?"

"This, Sam." I took the velvety box out of my pocket and placed it in her hand. I pursed my lips together, waiting for her reaction. I had been ready to give it to her since she'd walked through the door, but I had wanted to show her everything else, and now, somehow, she'd managed to beat me to it.

"This? This was in your pocket the entire time? And I thought you were just happy to see me," she joked, accompanying her words with a disappointed sigh, but then smiled at me. *Such an actress,* I thought, shaking my head. She stared at the box in the palm of her hand with the utmost curiosity but didn't open it, as if it were an abstract object.

"Okay, knock it off, funny girl," I joked. "Open the box."

Her gaze darted between me and the box, and with a sharp intake of breath, she lifted the lid. "Oh my gosh," she said with a sigh. "Hugh, it's beautiful."

"It's been in my family for more than a hundred years.

My great-grandma had it first. My mother wore it last." The floral diamond cluster ring had been passed down in my family. I had seen pictures of my great-grandma and grandma wearing it, and I had distinct memories of my mum wearing it when I was a kid.

"I've wanted to give you this for a while," I said, taking the ring out of the box.

"A while?" she asked, confused. I knelt in front of her, and her eyes widened as her lips parted, accentuating the surprise on her face. I took her hand in mine, and as I locked eyes with her, I attempted to do this right.

Hopefully, I wouldn't mess up my lines.

"Samhain, I've wanted you since I first laid eyes on you. I craved your friendship and your love before you were even mine. I fell for you so fast. I didn't even think it was possible to fall in love like this. I never want anything to keep us apart ever again. I love you, and I want to love you until the end of my days. Will you do me the honor of becoming my wife?"

SAM

His accent was thick on the last sentence, and it drove me insane. We had been apart for weeks, and I was aching for him. His words had my head swimming in a sea of feelings and I felt light, as if I were levitating on a cloud of cotton candy.

Prior to that day, I hadn't thought I could love him more than I did, but I had been wrong. There were not enough words for how amazing he was, for how precious he was to me.

"Hugh MacLeod, you're everything to me. You know

that, right? The world might know you because you're gorgeous and good at what you do, but you are *so much more*," I said with a sigh, briefly glancing around the place, taking in what he'd done—what he'd done *for me*. His eyes were fixed on my face, and he looked up with a certain impatience. "You're smart and funny. You're beautiful and have a heart of gold. You're the only one I would ever want to spend a lifetime with. I would be honored to become your wife."

He slid the ring on my finger, kissing it. Then, he proceeded to kiss each one of my fingers, and when he got up, he crushed his lips on mine. I welcomed him, eager. When I had arrived in Scotland the previous year, I'd had no idea what my future would look like. Now, I knew there would be some days of constant rain and dreadful cold. I knew there would be days when my life looked like one big, endless storm, but I also knew I'd have the sunny days and then some. I knew that with Hugh by my side, the future was looking bright.

Acknowledgements

A little over two years ago, I was writing my very first romance novel when I fell in love with a certain TV show: the cinematography was spectacular, the characters compelling and the acting superb (don't even get me started on the scripts, costumes and set ...I could go on). Scotland looked stunning, even just from a TV screen, and I was...smitten. As my love for *Outlander* grew, I wanted to write a story that took place in Scotland. Being the inexperienced writer that I was, I told myself I could start writing that story once I'd finish *Prude*. Now, here I am, more than two years and four books later. So now you know I've wanted to write *Lost in Scotland* for a long time, and I hope you love Sam and Hugh as much as I do. *Lost in Scotland* encapsulates my love for movies, TV shows, traveling, my fascination with gossip in modern society and *Outlander*. I don't think I would have been even remotely inspired to write this book if I hadn't stumbled across Diana Gabaldon's series, so my humblest thank you goes to Herself for creating the ultimate book hero, responsible for making generations upon generations of women swoon.

And now, I must thank those who help me grow each day as a person and a writer. I have a lot of people to thank for their love and encouragement.

Thanks to Emily, for loving this story when it was just a bunch of scenes all over the place. Thanks to Mae Wood, for loving this Scottish romance when it was still super dirty pre-edits.

Thank you, Katie Pettigrew, for accidentally providing me with the inspiration for the ultimate romance epilogue.

To Caitlin with Editing by C. Marie: thank you for making my words better. You're THE BEST. I love working with you.

Samantha with Samantha Leigh Design: thank you for working SO HARD on this cover. You know I LOVE IT. It's just what I wanted.

Julie Deaton: thank you so much for your proofreading on Lost in Scotland. I love reading your notes!

Thanks to Alexandria with AB Formatting for her excellent work.

Marla Selkow Esposito, thank you for being so sweet and giving me peace of mind with another read-through. Thanks to my darling E.S. Carter, for making sure Cecilia spoke like a true Brit. Thank you to my betas: Shawn Garcia, Dina Pisotti Maio, Amanda Lee, Lora Jarvis, Megan Addison and Barbara Sinnott.

Thanks to Zeia Jameson, Andrea Johnston, Jiff Simpson, Andee Michelle, MR Manfield, Cassie Graham for loving these characters as much as I do. Thanks to my BFF of the intranets, Shirl Rickman. Thanks to Lauren, who's still yelling at me to finish *Outlander* – I will get there...eventually. Maybe when the last book comes out?

Thanks to Carrie Tenney for messaging me: our mutual obsessions were bound to make us cross paths. Thanks for introducing me to Samantha Patterson. Samantha, thanks for reading and making sure I'd written Hugh like a proper Scotsman. Thanks to the Manuscript Minxes for their friendship and daily encouragement. You guys are the

BEST! Thanks to Erin Spencer, who's always a message away. Thanks to the amazing Southern Belle Book Blog and Enticing Journey for handling the promo. Thanks to the bloggers who rock my socks off and work tirelessly to promote the work of indie authors. A special thank you to Abeautifulbookblog, Schmexy Girl Book Blog, Maryse Book Blog, Typical Distractions, Aaly and The Books, Obsessed with Romance, Reviews by Reds, Disheveled Book Blog, Reading in Sarah's Corner, MustReadBooksorDie, Book Junky Girls, A Page to Turn Reviews, ItaPixie's Book Corner, Marieke's Books and Itsy Bitsy Book Bits. Thank you for supporting me!

Playlist

This is just a small selection of the music I listened to while writing Lost in Scotland. You can play the entire playlist on Spotify!

Comeback Queen – LOLO
High Heels – JoJo
Hell No – Ingrid Michaelson
Why Should I Be Sad – Britney Spears
Outside – Calvin Harris & Ellie Goulding
Don't Stop Me Now – Queen
Send My Love (To Your New Lover) - Adele
Fuck With Myself – Banks
Shut Up Kiss Me – Angel Olsen
Good Girls – Nick Jonas
Jump – Rihanna
Pony – Ginuwine
Starving – Hailee Steinfeld
Pink + White – Frank Ocean
Higher Love – Alex Vargas
Damn Sam (I Love a Woman That Rains) – Ryan Adams
Edibles – JoJo
Hold Up – Cavillo Sisters (Beyoncé Cover)
Peace of Mind – The Killers
A 1000 Times – Hamilton Leithauser + Rostam
Black Magic – Little Mix
Brown Eyed Girl – Van Morrison

About the Author

Hilaria Alexander was born and raised in the south of Italy, where her family still lives. She was bit by the travel bug early on and lived in Tokyo and Orlando for a while before settling down in Oklahoma City with her husband and kids. She loves books - obviously - as well as movies and TV, and is addicted to award shows. She can't play an instrument to save her life, but she loves music, which is one of her biggest inspirations when plotting new stories. If you have questions about her or her books, ask her on Facebook and Twitter, or email her at hilaria_alexander@outlook.com.

ALSO AVAILABLE BY HILARIA ALEXANDER

Prude

My editor, who also happens to be my best friend, told me she thinks I write like a prude. That EVERYONE thinks I write like a prude. She made it clear that my next book will not be published if I don't "spice things up".

Instead of replying calmly, like the "old" Prudence Clearwater would have, I stormed out of her office and told her to go to hell.

After a few days spent wallowing, unsure about my future, I decided that I should:

1. Ignore the naysayers and backstabbing.
2. Re-evaluate my inner circle, especially my deceitful BFF.
3. Focus on my writing and figure out where I went wrong.
4. Accept any help I can get, especially from my old college crush, who happens to be a successful book agent and looks like a Viking God.
5. Keep my friendship with the aforementioned Viking God platonic, even when he makes me tingle in all the right places.

Or maybe, since I'm not a prude, I should just live a little...and surrender to the charming Ben Hallstrom.

What's the worst that could happen?

This Love

Music brought them together,
But it just might tear them apart.

Leaving New York.
It was the best decision I ever made.
Packing up and moving to the other side of the world changed me.
I turned a new page, leaving the past behind.

Amsterdam felt like home–for a while.
But I was still stuck.
Unable to move forward.

Then, Lou Rivers showed up,
Instantly, I felt my life shift again.
A constant reminder of the life I once had,
The mistakes I left behind.
He's the musician I dreamed of being...
If I were stronger, bolder, braver.
But I wasn't.

He taught me how to love music again,
And for the first time, I feel like I know what to do.
But how can I?
How can I become myself without giving up on us?

FU Cancer

Lucy has always been a good girl. The most hardcore thing she's done in her life was falling for a divorced man ten years her senior.

But he was the love of her life, and she married him. When her Peter Pan of a husband decided to divorce her, she thought it was her chance to start anew. That was until she was diagnosed with breast cancer. Besides looking like Britney circa 2007, she is taking it well, real well. You might see her walk around the hospital during chemo sessions with bright colored wigs and outrageous t-shirts that seem to shock the most conservative employees. One of them reads FU CANCER.

Not About Love

Strong and independent,
Wrong for each other in every way.
But the heat, the passion, the pull.
Undeniable.
Irresistible.
When we were together,
The chaos turned to desire,
Need.
Bliss.
I was his.
He was mine.
For the time-being.
Different countries.
Different worlds.
Just sex.
No strings attached.
That's how Boyd Rivers wanted it.
And exactly how I liked it.
But sometimes, fate has other plans...
Can it really be not about love?

66549887R00195

Made in the USA
Charleston, SC
22 January 2017